Christian White is an Australian author and screenwriter whose credits include the feature film *Relic* and the Netflix series *Clickbait*. His debut novel, *The Nowhere Child*, was one of Australia's bestselling debut novels ever. Rights were sold in 17 international territories, and it has been acquired for a major screen deal. Christian's second book, *The Wife and the Widow*, was published in 2019 and became an instant bestseller. *Wild Place* is his third novel.

Christian lives on the Mornington Peninsula, Victoria, with his wife, Summer DeRoche, and their adopted greyhound, Issy.

WILD PLACE

CHRISTIAN WHITE

books that leave an impression

Published by Affirm Press in 2021
28 Thistlethwaite Street, South Melbourne,
Boon Wurrung Country, VIC 3205
affirmpress.com.au

Text and copyright © Christian White, 2021
All rights reserved. No part of this publication may be reproduced without prior permission of the publisher.

Title: Wild Place / Christian White, author
ISBN: 9781922626103 (paperback)

 A catalogue record for this book is available from the National Library of Australia

Cover design by Christa Moffitt, Christabella Design
Cover image from iStock, credit Kalulu
Typeset by J&M Typesetting
Proudly printed in Australia by Griffin Press

For my siblings, Niki, Peter and Jamie

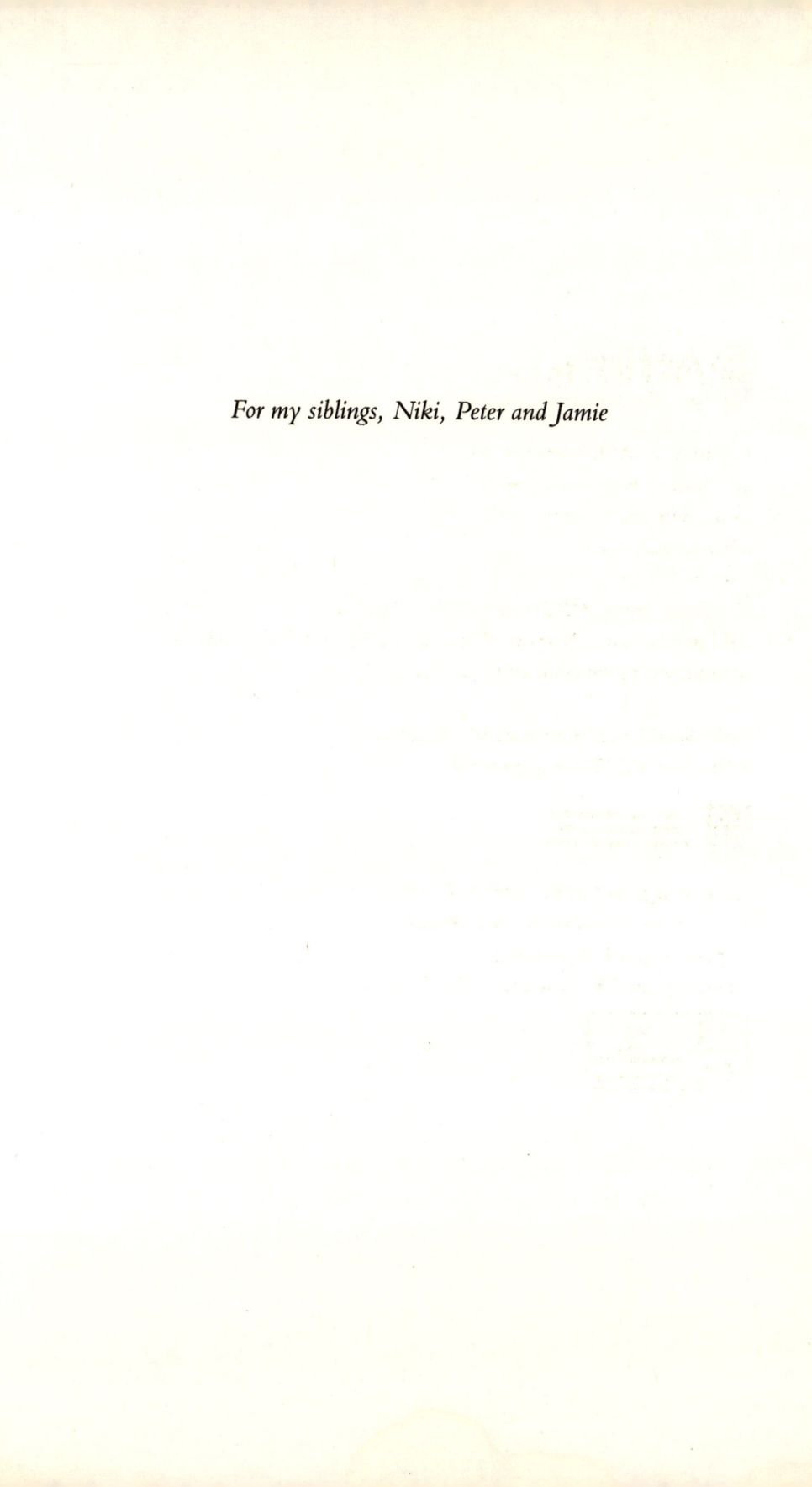

PROLOGUE

Friday

8 December 1989

'The existence of Satan is a matter of belief, but the existence of Satanism is undeniable. Darkness lurks behind the lyrics of your child's favourite song, on the shelves of your local video store, in the homes, schools and parks of every small town across the country. In tonight's Special Look, we'll be diving deep into the dangerous and troubling world of devil worship. It's an epidemic and spreading fast. Nobody is safe. Especially not your—'

Nancy Reed muted the TV. It didn't make much difference. There was still plenty of noise in her head. She was doing the two things guaranteed to bum a person out on a Friday night: drinking alone and reflecting on her life.

Somewhere along the way, something had gone wrong. She was forty-one, unemployed, and staring down the barrel of a divorce. But when she looked back, performing a kind of post-mortem on her life, there were no obvious signs of trouble. There was just a series of wrong turns and bad decisions. The cause of death, it seemed, was life.

It was coming up on 11pm. That was late, for suburbia. Her daughter was sleeping over at a friend's house and her husband – *ex*, she reminded herself – was in a budget room at the Camp Hill Motor Inn, where he'd moved while they finalised the divorce. Nancy was alone, free to fall into a pit of despair and self-pity.

On the coffee table in front of her lay *The Camp Hill Leader*, open to the employment section. Her yellow highlighter sat beside it. She hadn't even needed to take the cap off. The only jobs she seemed qualified for were night filler, check-out chick and flipper of burgers, and she wasn't that desperate. Yet. The problem with being a stay-at-home mother was that none of her skills translated to the workplace. Seventeen years of child rearing should have qualified her for a job as a hostage negotiator or an upper-management position in a psychiatric hospital.

It was Owen's fault. He had insisted Nancy stop work. He was old-fashioned that way. Or maybe he just needed something to excuse his bad behaviour. Maybe he knew that when someone depends on you for everything, it's harder for them to leave.

Feeling bitter, she drank more.

Creak.

The noise came from somewhere behind her. She spun around to look over the armchair. Most of the lights in the house were off – she'd be paying the electricity bills herself soon and wanted to get used to keeping costs down. The TV cast wavering shadows across the walls. There was nobody there. At least nobody she could see.

Nancy stood in the dark and listened. There it was again: a soft metallic *click*, a long, slow *creak*. A window in one of the other rooms was being slid open from the outside. She crept through the kitchen and stood in the mouth of the hallway.

Silence.

Before creeping down to the end of the house to investigate, she went right past the rack of hefty frying pans and the block of Ginsu kitchen knives, which were sharp enough to slice through a leather shoe – *but wait, there's more!* – and armed herself with the *Yellow Pages*.

A gun would work better. There was one in the house, a rifle Owen used to hunt rabbits when he visited his cousins – they lived up north, directly in the middle of arse-fuck and nowhere – but the gun was at the other end of the house, on the top shelf of her wardrobe, in a locked case. The key was in the pocket of her ex-husband's jeans, which were now, no doubt, slung over a chair in a room at the motor inn.

Nancy briefly considered calling him, but decided she'd rather be dismembered and left in a shallow grave than give him the satisfaction. As much as she hated to admit it – and never would, out loud – Nancy missed having a man around at times like this. She was getting the hang of being a single mother, but sometimes wished it came with an add-on option. A male she could send blindly ahead of her, into danger.

She reached into the dark and flicked on the light, relieved to find there was no psycho killer waiting there for her. She held the phone book aloft and moved steadily down the hall. Halfway, she heard movement. A light blinked on somewhere. A pencil-thin sliver glowed beneath one of the doors. Tracie's bedroom. Two more steps, then the sound of drawers being opened and rifled through. If they – whoever *they* were – had been ransacking any of the other rooms, Nancy might have snuck to a neighbour's house to call triple zero.

But they were in her daughter's room. Common sense abandoned her and white-hot rage swept in. She raised the phone book high with her right hand. With her left, she took hold of the knob and swung the door open.

In the middle of the room stood a small, slight woman with a striking sweep of blonde hair, bleached so recently that Nancy could smell the chemicals wafting off her.

'Tracie?'

Nancy's daughter let out a court-room gasp, scrambled backwards so fast she knocked a stack of cassettes off her side table, then sighed with relief. 'Jesus, Mum, you scared me.'

'*I* scared *you*? I thought you were an intruder.'

'And you were planning on calling him a taxi?'

Nancy exhaled, smirked and lowered the phone book. 'What happened to your hair?'

When Tracie had left earlier that evening, she'd been a brunette. A pretty, effortlessly natural brunette. She'd come home looking like Debbie Harry. 'I felt like a change. Like a statement. Do you like it?'

'I do.' She didn't. 'You know, most kids sneak *out* of their bedroom window. Not the other way around.'

'I forgot my key and didn't want to wake you.'

'I thought you were spending the night at Cassie's.'

'We had a fight.' Tracie stepped out of her sneakers. 'How's the job hunt going?'

'It isn't.'

'Good,' Tracie said. 'You don't need to find a job; you need to find a man.'

'I'd rather blow my own brains out, but thanks anyway.'

'Come on, Mum. You're still pretty and funny and young. Ish.'

'Your dad's side of the bed is still warm.'

'But I won't be around forever,' Tracie said.

That stung in a way Nancy hadn't been expecting. It was true, of course. Tracie had just finished high school. She was off to university next year, and then there would be work and boyfriends and weddings and children, and Nancy would eventually die alone.

But that's not what bothered her. Correction: that's not what was bothering her in that moment. It was something in Tracie's tone. *I won't be around forever.* It was the kind of thing a parent said to a child, not the other way around. Since the separation, Tracie had aged. That was a strange thing to say about a seventeen-year-old, but it was true. Her eyes had darkened.

'Your father and I will be fine,' she said. 'You don't have to worry about us.'

'I'm not worried about Dad. Not in that way, at least. He'll marry the first bimbo he meets.'

'He's not like that.'

'He's a survivor, Mum.'

'If he's a survivor, what does that make me?' Nancy asked.

Tracie shook her head. 'I just hate to think of you living in this big house all by yourself.'

Nancy sighed, then sat down on the bed and helped Tracie under the covers. A whisper of warm air drifted in through the open window.

'So,' Nancy said. 'Talk to me about the hair.'

'What about it?'

'Usually when a woman does something this dramatic, it's because she's lost control of something major in her life and this is her way of taking back that control. Oh no, you did that because of the divorce, didn't you?'

Tracie raised a smile but it fell away fast. 'It has nothing to do with you, Mum. This'll probably sound crazy, but I wanted to look like someone else. I … I think someone's been following me.'

Nancy sat forward.

'A few nights ago, someone called the house,' Tracie explained. 'When I picked up, whoever was on the other end of the line didn't say anything, but I could hear them breathing. And since then I've just had this feeling, you know, like I was being watched. The other day, at the roller rink. And then again tonight at the movies.'

Nancy waited. Then she asked, 'Is that it?'

'Is that it?'

'Did you actually see anyone?'

Tracie glared at her. 'Not exactly.'

'Is it possible all your spying has made you a little paranoid?'

'I don't *spy*, Mum. I capture truth. That's like, journalism 101.'

'I'm sorry, honey, but you often do this.'

'Do what?'

'Last month you were convinced someone was outside your window, scratching on the glass, but the noise magically went away when I pruned the lemon tree. The month before that, you thought a poltergeist was moving things around the house, until we discovered the window in the spare bedroom had been left open. You have a rich imagination, Trace. It's one of the things that makes you unique. But it also makes you …' Nancy chose her next word wisely. 'Reactive.'

'You sound like Cassie. She says it's because I'm an only child and we need more attention.'

'I hate to say it—'

'Then don't.'

'—but Cassie might have a point.'

'I hate you.'

'I love you too. Is that what you and Cassie fought about?'

'Actually, the fight was about you and Dad.' Tracie's expression hardened. 'Mum, I'm going to ask you a question now and I want you to tell me the truth. Don't sugar-coat it, don't placate, and don't give me some vague, rambling non-answer like you and Dad usually do.'

'I'm not even sure I know what *placate* means.'

'Mum. I'm serious.'

She meant it. Nancy could see that, and it made her nervous.

'It's about the divorce,' Tracie said. 'Did Dad … Was he …' She paused to compose herself. 'Was there someone else?'

Tracie Reed went missing the next day.

1

Thursday

28 December 1989

Tom Witter taught English at Camp Hill Christian College. He was forty-four in the summer of 1989, when Tracie Reed went missing. He heard about it at a neighbourhood watch meeting, three days after Christmas. These meetings were held twice a month at Lydia Chow's place. A representative from every household on Keel Street was expected to attend. That night, he'd drawn the short straw.

Bill Davis had him cornered at the refreshment table. Bill lived in the big house at number four. He was roughly the same shape and size as a grizzly bear. Connie – Tom's wife – called Bill a social vampire, because when you got stuck in a conversation with him, he sucked you dry before moving on to his next victim.

'Are you and the missus still coming to our New Year's Eve bash?' Bill asked. 'Vicky never got your RSVP.'

'I'm not sure we'll make it this year, Bill. Connie wants a quiet one in.'

'She's still mad about the award, isn't she?'

Tom didn't respond.

At Bill and Vicky's last New Year's bash, Bill had doled out handmade awards to everyone in attendance. Tom was named *Brainiest Man on Keel Street*, which he accepted with no small amount of pride. Connie, on the other hand, was given *Best Bum*. She was quick to point out that while technically true, Bill had ignored what she considered her greater assets: intelligence and sense of humour.

Now Bill looked around the room and sighed. 'What's that spot between your balls and arsehole called?' he asked.

'Perineum,' Tom said.

'*Perineum*.' Bill rolled the word in his mouth. 'These meetings are as pointless as a perineum.'

'You could have gone with the appendix or earlobe. But, yeah. I get it.'

Lydia, their host, inserted herself between them. 'The perineum is actually very important,' she said. 'It keeps the dick and the arsehole apart, just like I'm doing right now.'

Tom managed a half smile. Bill laughed outright, his eyes crawling down Lydia's rear end as she bustled away.

Lydia was a slim woman in her mid-forties, with a high and tight ponytail that swished back and forth with each quick little step she took. She wore low necklines and high hemlines and was known as a bit of a flirt. All that really meant was she was bored, which made her the perfect facilitator for these meetings. Not a whole lot happened in Camp Hill, but if there was a molehill in town, you could count on Lydia to make it a mountain.

'I need everyone in the living room,' she called. 'We're about to get started.'

Tom and Bill did as they were told.

All the furniture in the living room had been cleared to make way for three rows of plastic chairs. Most of the other attendees were already seated, with varying degrees of enthusiasm. Lydia's husband, Rob, was in the back row, nursing a vodka tonic and struggling to keep his eyes open. Ellie Sipple from number six sat up front, clicking and un-clicking a ballpoint pen. Next to her was Donnie Hines. He ran his own real estate business and was onto his third — or was it fourth? — wife.

Tom found a seat in the middle. Bill sat in the row behind. Lydia went to the front of the room and — in lieu of a gavel — clapped her hands once. Hard and loud.

'Welcome, members of the Keel Street Neighbourhood Watch,' she said. 'The date is December twenty-eighth, Ellie will be taking minutes, as per, and this meeting is now in session.'

She paused, as if waiting for applause. There wasn't any.

'First item on the agenda,' she went on. 'We still need more signatures on the petition to have the council install a speed bump on Johnson Avenue. I cannot stress how important this is. That street has become a hoon-magnet and it's only a matter of time before someone's pet — or, God forbid, child — gets run over.'

Lydia's husband yawned from the back row.

'Am I keeping you up, Rob?' Lydia asked.

A murmur of laughter from the audience.

'Next, we've received a report of a break-in over in Mount Eliza. An unseen assailant smashed the window of a work ute and got away with over three hundred dollars' worth of tools. It's a good reminder to bring our cars inside at night, which, incidentally, might save us a few ugly black stains on the bitumen. Yes, I'm looking at you, Gary.'

Gary Henskee, from number nine, drove a '79 Mitsubishi Scorpion that was forever leaking oil at the bottom of his driveway. He said, 'I'm not sure my car falls under your jurisdiction, Lydia.'

'Oh, come on, Gary, cleanliness and godliness and all that. And while I'm picking on you, you still haven't fixed your porch light. A lit street is a safe street. And I know what you're all thinking. That would have sounded a lot catchier if it rhymed, but you get what you're given in this life.'

Norma Spurr-Smith, from number eight, cleared her throat.

'Right,' Lydia said, taking the cue. 'Norma's Christmas gnome is still missing. If you have any information, please speak to Norma after the meeting.'

Bill tapped Tom on the shoulder and whispered, 'What'd I tell you? Pointless as a perineum.'

Lydia said, 'The third and final item on the agenda is a big one. Ellie, would you mind?'

Ellie Sipple tucked her pen behind her ear and stood. She flipped open a manila folder, took out a stack of photocopies, and handed them out.

Tom assumed it would be an updated list of everyone's

contact details, or point-by-point instructions on how to get the perfect edges when cutting one's lawn. But it was a colour photo of a teenage girl with dark curly hair and deep-set eyes. The girl was smiling. A bright, genuine smile. Slung around her neck was a pair of headphones – the kind you'd find attached to a Walkman – with a strip of red tape holding one of the ear pads on.

Below the photo was:

MISSING PERSON

Tracie Reed, 17 years old, was last seen in her home on Bright Street, Camp Hill, on Friday 8 December 1989. If you have seen this girl, know of her whereabouts, or have any information that might help, please contact the number below or dial triple zero.

HELP BRING TRACIE HOME!

Tom stared at the girl's face, only half listening as the group got their bearings.

'She's been gone almost three weeks,' Lydia said. 'As the crow flies, Bright Street is right on the other side of Wild Place.'

Wild Place was what locals called the community forest that formed a natural barrier between neighbourhoods. It wasn't expansive, but it was dense. It ran a little over a kilometre from start to end, and about half of that across. The trees – spotted and sweet gums, mostly – were tightly packed and brimming with birdlife. All the houses on Tom's side of the street backed onto Wild Place, with little gates that gave into the forest.

'Is everything all right, Tom?' Lydia asked.

He must have been making a face, because she was staring at him. This wasn't all that uncommon. Tom had Tourette syndrome. When most people heard that, they pictured someone shouting *shit fuck motherfucker* in the middle of a crowded supermarket, or while riding the bus. But for most people – like Tom – it was more subtle: tics, twitches and small, uncontrollable movements. Tom blinked in rapid-fire bursts, made strange sounds in the back of his throat and, sometimes, his neck would jerk suddenly left and right. Still, over the years, he'd learnt to hide most of the signs. He could bottle up the tics and let them out when he was alone. Sometimes, though, if he was feeling particularly stressed or anxious or excited, they took over.

'I'm fine,' he said. 'But I know this girl. She was in my literature class.'

Lydia's face lit up. 'What was she like?'

'I don't remember a whole lot about her,' he said.

Lydia went on: 'Well, the police have no idea where she is, so her family has turned to the public – us – for help. Let's face it, this is Camp Hill so the chances of us having a roaming child killer on the loose are pretty slim. Knowing girls her age, she probably ran off with some boy and the pair of them are having unprotected intercourse right now, as passionate as it is brief. Even still, we should be on the lookout for any suspicious activity.'

Cheree Gifford, who lived in the house with the blue door

at number fourteen, asked, 'What sort of suspicious activity?'

'Strangers in the area, mysterious vehicles, anything out of place. In the meantime, I'm going to need someone to put these posters up around the neighbourhood. I'd do it myself but I'm busy with the Johnson Avenue speed bump petition. Now, we all know what happens when I ask people to volunteer. Poor Ellie here is the only one who puts her hand up and gets saddled with all the work.'

'I don't mind, really,' Ellie Sipple said.

Ignoring her, Lydia said, 'Tom, how about you?'

He looked up. 'Me?'

'As her teacher, you obviously have a connection with this girl, and plenty of time on your hands.'

Tom couldn't argue with that part. The high school was on break for Christmas holidays. Tom had five long weeks of summer stretching out ahead of him.

'So,' Lydia said. 'What do you say?'

What *could* he say?

2

After the meeting, Tom stepped out into the warm evening air and started home. His house was four doors down and across the street from Lydia's, so it was a short walk. Bill walked with him, smoking a cigarette like his life depended on it.

'If I walk slow enough, I might get through the whole thing before I get home,' he said. 'Vicky won't let me smoke in the house. She bought one of those little no-smoking signs from What's New and hung it inside the front door. Makes me feel like a stranger in my own home.'

Keel Street was lined with big, single-family houses, set back across wide green lawns. Veranda lights were on, cars were parked neatly in driveways (aside from Gary Henskee's Scorpion) and a sluggish summer breeze was drifting along the footpath.

Mark Devlin was drinking beer in his garage with the doors rolled up. He waved as they passed. Now here came Irene Borschmann walking her dogs, Lola and Dude: a rottweiler and a chihuahua, like Arnold Schwarzenegger and Danny DeVito in *Twins*.

Bill said, 'Hey, Reenie, what's good for an ingrown toenail?'

Irene and her husband Red lived two doors down from Tom. They ran the local pharmacy, which meant they knew far too many intimate details about the neighbourhood. Example: Tom's great haemorrhoid battle of '87. Before his vasectomy, he'd drive all the way to Frankston to buy condoms.

'Nail softener helps,' Irene said. 'Come in tomorrow and I'll do you a deal.'

'You don't need to see the nail?'

'I have enough trouble sleeping already, thank you.'

Lola had starting shitting on Patti Devlin's agapanthus, so Tom and Bill moved on.

Tom was carrying the stack of posters Ellie had given him. He angled them towards the streetlight so he could see Tracie Reed's face. Bill noticed, and asked, 'What do you think happened to her?'

'I don't know,' Tom said. 'She might have run away. Camp Hill's like a prison for kids her age.'

'Maybe she was murdered.'

'Jesus, Bill.'

'I'm just saying. A pretty girl like that. It's hard not to think the worst. Feel like a nightcap? You haven't seen the new pool table.'

'Next time,' Tom said.

He crossed the street towards home. Bill drifted on down Keel Street, taking slow steps and long puffs of his cigarette, turning to look over his shoulder every now and then in case Tom changed his mind. He didn't.

Tom was halfway up the front steps when he heard a small voice mutter, 'Motherfucker.'

He looked over his fence. His next-door neighbour, Debbie Fryman, was kneeling by her front door with a screwdriver in her hand.

Tom called out, 'Everything all right over there, Deb?'

'Depends on your definition,' she said. 'I'm trying to get this deadlock thingy in. The guy at the hardware shop said it was easy to install. I'm starting to think he was being sarcastic.'

'Nobody locks their doors in Camp Hill,' Tom said.

'Even so, the option would be nice.'

'Let me take a look.'

Tom set the posters down on his own doorstep, then trotted back down the steps and over to Debbie's place. She greeted him with a warm, weary smile, then handed him her 'toolbox': an old ice-cream container filled with miscellaneous screws, an unopened packet of nails and two spanners. Tom armed himself with the screwdriver. He had no idea what he was doing – he couldn't screw his way out of a wet paper bag, no pun intended – but man-code dictated he should give it a try.

'Why didn't I see you at the neighbourhood watch meeting tonight?' Tom asked.

'I was busy' – she lowered her voice – 'driving nails into my ears.'

Tom laughed.

'It's not the boredom I can't handle,' she explained. 'It's the long hateful glares I get from Lydia.'

'Lydia doesn't hate you.'

'Well, fine, maybe she doesn't hate me. But she doesn't like me, either. I'm a single mother working crazy hours in the middle of suburbia. That's enough to make me an *other* in some people's eyes.'

'I hope you don't think I see you that way.'

'You're one of the good ones, Tom.'

But that wasn't exactly true. Tom had never made any real effort to connect with Debbie. It was strange, considering how close their boys had once been: her son Sean and his eldest boy Marty grew up together and, for a while there, had been best friends. It might have been the age difference – Tom and Connie were a full ten years older than Debbie – but, as much as he hated to admit it, the fact she was a single woman didn't help. It created a strange dynamic. There's a reason tables have four legs.

She stood over him, hands on hips. Bathed in the warm orange glow of the veranda light, Debbie looked – there was no other way to put it – beautiful. Her hair was soft and red, her eyes a piercing shade of green. Her skin looked so soft and pale it made Tom picture a splash of cold milk in a cup of black coffee.

'How's Marty?'

'Moving out,' Tom said.

'You're kidding.'

He shook his head longingly, then turned to look up at his house. 'He told us a few weeks ago. He's found a flat to rent in Frankston with a mate. He wants to be closer to uni. That's how he sold it to Connie and me, anyway. He's still studying architecture. The kid who didn't pick up a crayon before he was seven is going to draw houses for a living.'

'How do you feel about him moving?'

'I feel a midlife crisis coming on,' Tom said. 'What do you think? Should I buy a convertible or have an affair?'

'Convertible, definitely. That, Connie might forgive you for.'

Then, because when people ask about your kid, it usually means they want to talk about their own, Tom asked, 'And Sean?'

She shook her head, and for the first time since Tom arrived, her smile faded. 'I've been putting pressure on him to apply for TAFE or get a job. He has so much talent and it's all just being … wasted.' She looked up at her house and sighed. 'I don't know what I'm going to do about him, Tom.'

Even though Marty and Sean had been close, they couldn't have turned out more different. Marty was bright, motivated and athletic. Sean had gone goth. His hair was long and greasy, box-dyed black. He got around in trench coats and baggy T-shirts for bands Tom had never heard of.

Tom didn't know what to say, so he said, 'It's probably just a phase.'

Debbie stopped just short of rolling her eyes. She might have heard that a few hundred times already. 'Yeah, maybe.'

'I need to confess something to you, Deb.'

'Okay.'

'I have no idea what I'm doing with this screwdriver.'

The weary smile returned to her face. 'That makes two of us. Thanks for trying.'

He said goodnight and crossed back to his place. He paused at his front door to look back. Debbie was on her knees again, fiddling with the deadlock. In a nearby window, a curtain shifted and a silhouette appeared. It was Sean. Tom gave a small wave, but the kid didn't wave back. It was a little creepy, but that was Sean's schtick: a monochrome teenager in day-glo suburbia.

He slipped away and the curtain closed.

Home was a four-bedroom split-level, decorated in shades of brown and yellow. The walls were busy with framed family photos. A particularly gruesome one hung in the entrance way, just inside the front door. A glamour shot of Tom and Connie. They paid a professional photographer to take it, so it was all soft focus and smouldering looks to camera.

Connie looked great: soft skin, straight blonde hair, her trademark know-it-all smile. Tom, not so much. He looked like a middle-aged suburbanite, which, to be fair, was exactly what he was. Worse, he'd worn horizonal stripes the day of the photo and was now forced to relive that mistake over and over, every time he stepped inside.

He closed the front door behind him, kicked off his sneakers, and went into the living room. Connie was working out to the Jane Fonda tape she'd got for Christmas from her sister. She didn't turn around when he came in.

'Dinner's in the oven,' she said, between breaths. 'I hope you're not sick of Christmas leftovers yet. We have enough to get us into the nineties. I'm not even exaggerating.'

'How's the workout?'

She flailed her arms around in the air — at least that's what it looked like to Tom — and said, 'Apparently this is how you get rid of the, quote, *wobbly wobble*, unquote, beneath your arms. Wine helps.'

She paused to sip from a glass of white wine on the coffee table.

'I'm not sure you're supposed to combine alcohol and aerobics,' Tom said.

'It's a workout, not aerobics.'

Keiran, their youngest, was sitting on the sofa, entranced by Jane Fonda. He was thirteen. During the school year he looked like a normal, clean-cut kid. During the holidays he turned into something from *Lord of the Flies*. His short hair was tangled and sweaty. There was dirt on his cheeks and more beneath his fingernails. A wild kid at a wild age.

'Hi, kid,' Tom said. 'You seem to be enjoying the video too.'

'Mum said I can watch TV when she's done. *Knight Rider*'s on.' Keiran dragged his eyes away from Jane Fonda's leggings long enough to clock the posters under Tom's arm. He turned his head sideways to read the bold capitals aloud. '"Missing Person"?' His eyes widened. 'Oh, shit.'

In unison, Tom and Connie said, '*Language*.'

'Right. Sorry. But this girl. I know her. Well, I don't *know* her know her. But she goes to my school.'

'And she was one of my students,' Tom said. 'She was in the

year below Marty. Where is he?'

'Packing,' Connie said.

He grunted.

'You asked,' Connie said. She took a break from her workout to sink more wine and look at the posters. 'What are you doing with these?'

'Lydia volunteered me to put them up around town.'

Connie slammed back the rest of her wine. She'd been drinking more since Marty decided he was moving out.

'Do I need to show you the list again?' she asked.

Connie had given him a list of all the things that needed fixing before he went back to work in January. The upstairs bathroom had a leak, the sewing room needed a fresh coat of paint, and the screen door thudded through the night like a heartbeat.

'What happened to her?' Keiran asked. 'Is there, like, a psycho killer on the loose or something?'

'No,' Tom said. 'But just in case, I don't want you playing in Wild Place for a while.'

'I'm thirteen, Dad. I don't *play*.'

'What do you do?'

'Hang. Chill.'

'In that order?'

'Depends.'

'Fine. I don't want you hanging or chilling in Wild Place.'

Keiran rolled his eyes. 'Has anyone ever told you you're, like, really paranoid? You should probably see someone about that.'

'The kid has a point, Tom,' Connie said. 'After the Tylenol murders in America, you didn't allow painkillers in the house for months. I had to smuggle in ibuprofen like a drug mule whenever I got my period.'

'Ew, Mum. Don't say *period*.'

To Keiran, Tom said, 'Just promise me you'll stay out of the bush for a while.'

Keiran looked to Connie. 'Mum?'

She spread her hands. He looked back at Tom.

'Fine,' he said. 'I promise.'

After dinner, Tom went upstairs to Marty's room. He was rolling up a movie poster: *Full Metal Jacket*. Aside from his clothes, the poster seemed to be the only thing he was taking with him. He was apparently abandoning his Enid Blyton collection, and the little plastic basketball hoop suction-cupped to the door of his wardrobe. He was, of course, abandoning his father as well.

Without looking up, Marty said, 'How was the meeting? Did they find Norma's gnome yet, or are they still waiting for the kidnapper's ransom demand?'

'Don't you mean gnome-napper?' Tom said.

Marty made a sour face. 'Oh, Dad, that was bad.'

'You'll miss my jokes when you're gone.'

'If you say so.'

A small AM/FM radio sat on the windowsill, whispering a Fleetwood Mac song. Marty hummed along. He was a good-looking kid, with a firm jaw, clear skin and a sweep of blond hair that always seemed to fall just right. He got all that from Connie. Tom didn't have a whole lot of hair left.

'How does it feel to be leaving your old room?' Tom asked. 'I bet you'll miss this place when you're living with six other dudes.'

'I'm moving in with one housemate. And don't say *dude*. It makes you sound like a ...'

'Let me guess. An old man?'

'A pervert.'

Tom sat down on the bed and watched his son pack. 'Are you sure you've thought this move through, Marty?'

'Please don't start, Dad.'

'I'm not starting anything. I think your mum and I just assumed we'd get to hang on to you for a few more years. At least until you got through uni. It feels sudden. Did something ... change?'

Marty ran a strip of masking tape over one of the packing boxes and looked at his father. 'I changed, Dad. When I was a kid, Camp Hill felt like the whole world. Now it feels like just a tiny part of it.'

'You're still a kid, Marty,' Tom said.

'Then why did they give me a driver's licence?'

'Touché,' Tom said. 'Hey, do you know Tracie Reed?'

'From Camp Hill College?'

'She was a year below you, yeah. She's gone missing.'

Marty raised his eyebrows. 'Missing?'

Tom gave him one of the posters. 'Maybe you could ask

around about her. One of your friends might have seen her, or heard from her.'

'Maybe,' Marty said. 'But we're not really in the same crowd.'

'You didn't know her?'

'We were in one class together. They let her take year twelve media because I guess she was smart. She knew it, too.'

'How do you mean?'

He shrugged. 'She was just one of those girls who acted like she was better than everyone else.' He frowned. 'Do you think she's okay?'

'I hope so,' Tom said.

Tom went to the window and looked out. The back lawn sloped gently to the wooden fence and gate. Beyond that was Wild Place, deep and dark and full of shadows. The bushland shifted in the breeze. A strange, unsettling image came to Tom, drifting in like a memory or a psychic vision. He saw a faceless man lurking beneath the trees, saw him reaching out and taking hold of Tracie Reed, dragging her into the dark. He pictured the man's mouth, big and oily, opening wide to devour her.

After saying goodnight to Marty, Tom went back downstairs. Then, for the first time since he could remember, he locked the front door.

3

Friday

29 December 1989

At 7am, Owen Reed sat on a wooden bench in an air-conditioned hallway, in the mortuary behind the Coroners Court. He checked his watch. A detective was supposed to have met him here three minutes ago. He was late.

Nearby, there was a small white coffee table with a spread of magazines, newspapers and books. *Reader's Digest, Time, Vogue, The Very Hungry Caterpillar.* That last one choked him up. Who would sit and leaf through reading material in a place like this?

Owen checked his watch again. Four minutes late.

He was a big man. No. *Big* didn't do him justice. The guy was huge. Well over six foot, with wide, rugby-player shoulders and a boxer's nose. He was usually clean shaven, with speckled grey hair cut military short, but since Tracie had gone, he'd stopped taking care of his appearance. His beard was shaggy and dark, his hair a fluffy and expanding Chia Pet.

He stared at the white wall opposite, and waited. Somewhere beyond that wall, he knew, there were bodies. He had no idea how many. Dozens? Hundreds? He pictured them all laid out side by side on steel gurneys, like floor stock at a hardware store. Or maybe they were slotted away in those coffin-shaped drawers, like in the movies.

'Mr Reed.'

Detective Rambaldini, the cop who'd been handling his daughter's case, strode towards him. Rambaldini was meaty and soft, with a fluffy tuft of red hair on his head, and a little more under his nose. He wore a short-sleeved yellow shirt that didn't seem to fit right. Owen only ever wore long sleeves. Short sleeves made him feel like he was forgetting something.

It was a strange thing to think about, under the circumstances. But as the days since Tracie went missing had turned into weeks, Owen had found his mind drifting more and more. He'd catch himself wondering when his car was due for its next service, or remarking about the high price of tomatoes at the Camp Hill Safeway. These moments were always fleeting. It was a coping mechanism, he guessed. A mind could only run on raw fear and panic for so long before it needed a break.

Owen stood up.

'Thanks for coming down at such short notice,' Rambaldini said. 'This is a long shot, Mr Reed. Let me make that clear. There's a very good chance you came all this way for nothing.'

'Can I see her?'

'It's against regulations to allow you to see the body in person before a formal identification has been made.' He looked down at an unmarked, yellow envelope in his hands. 'But I have a photo here to show you.'

Owen stared at the envelope. He didn't reach for it. Instead, he sat back down. His legs felt suddenly heavy. Detective Rambaldini sat down next to him.

'Where did you find her?' he asked.

'The Yarra River. She got tangled in some fishing debris a short distance from the Oakbank Bridge. It's a popular suicide hotspot.'

'Is that how she died? She jumped from the bridge?'

'We don't know yet,' Rambaldini said. 'Unfortunately, the body spent a lot of time in the water, so determining her identity and cause of death will take some time. You should try to prepare yourself, Mr Reed. Her appearance is … disturbing. If it is her, even after seeing the photo, there's a chance you may not be able to identify her.' He paused. 'Did your daughter ever have any issues with addictive behaviour?'

'*Does*,' he corrected.

'I'm sorry?'

'You're talking about her in the past tense.' He looked again at the envelope in the detective's hand. Before he saw the photo, before he *knew*, Tracie was an *is*, not a *was*. 'And I don't know what you mean by addictive behaviour.'

'Did she—' Rambaldini caught himself. '*Does* she drink?'

'No.'

'Any history with drugs?'

'Never. Tracie isn't like that. She's a good girl.' He shook his head, then thought about it. 'She came home from a party a few years ago smelling like pot. Her mum and I rode her pretty hard about it. I know all that talk about it being a gateway drug is cheesy, but it is based on fact. She admitted there was weed at the party but swore she didn't have any.' He looked the detective in the eye. 'I believed her.'

A crease appeared on Detective Rambaldini's forehead. 'A toxicology report showed heroin in our victim's system. A lot of it.'

'She wouldn't,' Owen stammered. 'She has a cousin who died of an overdose. She's terrified of drugs. If that was in her system, then someone else forced her to take it.'

Rambaldini looked sceptical. Owen couldn't blame him. It would be hard to find a father who didn't think his daughter was a good girl, but in Owen's case, it happened to be true.

'Are you ready?' Rambaldini asked.

No.

'Yes.'

Rambaldini handed over the envelope. It was sealed. He tore it open with his index finger and let the photo fall out onto the palm of his hand. It was a Polaroid, facing down. He turned the photo over, then drew in a tight breath. His instincts kicked in: told him to look away. Turn away. Run away. But if he didn't do this, his wife would have to. Ex. Whatever.

So he looked. The dead girl's face was bloated, bruised and waterlogged.

'What are all those little nicks in the skin?' he asked. 'They look like stab wounds.'

'She was in the water for some time,' Rambaldini said. 'Those are fish bites.'

He felt cold. Numb.

Detective Rambaldini asked, 'Is it your daughter, Mr Reed?'

Owen looked up.

'Have you ever heard of Puzzle Park?'

Rambaldini looked at him with a bewildered expression, then shook his head.

'It's an amusement park out past Yarra Junction. It's run by a couple of hillbillies. Safety codes be damned. I don't even know if it's still there. The council probably closed the place down.'

'Mr Reed, I don't think I'm following,' Rambaldini said.

'When Tracie was five, maybe six, whenever the ad for it came on TV, she'd lose her mind. Eventually my wife and I bit the bullet and took her out there for the day. There was this slide there. The Big Dipper. No, that's not it. The Big Screamer. It must have been forty, fifty feet high.'

His gaze shifted back to the girl in the photo.

'To say Tracie *wanted* to go on this slide doesn't do the story justice. She *needed* to. *Yearned* to. When she looked up at that thing, it was as if she knew it was her destiny to ride it. Tracie's mum thought it was too dangerous, and that Tracie was too little. She was right, of course, but Tracie wouldn't take no for an answer.'

Rambaldini waited.

Owen smiled at the memory. That mustn't happen too often in a place like this. 'Tracie started crying and screaming. She threw herself down in the sawdust and started kicking her legs. So we did what any good parent does when their kid throws a tantrum: we gave in.'

'Mr Reed,' Rambaldini said. 'Owen. I really need you to—'

'Five minutes later there was blood pouring down Tracie's face,' he said. 'She'd come off the side and shot headfirst into the wire fence. She had to get stitches. It left a scar. Right here on her forehead.'

He pointed to the place. The detective got it. He leaned in to get a closer look at the photo.

'... Are you sure?'

'This isn't her,' Owen said. 'This isn't my daughter.'

It took Owen nearly two hours to get back to Camp Hill. He spent most of that time stop-starting in his bright yellow convertible. Even this early in the day, traffic was bad. Summer tourists were flowing to the Mornington Peninsula in droves. He spent a lot of that drive thinking about the girl in the photo. The girl who wasn't Tracie. He pictured her father, looking and hoping and praying in vain.

Damn, he thought. He was crying again. He got home a little after 9.30am. No. *Home* was currently the motor inn just off Nepean Highway, with a view of a swimming pool so green he couldn't see the bottom. But home used to be – and in a sad, nostalgic sort of way, always would be – number ten Bright Street.

On his way to the front door, he smelled barbeque smoke wafting over from neighbouring yards and pop music drifting over fences. Life went on in this little suburban paradise under a clear blue sky, with or without Tracie. Owen supposed his house – *Nancy's* house – was the dark cloud in that sky.

In the days after Tracie disappeared, he and Nancy had taken on a sort of macabre celebrity status. Everyone wanted to tell their friends they knew the parents of the missing girl. But when the police decided Tracie was a runaway, everyone else did too. Almost overnight, he and Nancy went from being someone to feel sorry for to someone to blame.

Nancy met Owen at the front door. She looked pale and skinny: the ghost of the woman he knew before all this happened. Her eyes were sunken dark shapes. Her lips were stained from last night's red wine. At least, Owen hoped it was from last night.

'Bad news or no news,' Nancy asked.

'It wasn't her, Nance.'

'I could have told you that and saved you the drive,' she said. 'If she was dead, I would have felt it. You look tired.'

He gave her a weary smile. 'You got any coffee?'

She nodded, and walked back into the house. He followed her in. When Owen lived here, this place had been spotless. Nancy had been obsessively neat. But now it was a mess, and getting messier. As far as Owen could tell, Nancy hadn't been outside since Tracie left. She wanted to stay close to the phone in case someone – Tracie, the police, some deep-voiced kidnapper looking for a ransom – called. That was part of it, anyway.

The other part, Owen guessed, was that this house had become a grim sort of sanctuary. Each room held precious memories and artifacts. Nancy could drift around and visit each one. She could relive moments, over and over. Here Tracie was at thirteen, sitting at the kitchen table, rushing her before-school breakfast and finishing her homework. There she was at seven, lazing in the lounge room on a Friday night watching a video. There she was in the laundry sink, giggling through soap suds, when she was small enough to fit in it. Small enough to fit in the crook of Nancy's arm.

They sat down at the kitchen table and drank stale coffee. It was still early, but already hot. Nancy slung open a window but it didn't do much. For a while, neither of them talked. The refrigerator hummed. The tap dripped. Somewhere in the neighbourhood, someone was mowing their lawn.

'It's like being stuck in a holding pattern, isn't it?' Owen said, when the silence got too much. 'Like circling the tarmac.'

Nancy got up and went to the sink. She emptied her coffee mug and gave it a quick rinse. It was one of the mugs he'd swiped from work, with *ARB Insurance* printed on the side. Nancy then took a bottle of white wine from the fridge, filled the mug, and returned to the table without comment.

'It's a little early, Nance,' Owen said.

She glared at him, and drank.

'The days are long and the nights are longer.' Nancy raised the mug. 'This helps.'

He nodded slowly. He had his own ways of coping.

'You want to hear something creepy?'

'I would *love* to hear something creepy, Owen,' she said. 'You always had a knack for reading the room.'

Owen ignored the sarcasm. 'When I moved out, I started

taking long walks. I've always found it easier to think while moving. It didn't hurt to get out of my depressing little motel room, either. So I walked. And when my legs got sore, I drove. Sometimes I'd drive over here.'

Nancy looked up.

'I'd park across the street,' he said. 'Behind Mike Carson's gum tree so you couldn't see me if you looked out the window.'

'You're right,' she said. 'That is creepy.'

He smiled. 'I just wanted to make sure I was close by. In case something happened. In case you needed me.' He looked up, blinked moisture from his eyes. 'If I had been there that night …'

'But you weren't, Owen,' Nancy said. 'You weren't here.'

'I could be now, Nance.'

'Owen.'

'I could move back into the house. There's no reason either of us has to go through this alone.'

'Please,' she said. 'Just don't.'

'Doesn't it all seem smaller to you, Nancy?' he asked. 'All the problems we had in our marriage before. Now that Tracie's gone, it puts things in perspective. Doesn't it feel that way? If you let me come home, we can shoulder this together. Like the old days.'

She finished her wine and set the mug down on the table.

'Our problems don't seem smaller to me,' she said. 'Owen, there's something I haven't told you.' Pause. Deep breath. 'The night she disappeared, Tracie asked me about what went wrong between us. She asked me point blank if you were seeing someone else. I know we both agreed she didn't need to hear all the gory details, but ...'

'What did you tell her?'

'Tracie asked for the truth,' Nancy said. 'So, I gave it to her.'

4

The first thing Keiran Witter saw when he woke that morning – the first thing he saw *every* morning – was the dark green netting that formed a canopy over the bed.

Keiran's whole room was decked out with military gear. His bedsheets were patterned with camouflage. A *Platoon* movie poster was stuck on the back of his door (the double 'o' in the title was a pair of dog tags, which was just about the coolest thing Keiran had ever seen). There were no glow-stars on his ceiling, but there were glow-tanks and glow-soldiers and glow-bombers. There were *Howling Commandos* and *Battle* comics strewn over his desk and dresser and, hidden in a trunk beneath his bed, all his old G.I. Joe action figures.

He still dragged them out sometimes, late at night, when he knew nobody would catch him. Over the past few months, Keiran had become dimly aware that he had entered a whole new transitional part of his life. Technically, he was too old to play with toys, but not too old that he didn't want to. He was old enough to want to touch a girl, but too young to actually touch one. If he could touch one, it would be Hannah Kehlmann, who sat three rows ahead of him in science and the row behind in maths. Hannah had hair the colour of dead leaves. Now that Keiran thought about it, that made her hair sound dirty, but the shade was, in fact, wonderful. Hannah was wonderful.

He sat up and lifted his pillow. He'd stashed Tracie Reed's missing-person poster beneath it the night before. He took the poster out now and stared at it, then picked up the phone on his bedside table and punched in the number of his best friend, Ricky Neville. He'd got the phone for his birthday that year. It was bright yellow and shaped like a banana.

'Neville residence,' said a singsong voice on the other end of the line.

Ricky's mum. Damn.

'Hi, Mrs Neville,' Keiran said. 'Is Ricky there, please?'

'Is that you, Keiran?'

'Yep.'

'How was your Christmas?'

'Good.'

'Are you enjoying the holidays?'

'Uh-huh.'

'And how are your parents?'

'They're fine, Mrs Neville,' Keiran said.

'Got any big plans for New Year's Eve?'

Jesus Christ. Keiran told Ricky's mother he had no plans, and agreed with her that, yes, it was good beach weather, but, yes, if he went to the beach he'd have to *slip, slop, slap* because of the hole in the ozone layer and, yes, it was kind of funny that they didn't worry about things like ozone layers and acid rain and AIDS when she was Keiran's age. The times, they were a-changing.

Approximately sixty-five years later, she put Ricky on the phone.

'Ricky, dude, you have to do something about your mum,' Keiran said.

'Sorry. She's been lonely ever since my dad started doing shiftwork again.' Then, calling out, he said, 'Yes, Mum, I'm talking about you. Quit bogarting my friends.' Back to Keiran: 'Did you see *Knight Rider* last night?'

Keiran had watched last night's episode of *Knight Rider* and, even though it was a repeat, he'd enjoyed it. But there was no time for that now. 'Can you meet me at the club house?'

'When?'

'Now?'

'My Aunt Miriam is coming over this morning,' Ricky said. 'So, for the love of God, yes, I can meet you. You sound freaked. Is everything all right?'

He looked at the poster. Tracie Reed looked back.

Keiran said, 'No.'

Keiran hurriedly took a leak, brushed his teeth and got dressed. He was on his way downstairs when he heard Marty talking in soft tones. Keiran crept over to his bedroom door. It was open. The blinds were still drawn, but Keiran could make his brother out. Marty was lying on his bed, one hand tucked behind his head, staring at the ceiling, talking on the phone. Marty had got a phone for his birthday too. He'd even got his own phone line.

'Dad told me last night,' Marty was saying. 'Did you know?'

Keiran gave the door a light tap. Marty looked over.

Into the phone, Marty said, 'I have to go, Cass.' Then, to Keiran: 'Morning, dickhead.'

'Hello, arsehole,' Keiran said. 'Who you talking to on the phone so early?'

'None of your beeswax.'

Keiran lingered. 'Looks like you're all packed.'

'Pretty much.'

Keiran felt a genuine and slightly confusing sadness as he scanned the packing boxes around Marty's bed. His big bro was moving out. Part of him was thrilled. With Marty gone, Keiran would get the big room. There was space enough for a double bed in there. But he didn't like to think about how the house might feel after Marty was gone. It made him feel strange and old and something else. Something a grown-up might call a fancy word like nostalgia or melancholy. Keiran just called it feeling shitty.

'I can't believe you're leaving me with them,' Keiran said.

Marty made a strained, defeated face. He might have been feeling shitty too. 'I'm just clearing a path, little dude. You'll thank me one day. What are you doing with that?'

He pointed to the poster in Keiran's hand. Tracie Reed. Keiran rolled it up and shoved it into his back pocket. 'Nothing.'

'There are way better things in this house to wank over, Keiran.'

'Gross. Shut up. Like what?'

'There's a stack of underwear catalogues on top of the fridge,' Marty said.

'See, what am I going to do without you?'

Keiran had promised his dad he wouldn't go into Wild Place, but that's where the club house was. It was a problem, but not a big one. Usually Keiran could step right through the back gate and into the bush. But that wasn't the only way in. This just meant he needed to be a little sneakier.

So he walked to the end of his street, took a left on Novak, then headed up to where the stormwater drain was. It was just after 8am, but everyone got up early in suburbia. People were out mowing lawns, washing cars and watering garden beds, and all of them had great big smiles on their faces.

It made Keiran think of something Sean Fryman told him: *adulthood is like polishing the deck of the* Titanic. What he meant, Keiran thought, was that later, when these people's lawns grew long again, and their cars got dirty, and their flowers got thirsty, they'd do it all over again, until one day, *bam* – the big dirt sandwich!

They didn't see it that way, of course – if they did, they'd be screaming around looking for lifeboats – but Sean did. Sean lived next door to Keiran, and was probably the only actual cool person in Camp Hill. He wasn't dark-sunglasses cool, but *worldly* cool. He was sort of mysterious and a little bit dangerous, like Kiefer Sutherland in *The Lost Boys*.

Sean had taught Keiran a lot. No, *taught* wasn't quite right. Sean had opened Keiran's eyes. For example: the Bible was pretty dumb, when you stopped to think about it. It wasn't just Noah's ark, which was obviously flawed because how the hell would anyone fit two of every animal – *every animal!* – on a boat and, by the way, how did all the freshwater fish survive? But it was the whole Jesus story too. Jesus was God, which meant, as Sean pointed out, that God sent himself down to earth, to sacrifice himself, to himself, to reset a system that he made himself. It made zero sense. Yet all of Keiran's teachers, and most of the adults in his life, talked about Jesus and the Bible as if the whole thing happened. If they were wrong about that, they could be wrong about anything ... or *everything* ...

Halfway up Novak Street, he reached the drain. It was at the end of a narrow laneway that cut between houses. There were steep grassy slopes on either side of the drain. Keiran took the left one, up and over and into the bushland.

Wild Place was summed up in the name: a wild patch of land in the middle of the most un-wild place you could imagine. It wasn't big, exactly, but it was big enough. Any bigger, and it might roll out into the neighbourhood and consume the houses like in *The Blob*.

According to legend, the bushland was home to a killer clown, was the secret burial place of the Beaumont children, and contained a hidden pit filled with venomous snakes. Keiran didn't really believe any of that, but he lived in hope.

The air was hot and sticky outside, but the temperature dropped a few degrees the second Keiran stepped into the trees. They were gum trees mostly, tightly packed and twisted – a typical Australian landscape, to the outside observer, anyway. But in Keiran's mind, they became the muggy jungles of Vietnam.

Keiran liked movies about most wars, but the ones set in Vietnam were the best. He wasn't sure why. It may have been the exotic location or the stealth of the enemy, or it might have been because *Platoon* and *Tour of Duty* and *Rambo: First Blood Part II* were all set there. He knew all the lingo. He called helicopters *birds* and small aeroplanes *bird dogs*. He knew that *AIT* stood for Advanced Infantry Training. As a joke, he'd once called Ricky *4-F*, which was the classification given to those deemed unfit for military service.

As he followed a narrow dirt trail through the trees, he armed himself with Tracie Reed's Missing poster. It was now an M16 rifle, and he was going to need it. He was deep in enemy territory. The rest of his platoon was dead. He was going to have to shoot his way out. But that was fine, because he was a one-man army and he'd set timed charges in the trees and any second now—

'Oh.'

He was at the club house. He'd been so engrossed in his fantasy that he hadn't even noticed until he was standing right in it. It wasn't a building, exactly. It was a small clearing hidden off one of the trails, where a big tree had fallen against an even bigger tree. Keiran had draped an old picnic blanket he'd found in the garage over some of the branches to create a sheltered nook. It shielded them from the cold and wet of winter, and kept them cool on hot days like this one. Last summer, they found a truck tyre in the mouth of the stormwater drain and rolled it all the way over. They'd planned on using it to sit on, but it made a better fire-pit. Although the burning rubber smell took a bit of getting used to.

There was no sign of Ricky yet, so Keiran went over to a knotted hollow in one of the trees. It was their secret hiding place, plugged with the gnome he and Ricky had swiped from Norma Spurr-Smith's house. They'd painted it dark green and put a little red fabric headband around his hat like Rambo. It was supposed to be a conversation-starter for when they brought girls to the club. So far that hadn't happened. He removed the gnome, reached behind it, and took out a waterlogged *Playboy*. Ricky had pinched it from his cousin.

Around fifteen minutes later – Keiran couldn't be sure because he'd left his watch on his bedside table – Ricky arrived. He stumbled into the clearing like some big, lumbering woodland creature, drenched with sweat.

'How are you already *that* sweaty?' Keiran asked.

'I can't help it, dickwad,' Ricky said. 'I have big sweat glands. It just pours out. You know what they say about people with big sweat glands, though, right?'

'What?'

'It correlates to penis size.'

'Nobody says that.'

Ricky dropped onto the grass and crossed his legs. He

was, to use the technical term, *humongous*. His T-shirt could barely contain his torso. He was famous at Camp Hill Christian College for having bigger gazongas than Terry-Ann Colson, whose doctor, if the rumours were to be believed, had suggested reductive surgery.

'So, what's the big emergency?' Ricky asked.

Keiran handed Ricky the rolled-up poster.

Ricky unfurled it, then asked, 'Is this real?'

'Dad brought it home last night.'

'What happened to her?'

'Nobody knows.'

'Holy shit,' Ricky said. 'Do you think someone kidnapped her, or murdered her? Or maybe she's being held in a dungeon someplace? Man, you hear about this stuff happening, but we know her! We actually know her!'

'Look at the date,' said Keiran, pointing.

Ricky read aloud. 'Friday eighth of December 1989. What about it?'

'It was the same night.'

'As what?' Then the penny dropped. 'As our séance?'

Gravely, Keiran nodded.

'Are you sure?'

'I triple-checked,' Keiran said.

Ricky left the poster on the ground and stepped backwards, as if distancing himself from Tracie Reed. 'This is fucking creepy, dude, but it's a coincidence. I mean, it has to be a coincidence, right?'

'What if it isn't?' Keiran said.

'Dude! Don't say that! I didn't bring a spare change of undies.'

'What do we do? It says on the poster that if you have any information about her disappearance then you should tell the cops.'

Ricky paced left, then right, then snatched up the poster and stuffed it into the pocket of his shorts. 'Come on.'

'Where?'

'Sean will know what to do.'

'Don't do anything,' Sean said.

Keiran and Ricky stood nervously in the middle of the room while Sean sat before them in his desk chair, like a king holding court. Sean was dressed in black, like always. His hair, which seemed somehow blacker than his clothes, hung down to his shoulders.

'That's what I told him,' Ricky said, gesturing at Keiran.

'No, you didn't,' Keiran said.

'Well, I *thought* it.'

Sean's bedroom was dark with a capital 'D'. Keiran had only been in there a handful of times, but he'd never seen the curtains open. The only light came from a gooseneck lamp in the corner with a red cut of fabric over the top, and the heat lamp inside his pet snake's terrarium.

Whatever space wasn't stacked with heavy metal records was cluttered with spooky little artifacts: a pickled cane toad in a jar, a screaming face carved from wood, an antique set of pinned butterflies in a frame and, curiously, a passenger-plane emergency booklet. There were candles melted down to their wicks and half-burnt incense sticks. It was pretty much exactly like that old man's shop in *Gremlins*.

In the middle of it all, on the dresser, was an old chess set. The pawns were angels and demons, the kings were God and Satan.

'Hey, Sean,' Keiran said. 'What actually happened that night?'

'You were there,' Sean said.

'No, I mean after.' He swallowed. 'We were worried about you.'

'No, we weren't,' Ricky said.

'Fine,' Keiran told him. '*I* was worried.'

A sinister smile crept over Sean's face. 'Oh, now I get it. You think I had something to do with what happened to Tracie.'

'No, I just thought …' Keiran looked at the demonic little creatures on Sean's chess set. 'What if what we did that night … worked?'

Sean stood slowly. He was Marty's age, but taller and stronger and, somehow, older. He put a hand on Keiran's shoulder. It felt heavy.

'If it worked,' he said. 'Then that's all the more reason to keep it a secret.'

5

Tom woke early and whipped up a quick breakfast: toast, fried eggs, a cup of Nescafé – Connie only liked the instant stuff – and fresh OJ. He was, of course, overcompensating. This time of year never seemed fair. While Connie nine-to-fived at the Camp Hill Savings & Loans, Tom lazed around and did whatever he could to fill his time.

She came downstairs around eight-thirty, in an unflattering dark grey dress that made her look, in a word, *bankish*. When she saw he'd made breakfast she offered up one of her trademark crooked smiles and said, 'My hero.'

'Don't be shy,' he told her. 'I made way too much toast and Keiran was gone before I got up.'

Tom joined her at the table. He'd already eaten but there was always room for more coffee. Morning sunlight spilled in through the window, casting everything in a dazzling yellow.

'Do you ever notice what a struggle it is to get that kid up and ready for school, but when he's on holidays he's up and out at the arse-crack of dawn?'

'*Arse-crack of dawn*,' Connie echoed. 'That's good, Tom. I might steal that one.'

'I heard it from one of the kids at school and have been dying to use it ever since.' He sipped his coffee. 'What do you think Keiran does all day?'

'He's thirteen, Tom. I don't *want* to know what he does all day. Oh, and before I forget, I told Marty we'd help him move on Saturday. He's not taking a lot of stuff but I think we'll still need both cars. And afterwards, I thought you and I could strip naked and try out Bill and Vicky's new hot tub.'

'… Huh?'

'You know, when we were dating, you'd at least pretend to listen.'

'Marty's moving on Saturday. I got it. I'm just thinking about Keiran. Do you really think he'll stay out of Wild Place?'

'Honestly, no. But he's a smart kid. I'm not saying don't worry about him. I'm just saying, worry less.'

'Easier said than done.'

'Uh-huh.' She paused. 'Is everything all right, Tom? You're twitching.'

'I always twitch.'

'You're doing The Owl.'

The Owl was one of Tom's stranger moves: a sudden bulging of the eyes, drawing down of the lips and a flaring of the nostrils. *Tu-whit tu-whoo!*

And here Tom was thinking he was being subtle.

'Must be the coffee,' he said.

From the kitchen window, Tom watched Connie's Toyota Corolla hatchback – known lovingly around the Witter house as Lil' Red – hurtle out of the driveway and onto Keel Street. He got changed out of his pyjamas and into jeans and a crisp white T-shirt, then dug his old backpack out of the sewing room. He filled it with Tracie Reed's posters, a staple gun, some tape and a ham-and-cheese sandwich.

Then he hit the streets.

It was a bright, sun-drenched morning. Keel Street was a postcard. Kids on brand-new bikes blazed along the footpath. Young couples ambled, hand in hand. Big cars filled with camping gear rolled out of Camp Hill. Christmas decorations were still up in most of the houses, but already they were looking limp and forgotten.

Starting on Keel Street, he stopped at every third or fourth telephone pole in the neighbourhood, along with bus shelters and noticeboards. He walked all the way from the overpass to the Esplanade, from the Camp Hill Milk Bar to the Good Shepherd Lutheran Church. His church.

Tom had a complicated relationship with his religion. He worked at a Christian high school and was raised on Jesus and Satan, but he was well aware of the moral hypocrisy of the Bible, not to mention the twisted, and at times nonsensical logic. Despite all that, He always seemed to be there for the big stuff.

He put a poster up on the community board just outside the entrance. It was busy with ads for piano lessons, Christmas messages, a few notices about missing pets, and a handwritten sign declaring: *When you sling mud at others, you're the one who loses ground. Sunday Worship 10am.*

He looked up at the cross and said a quiet prayer.

Each time he put a poster up, he was careful to keep the staple away from Tracie Reed's face. He spent the better part of the morning looking into her dark eyes, feeling stirred by them.

As the sun rose higher, he started to regret leaving the house in jeans instead of shorts. Sweat gathered on his neck and on the backs of his legs. By the time he reached the village he was hot and thirsty, so he ducked into the Safeway to buy a Coke.

Camp Hill Shopping Village was a big square of small-town staples: butcher, baker (no candlestick maker), newsagent, post office, bottle shop, the Borschmanns' pharmacy, and a few little boutique stores selling miscellaneous *stuff* like maps and crystals. He always wondered how places like that sold enough to stay afloat.

There was a busy bus shelter outside the supermarket, used by three different routes. A heavy foot traffic area. He put a poster up at eye level, then parked himself on a bench across the street to drink his Coke and eat his ham-and-cheese.

He watched people gather in the bus stop, waiting for the 11.03am 781 to Frankston. There were two teenagers playing thumb-war, another reading a comic book, and an elderly couple dressed in what you'd see in the window of a Salvation Army shop. None of them looked at the poster. None of them seemed to notice. Were they just too caught up in their day, or did they not see Tracie the way he did?

Feeling inconsequential, he started back, hitting telephone poles and bus stops with the last of the posters. He was walking past a huge two-storey house on Tobey Street when someone called his name. Well, it wasn't *exactly* his name ...

'Twitchy?'

Tom turned. A hefty shirtless man was standing in the driveway, a hose in one hand, a bucket of soapy water in the other. He was part way through cleaning a BMW sporting personalised plates: *STVMCD*.

Steve McDougal.

One of the problems of sticking around your home town was the bullies usually stuck around too. McDougal and two other boys had made Tom's life hell during high school. Tom had made a particularly good target because of his spasms, which he had only begun learning to conceal in later years. He wasn't officially diagnosed until his thirties. If McDougal had known, he might have come up with something more creative than *Twitchy. Tommy Tourette's* sprang to mind.

A familiar brand of anxiety swept over Tom. He tried not to jerk, which only made him jerk more.

'Hi, Steve,' Tom said.

McDougal put the bucket down, turned off the hose, and came up the drive to meet him. 'What are you up to nowadays, Twitchy?'

'Ha. It's Tom. And, you know, not much. Married. Kids. The usual. How about you?'

'Spent some time in Perth. Made a mint. Gave marriage a go, but she turned out to be a bitch-queen from hell. You probably remember her. Amy Matheson.'

Tom did. Amy was the female equivalent of Steve: beautiful, athletic and cruel. That those two had found each other – and lost each other – seemed like proof that there was some sort of cosmic order to the universe.

'Sorry it didn't work out,' Tom said.

'Don't be. She packed on the kay-gees after kid number one, then totally gave up after kid number three. She's nothing like she was in high school. Speaking of high school, I heard a rumour about you. Are you teaching at Camp Hill Christian College?'

Tom nodded. 'Yeah, but it's a little different now. I'm allowed in the teachers' lounge and I hardly ever get detention anymore.'

McDougal didn't laugh. 'Does Miss Woods still work there? Remember those low-cut tops? Wow. I learnt fuck-all in her maths class, but those tits were an education.'

He gestured a chef's kiss.

'She's Mrs Parker now,' Tom pointed out. 'She's on my pub trivia team. And in her fifties.'

'I'd still give 'em a squeeze. Do me a favour and tell her that next time you see her. It'll probably make her day.'

'I'm sure it will.'

'Did you hear what happened to Benny Cotter?'

Benny Cotter was one of McDougal's fellow bullies. It seemed like only yesterday that Benny had snuck up behind Tom in the school canteen, jabbed him in the side with a fork, and then laughed hysterically when Tom dropped his meat pie.

Ah, memories.

There had been three bullies in total. McDougal, Cotter and Adam Bartlett. Tom called them the High School Carnivores. Just not to their faces.

'He's halfway through a six-year sentence,' McDougal said.

'He's in prison?'

'South Hallston Corrections.'

'What'd he do?'

'Got into a fight at some strip joint in Melbourne. The other guy pressed charges because he was basically a pussy and lost.'

'Wow,' Tom said. Then, because he couldn't help himself, added, 'I can't say I'm surprised.'

Dumb.

McDougal frowned. 'What do you mean by that?'

Tom had just stepped over a line he'd assumed was long gone. They were adults now, weren't they?

'Nothing,' he said.

'Nothing?' McDougal asked.

'Forget it.'

'Can't,' he said. 'I have a very good memory.'

'Ben had a temper. That's all I meant. I once saw him throw a chair at a teacher for asking for his homework.'

'So you think he deserves to be in prison.'

'I don't know the circumstances.' Tom took a step back. 'Maybe. I don't know. Probably not.'

McDougal loomed over him. The muscles in his neck were tight. His arms were slung out wide, like he was carrying invisible suitcases.

Tom's eyes bulged. His nostrils flared. His lips drew downwards, as if unseen hands were working him.

Tu-whit tu-whoo, he thought.

'Jesus,' said Steve, with a sinister smile. 'Did you just swallow a fly, or are you still this much of a freak?'

Tom's high school days had left a deep, itchy scar. McDougal had just picked at it. Underneath, all the old shame and insecurity and fear were waiting. There was rage there too: hot and raw. But the fear was stronger. It always had been. If it weren't, maybe Tom would have done something about the High School Carnivores. Maybe he wouldn't have backed down.

But he did. Then, and now.

'I'm sorry, Steve,' he said, in a pitiful little voice. 'Benny's a good guy.'

Pathetic.

'See ya, Twitchy.'

'Yeah,' Tom said. 'See ya.'

He walked on, feeling small.

When Tom got home, he poured himself a tall glass of water and drank the whole thing in four big gulps. He felt shaky and strange after his run-in with Steve, like he'd just avoided a traffic accident.

But he'd hung the posters. Someone might see Tracie's face and remember something. It might lead to a break in the case. She might come home safe and sound. She might not. The chances of finding a missing child alive decrease dramatically after twenty-four hours. He read that somewhere. Tracie had been gone for weeks.

Now what?

Tom knew *what*, of course. Connie's list.

He dug out his brand-new toolbox. It was a Christmas gift from Connie. Either she'd vastly overestimated his handyman skills or this was some sort of aspirational present. A spin on the cliché: dress for the job you want, not the one you have. *Buy gifts for the man you want, not the one you have.*

He dragged it into the upstairs bathroom. The hot tap was the one with the leak. He fished around for the adjustable spanner, then got to work unscrewing the handle. He'd never actually fixed a leaking tap before but he hoped the problem would be obvious when he took the thing apart, like a big STOP LEAK switch that had been thrown in the wrong direction.

While he worked, he gazed out the window above the tub. The community forest that foamed along the back fence was still and deep. Some days, the trees there looked hemmed in by the neighbourhood. Other days, like today, it seemed like they were bursting outward, forcing back the fences and the lawns and the houses to make way.

A lot of kids Tracie's age used Wild Place as a shortcut. There was a concrete laneway on Novak Street, where the 781 bus stopped. Cutting through the bush rather than walking all the way around would shave off precious minutes. If Tracie had run away, there was a good chance she'd gone that way. If someone snatched her, they'd probably have used the bushland to their advantage too. Had that place been properly searched?

Focus.

He turned his attention back to the tap, but he couldn't shake Tracie from his mind.

Tom was a naturally restless person. Connie had the incredible ability to just *be*. The kids did, too, from what he could tell. But Tom's mind was always buzzing. Maybe Keiran was right. Maybe he needed to see a professional. Or maybe he was just a realist. After all, life and happiness – all that good stuff – didn't stick around forever. Everything was temporary. Tom was always watching for the canary in the coalmine.

Then again, wasn't that what fathers were supposed to do?

He checked his watch. The day was still young. It wouldn't hurt to go and take a look around Wild Place. He'd be back in time to fix the tap before Connie got home. Maybe he'd find a clue. Maybe he'd find a body.

6

Tom unlatched the back gate and let it swing open. There was a shallow embankment on the other side. At the base was a narrow concrete culvert. During the colder months the channel was often full. Today it carried a trickle of brown water. Tom took a cursory look for snakes in the long grass on the other side, then stepped over it.

There were a handful of brown snake sightings in Wild Place each year and last summer Carlo Freeman swore he saw a tiger (snake, that is). Maybe that was what happened to Tracie. She might have been strolling through Wild Place and crossed paths with a brown or a red-bellied black, or Carlo Freeman's tiger snake. If she'd been bitten, she might have passed out and died before she had the chance to call for help. Tom pictured her small body pitching forward, disappearing into a bush, and imagined suns rising and setting, over and over.

At the top of the embankment, Tom found one of many trails that wound beneath the trees. The trails were narrow, intersecting in places, leading under low-hanging branches and over fallen trees. He chose one and followed it. It was cool away from the sun, beneath the canopy of trees. Wild Place was loud with the sound of insects, birds and frogs.

Tom kept an eye out for snakes and other hazards as he walked. But aside from a torn-up old porno mag, a truck tyre turned fire-pit, and some sort of lean-to fort made from dead branches and a picnic blanket, he found nothing unusual.

Wild Place was an internal community forest, officially known as Lot C. Enclosed by private residences, it gave homeowners access to a huge, mostly private swatch of nature. A big wild backyard for kids to explore and play in. It used to be one of several in Camp Hill. Now it was the only one left. The rest had been gutted and developed. The same thing would happen to this place eventually, Tom knew.

Everything is temporary.

As he walked, he thought about Tracie, which gave him a sharp pang of guilt. He was ashamed of how little he actually knew about her. He pictured her now: a prettyish but not too pretty girl, dressed in the blah colours of the Camp Hill Christian College uniform, bathed in dusty afternoon light falling in through his classroom window. How often would he have thought of her if she hadn't disappeared? How long before the memory faded?

The trail led across the community forest, to the backs of the houses on Bright Street. The embankment on this side was steeper. From the crest, Tom could see clear into all the homes. Into bedrooms and bathrooms and kitchens and lounges. From the ridge he could see a set of twins watching cartoons, a blonde woman vacuuming up the pine needles around her Christmas tree, a middle-aged man taking a nap in nothing but a sleeping mask and a pair of Y-fronts.

It was too easy to see into these people's lives like this. At night, under the cover of darkness, with the houses lit from the inside, it would be even easier. When he and Connie had bought their place on Keel Street, the idea of backing right onto a nature reserve had been appealing. It made the backyard feel private and tranquil. Now, all Tom could think about was what was hiding in the bush.

Up ahead, there was a second trail that would take him back through the guts of Wild Place and home again. So far, he'd found no clues, and no body, which probably wasn't a bad—

'Shit!'

Tom's left foot landed against something hard. He pitched forward, arms pinwheeling for balance, and landed on his knees in the soft grass. He turned back. It was an old coffee can, half-filled with nicotine-stained water and cigarette butts. He'd toppled the can when he kicked it, sending the butts skimming over the embankment and into the concrete channel below, like little brown boats on churning rapids. There were dozens of them, all smoked down to the filter.

Tom stood over them. They were all the same brand. Starling Red. He could tell because each filter had a tiny pink *S* on the side. Whoever smoked them spent a lot of time in this spot. He looked up. He was standing outside a large two-storey brick cube. From his vantage point high on the ridge, he had a clear and direct view into a bedroom.

It was a generous-sized room: neat and tidy. Above the bed was a big – and by the look of it, homemade – screen-print of Jack Kerouac. Most of the space was taken up by a large, floor-to-ceiling bookcase, packed tight. This had to be Tracie's room. She was what Steve McDougal might refer to as a book-geek. What Steve didn't know was that *book-geek* was a term of endearment to book-geeks. Tom knew from personal experience.

A dry branch snapped somewhere behind him. He turned. A small woman was standing on the trail, watching him. She was wearing an oversized knitted cardigan, which was a strange choice considering the heat.

'Mr Witter,' the woman said.

'I'm sorry, have we met?'

'Once. At a parent–teacher interview.'

Tom looked closer. The dark hair and deep-set eyes were familiar. She looked like an older, worn-down version of Tracie. 'You're Tracie's mum.'

'Yes,' she said. 'Now, would you mind telling me why you're lurking in the bushes behind my house?'

'I wouldn't call it lurking.'

'But you know how it looks.'

He did. He took a breath. He could tell her he was out taking a walk and move on, but he opted for honesty. 'I heard about Tracie. I'm out here trying to help.'

'Why?'

It was a good question. The short answer was: 'I have kids too.'

Nancy looked hard at him, then softened. 'Would you like to come inside, Mr Witter?'

'Call me Tom,' he said.

Nancy Reed's house was painted in different shades of green. All the blinds were drawn and most of the lights were off, so it took Tom's eyes a few seconds to adjust. When they did, he saw a cluttered and chaotic family home: dirty footprints up the hall, a stack of unopened mail on the side table, a sink full of dirty dishes.

'Watch your step,' Nancy said.

She gestured to a small mound of broken glass on the floor. The shards had been swept together and left there to gather dust, like a tiny crime scene. On the wall above the pile was an empty picture hook. Tom thought about asking what happened, but it seemed too personal a question somehow.

Nancy showed him to a wingback armchair in the living room, then stepped into the adjoining kitchen to boil the kettle. She moved like a zombie. Her eyes were swollen and red. Her lips were chapped and dry. Tom also noticed – while trying to not notice – that she wasn't wearing a bra.

'You used to have a beard, didn't you?' Nancy said.

'My wife made me shave it,' Tom said. 'She said it made me look pretentious.'

Nancy smiled. It was a sad, ghostly thing. 'Tracie said you were funny. She liked you. You were one of her favourite teachers. You and what's-her-name, the art lady.'

'Miss Millership.'

'Right.'

'That's always nice to hear.'

'You noticed her,' Nancy said. 'I think that's why. That might sound silly, but not a lot of the other people in her life did.'

Tom looked awkwardly down at his fingers, then noticed a small shrine to Tracie on the coffee table: a ring of dried flowers encircling a framed photograph. It was a picture of Tracie, taken when she was eleven or twelve. She was at a beach somewhere, standing knee-deep in water, grinning at the camera, pointing at a brightly coloured starfish on a rock. There was something helpless and hopeless about the photo. Tom felt a heavy sadness roll in and settle on his shoulders.

Beside the photo was the world's ugliest rag doll, and a Walkman sealed in a clear plastic bag. Printed on the side of the Walkman was *TCM-100B*.

'I found that in Wild Place after she went missing,' Nancy said. 'I bagged it because I thought they might want to check it for fingerprints, but they didn't bother. Instead, they sent a couple of constables to pick through the bushes near where it was. They were out there for sixteen minutes. I timed them. *Sixteen minutes.*'

Tom picked up the Walkman and, on instinct, checked the tape inside. Joni Mitchell's *Shadows and Light*.

'It's from my collection,' Nancy said over his shoulder. 'I used to love that album. Now I'm not sure I'll ever be able to play it again without thinking about the night she was taken.'

Taken?

'You want tea?' she asked.

Tom nodded. While Nancy went to make it, he thought about the last time he spoke to Tracie.

'Hey, Mr Witter, got a sec?'

It was November: Tracie Reed's last day of high school. The year twelvers left a little earlier than the rest of the students to prep for exams. Tom had hung back after sixth period to get a head start on report-writing. He was sitting at a desk in an empty classroom, trying to concentrate, when she knocked gently on the door.

'It's after four,' he said. 'What are you still doing here?'

'I saw your Sigma in the car park and wanted to come and say goodbye,' she said.

The Camp Hill Christian College colours were a drab grey and maroon, but Tracie wore them well.

'Are you all set for uni next year?' he asked.

Softly, almost begrudgingly, Tracie said, 'Yep. Journalism.'

'You don't sound too excited about it.'

'I am. I mean, I've always known that's what I want to do, but, I don't know. It's kind of scary, too. Leaving high school is, like, intense, isn't it?'

Tom put down his pen. 'What do you mean?'

'I spent the last six years wanting to get out of this place, but now that I'm finally going, I don't want to leave.'

Tom couldn't relate. On his last school day, he'd run home

without looking back. He thought of those years a lot, but never with nostalgia.

'Everyone has to leave the pond,' he said. 'Everything is temporary.'

'*Everything is temporary*,' Tracie repeated. 'That's, like, the most depressing thing I've ever heard, Mr Witter.'

He laughed. 'You can probably start calling me Tom, now.'

She half-smiled.

'Okay, *Tom*,' she said. 'That feels weird.'

Shuffling on the spot, she started again. 'I really enjoyed your class,' she said. '*Of Mice and Men* is, like, one of the best books I ever read. Although I still can't think about Lennie without crying. Oh, I finally got a chance to read *Slaughterhouse-Five*. I liked it. At least, I think I did. I've never read anything like it. That whole part where he's in an alien zoo with the porn star was, like: *what?*'

Tom laughed.

A week earlier, at the end of their last official class, Tracie had asked Tom for reading recommendations. The last kid to ask their teacher for reading recommendations was Tom, at Tracie's age.

'What did you think about *Nine Stories*?' he asked now. '*Catcher in the Rye* is Salinger's most famous work but, in my opinion, *Nine Stories* is just as profound.'

She nodded. 'That first story, "A Perfect Day for Bananafish", is a bit of a downer. That guy has, like, a great day – *a perfect day* – and then goes back to his hotel room and commits suicide.'

'Pretty messed up, right?'

'Sure, but I'm not sure I get it. Why does Seymour kill himself in the end?'

'Read it again in a decade or so,' Tom told her. 'You'll figure it out.'

When Nancy returned with the tea, Tom left the memory abruptly, like stepping out of a warm house and into the howling wind.

'What happened to her?' he asked.

Nancy looked at the photo on the coffee table and began to talk. Her tone was flat and even. There was no emotion in her voice. Tom got the sense she'd been over this story countless times already, both out loud and in her head. 'She came home late the night before. She'd been at the movies and was meant to be having a sleepover with a friend of hers, Cassie Clarke. You might know her from school.'

'She's not in any of my classes, but I know who she is,' he said.

'Tracie got home around eleven. She was normal. Or, I don't know, maybe she wasn't. When something like this happens, everything seems like a red flag, looking back. Every detail that might otherwise seem trivial feels ... significant.'

'Like what?'

'She'd dyed her hair blonde, for one thing. Bleached it within an inch of its life.' Nancy must have seen the so-what expression on Tom's face, because she added, 'You don't have daughters, do you?'

'Two boys,' Tom said.

'When a girl – well, any woman, really – does something big and bold and dramatic with their hair, there's usually something deeper going on. Like a break-up.'

'Do you think that's what happened to Tracie?'

She shrugged. 'I don't know what happened to her, Mr Witter. All I know is when I woke up the next morning, she was gone.' She viciously chewed on the nail of her pinkie. 'I called Cassie, Tracie's dad, her grandparents, anyone I could think of. Nobody had seen her. Then I called the police, and from there everything just sort of spiralled.'

She picked up the rag doll and held it to her nose.

'The cops think she ran away,' she said. 'Tracie's father and I are in the middle of a divorce. The police think that's reason enough for her to leave, but that's exactly how I know she wouldn't. Tracie knew I needed her. She knew I wouldn't survive without her. Someone took her, Mr Witter. I'm sure of it.'

Tom felt a chill.

'Who would do something like that?'

She reached into the pocket of her cardigan, pulled out a closed fist, then opened it. On her palm was a small pendant necklace.

'I found this under Tracie's pillow,' she said. 'It isn't hers. Tracie has a nickel allergy. Cheap jewellery like this gives her dermatitis. Itching, swelling, dry skin. I think it's a clue. She might have left it to send me a message, or it might be a calling card. Killers and kidnappers do that, you know. They leave something behind. They get off on it.'

Tom pictured a drowning woman, reaching for anything she could to keep from slipping under. It broke his heart a little.

'Did you tell the police about this?' he asked.

'Of course. The detective in charge, he pretended to listen, but I could tell he was just waiting for me to get off the phone.'

She handed the pendant to Tom. He turned it over in his hands. At the end of a simple silver chain, a five-pointed star within a circle.

'Do you know what that symbol is?' Nancy asked.

'No. But it looks familiar.'

'It's a pentagram.' She returned it to her pocket. 'A pentagram is to Satanists what the crucifix is to Christians.'

Tom frowned. 'Satanists? You mean, like, devil-worshippers?'

'I know how it sounds,' she said. 'You probably think I should be wearing a tinfoil hat. But in the weeks before she disappeared, someone was following my daughter.'

'What makes you say that?'

'Tracie told me. Well, she tried to. That night, at the movies, she felt as if someone was watching her. I told her she was imagining things. Cassie thought the same thing. She was with Tracie and said she didn't notice anything, but I should have believed Tracie. There are a lot of bad men in the world and, from my experience, most of them crave the same thing.'

She got up and went to the window. She drew the curtain back and blinked against the late morning sun. 'When a girl looks like my Tracie, it makes her a target. To perverts, Satanists, sex predators.' She paused. Tightened. Clasped her hands together. 'High school teachers.'

'... Excuse me?'

Still clasping the rag doll, she said, 'For the record, you seem like a nice enough guy, Mr Witter. But parent to parent, I'm sure you understand why I called them.'

Tom heard a car pull up outside. Nancy had been stalling him.

'Called who?' he asked.

7

Detective Sharon Guffey climbed one flight of rickety metal stairs, then she climbed another. The address she'd been given was on the third storey of a block of flats in Frankston. The climb took it out of her. She blamed the heat, but it might have been those extra kilos she put on over Christmas.

She reached the third floor and crossed a cramped space with a shared washing machine and dryer. On the other side, at the end of a short passage, was Graham Engstrom's flat. Flies buzzed by the front door. She cupped her hands against a dirty window and looked in. It was a one-bedroom place, cluttered with dirty dishes, empty bottles and an extravagant glass bong.

There were two men inside, both in their twenties, both shirtless. One was watching the other play a video game. Sharon leaned closer to the glass to get a better look at the gaming console. It was a brand-new Sega Master System. This was going to be easier than she thought.

She stepped back from the window, straightened herself to her full, imposing height, then knocked on the door. One of the men answered. He was skinny, with sharp collarbones and a sunburnt chest. He stank of pot. He craned his neck to look up at her and asked, 'What?'

'Are you Graham Engstrom?'

'Nup.'

'Is Graham Engstrom here?'

'Yep.'

Sharon sighed. 'Will you get him for me, please.'

The man offered a sleazy little smile, then called over his shoulder, 'It's for you.'

He padded back into the flat as the second man paused his game and came out to meet her. Engstrom was big. He had the wide, threatening presence of one of those obnoxious bull bars you saw on the front of four-wheel drives. His eyes were bloodshot. He was stoned.

'Graham Engstrom?'

He nodded. 'Who are you?'

'Detective Guffey, with the Frankston Police.' She showed her badge. 'There was a break-in on Christmas morning in one of the flats downstairs. A gaming console was stolen. A Sega Master System. Do you know anything about that?'

'Wasn't me,' Engstrom said.

'You were seen climbing out of a window with the console under your arm, Mr Engstrom.'

The guy didn't break a sweat. 'My word against theirs.'

'You were seen by several of your neighbours,' Sharon told him. 'A total of seven people. So it's your word against *theirs*. I should also tell you I can actually see the Sega right there.

You're making my job very easy, Mr Engstrom.'

'That's mine.'

'Got a receipt?'

'It was a gift.'

'So you wouldn't mind making a formal statement at the station?' She didn't wait for an answer. 'Put some clothes on, mate. I'll give you a ride.'

Engstrom didn't budge.

'Is it just you here?' he asked.

It went against procedure to show up at something like this by herself. Sharon was supposed to have waited for a couple of junior constables to meet her outside, but it was too hot to wait.

Thus: 'I'm here alone.'

Engstrom and Sharon were close to the same height, but he was carrying a lot more weight. He took a short step forward.

'Do you think you can drag me out of here by yourself?'

'I was hoping you'd walk.' Sharon held her ground. 'But the answer's yes. If I have to.'

His lips tightened. His jaw clenched. 'Is it really worth it, for a fucking video game?'

'Honestly,' Sharon said. 'Probably not.'

Engstrom raised a big, bright, shit-eating grin.

'That's what I thought,' he said.

He looked her in the eyes and scratched his balls.

Sharon grabbed him by the ear and took him to the ground.

The Frankston Police Station was layered with different shades of brown. The exterior, waiting room, chairs, walls, even the mysterious wet stains on the ceiling. Sharon was sure each shade had a name: walnut, coffee, cinnamon, tortilla, brunette. Shit. Somehow — and this was impossible — it even smelled brown.

It had AC, technically, but it was either broken or useless. Even the short walk from the front door to her desk was enough to raise a sweat on Sharon's brow. The good news was, there was a bottle of Johnnie Walker waiting there, with a little red ribbon around the neck. There was a card attached that read, *Merry Xmas: Dad. Dad* had been crossed out and in its place was *Guffey*.

'In the interest of full transparency, that's a bribe.'

It was Detective James Rambaldini. He was sitting a few desks over, dressed in his trademark mustard-coloured short-sleeved shirt and tie set that never fitted quite right. Rambaldini went by Rambi, Rambo, Jimbo and Rambles, but Sharon kept things simple.

'What do you want, Jim?'

Jim got up and wandered over. With his hands in his pockets and his gut pushed out, he rolled back on the balls of his feet and said, 'I need a favour.'

'Again.'

'It's a small one.'

'Okay.'

'But it might turn into a big one.'

'Jim. Bandaid. Off.'

'Right,' he said. 'I'm heading up north for five days with the family.'

'Don't rub it in.'

'Would you babysit one of my cases while I'm gone?'

'Which one?'

'A missing girl from Camp Hill. Tracie Reed.'

Sharon sat down and asked, 'The runaway?'

Jim nodded, then went on rocking on the balls of his feet. 'To be honest, a pair of fresh eyes might help.'

'Has something changed?' Sharon asked.

'No. I'm just sick of looking her parents in the eye and telling them that. I need a second opinion. Just in case. Do you mind?'

'I do mind, actually.' Sharon looked at the Scotch. 'But you know I can't say no to Mr Walker. Where's the file?'

He pointed. It was under the bottle. Jim ambled back to his desk. Sharon started to read.

Tracie Frances Reed, seventeen years old, had disappeared from her home on Bright Street, Camp Hill, on Friday 8 December 1989. Sharon had gone to school in Camp Hill. Her memories of the place were, at best, mixed. Aside from the throng of summer holidays, it was a quaint, sleepy little suburb, too small and too safe for its own cop shop, which is why the case came to them. Camp Hill was a short drive from Frankston, but it may as well have been another country.

Based on statements made by her parents, Tracie was a bright, quiet and well-adjusted young woman (whatever that meant). She didn't play any team sports, but liked swimming and running. She did well in school, had no criminal record, and no boyfriend.

She probably shat jellybeans too, Sharon thought.

Teenage girls were locked boxes and you could never count on Mum and Dad to have the key. Sharon flicked ahead in the report. Tracie had no brothers or sisters, but she did have a best friend: Cassie Clarke. According to Cassie, Tracie was kind and caring and the bestest best friend a girl could ever have, blah-blah-blah, but she was also prone to exaggeration. She liked attention. She'd even talked to Cassie about running away in the past.

Interesting. Maybe. She kept reading.

On the night in question, there was no evidence of foul play or a break-in, and zero signs of struggle. The doors were locked. Tracie's room was left neat and tidy. However, certain items were missing – some clothes, a backpack, a little cash – all consistent with a runaway.

Still, three weeks was a long time. Jim had checked hospitals and homeless shelters, and faxed Tracie's picture to just about every station in the state. Her parents had even gone out to local neighbourhood watch groups for help. So far, nothing. Vanishing without a trace was hard to do. Without help.

Sharon turned her attention back to the parents. The mum was a housewife who liked a drink. From the look of Jim's reports, she'd called nearly every day since Tracie disappeared. Last week, she had wanted a team of forensics sent out to fingerprint an old Walkman she claimed to have found in the bushland behind her house. A couple days before that, she was sure she'd found a mysterious boot print on a neighbour's garden bed. The week before that it was a list of licence plate numbers of suspicious cars she'd seen in the area. The week before that, it was about a mysterious necklace she'd found in her daughter's room that might be, according to her, linked to Satanism. Jim had drawn little red horns and a forked tail around the word *Satanism*.

The dad was a claims investigator for an insurance company, which was probably about as thrilling as it sounded. They were in the middle of a divorce. That meant a lot of anger, heightened tensions, emotions running hot. Not a great environment for a kid. Sharon could see why a teenage girl might want to escape all that.

There were several Polaroid photos in the file. Sharon set them down on her desk. One showed the back gate, which gave onto a nature reserve. Locals called it Wild Place. The gate was locked and there was no sign of tampering. There was another shot of the back door, and two of Tracie's bedroom window, inside and out. The window was open an inch or two, but that didn't mean much. It had been a hot summer.

Another photo showed Tracie's room. Sharon stared at that one for a while. There was a tall bookshelf crammed with literature and a screen-print of some guy she didn't recognise. Her wardrobe doors were wide-open. Sharon noted the empty coathangers. Just two. Below a packed space of dresses and jackets, to the left of a cassette tower, was a bright pink gym bag.

That was curious.

According to the mother – *what was her name again? Uh, here, Nancy* – Tracie didn't take much: a couple of pairs of underwear, two or three T-shirts, some spare cash and whatever clothes she was wearing. She had shoved it all into her school backpack when she could have used the roomier gym bag. That said one of two things to Sharon. Either she left in a hurry and didn't have time to stop and think about what to bring, or she wasn't planning on staying away this long.

Or maybe Sharon was just reaching. Jim had asked her for fresh eyes but maybe he didn't need them. Maybe Tracie ran away. End of story. Full stop. Case—

'Hey, Shaz?'

It was Constable Daniel Bradley-Shore from the front desk, a bulky twenty-something with a flat-top so perfectly square you might mistake him for a Lego man.

'I've warned you not to call me that, Danny,' Sharon said. 'You know I'm armed, right?'

'Have you seen Rambles?' he asked.

Jim's desk was empty.

'He was here a second ago,' Sharon said. 'What do you need?'

'It's about that missing girl.'

'What about her?'

'Her mum called triple zero,' he said. 'Something about a prowler.'

Twenty minutes later, Sharon pulled up outside a too-big suburban home in a street full of them.

A police car was already parked in the Reeds' driveway – Sharon had sent a couple of uniformed officers ahead of her – and it had drawn an audience. Neighbours watched from windows and doorways, then shrank back inside when Sharon looked at them, like shiny little cockroaches scuttling away from the light.

The front door was open. A short woman stood just inside, arms crossed. She stared at Sharon with narrow eyes. 'Where's Detective Rambaldini?'

'He's unavailable,' Sharon said. 'I'm his colleague, Detective Guffey. Are you Nancy?'

'I caught him lurking behind the house,' she said.

'Slow down. Who are you talking about, Mrs Reed?'

'The prowler. He was in Wild Place. Watching. Staring in through Tracie's bedroom.'

'This *prowler* ...' Sharon fought the urge to put air quotes around the word. 'Did you get a good look at him?'

'Well, yeah, of course. He's in my living room.'

'He's here?'

'I didn't want him to get away, so after I called you lot, I invited him for tea and kept him busy.' Nancy's face turned red.

'You invited a prowler in for a cuppa,' Sharon said. 'That's not something we'd generally recommend, Mrs Reed.'

Sharon looked over Nancy Reed's shoulder and into the house. A middle-aged man was in her living room. He was red-faced, pacing and agitated, but not bad-looking. She caught herself. Had it really come to this? Was her dating life so desperate that she'd stooped to checking out perps at work?

The two uniforms were trying to calm the guy down. His eyes popped open and shut – some sort of facial tic – and that's when Sharon saw it.

'Tom?'

8

It took Tom a moment to get his head around it. There was so much going on: two police officers telling him to calm down, rising nausea in his stomach, images of arrest and interrogation and false imprisonment playing on a flickering loop in his head.

The first officer, a youngish guy with wide eyes and a stubbly chin, put one hand out and the other on his firearm. 'Remain where you are, sir.'

Tom hadn't even realised he was pacing. He planted his feet on the carpet and took a deep breath. He fought the compulsion to stretch and contract his neck. He was searching for the right words to explain himself when the strikingly tall woman strode in. He looked at the gun on her hip. Then, finally, he looked at her face.

'Sharon?'

The towering woman's expression turned cold. 'Let's stick with *Detective Guffey* for now.'

Ouch.

'You two know each other?' Nancy asked.

'We went to high school together,' Sharon said.

There was, of course, a lot more to it than that. Sharon had been the closest thing Tom had had to a girlfriend when they went to Camp Hill Christian together.

He'd heard things about her over the years. He knew she was a cop. That the daughter of a criminal had joined the police force didn't surprise him one bit. Sharon had always worked to define herself in opposition to her parents. All kids did that, he guessed. But Sharon in particular had always had a knack for rising above.

Tom had wondered what it might be like to run into her, but never imagined it would happen like this.

Sharon Guffey. Wow. She looked great. Her eyes had taken on a wise, worldly sort of look but were the same pale blue planets he used to stare into. Age had hardened her soft edges, but she'd leaned into the greys and wrinkles, rather than away from them. It made her look beautifully confident.

'This is a misunderstanding,' he stammered. 'I can explain everything.'

'You'll get the opportunity to do that, Mr Witter. But first you and I are going to take a ride.'

Mr Witter?

A ride?

She led him outside.

When they reached her car – a black four-wheel drive – Sharon ushered him into the back seat, then got behind the wheel.

'Is this really necessary, Sharon?' He caught himself. '*Detective?* I'll answer your questions, but do we really need to do it at the police station?'

A thin smile crept onto her face. She lowered her voice. 'You can drop the *detective* thing now. That was for Mrs Reed. And we're not going to the police station, you dope. I'm driving you home.'

The drumbeat in his chest slowed.

'... Really?'

After turning off Bright Street, Sharon pulled over. Tom wiped his clammy hands on his jeans, then joined her up front. He told her where he lived, and they rolled slowly through the neighbourhood with the windows wound down.

'So, catch me up,' Sharon said. 'Married? Kids?'

'Yes, and yes,' Tom said. 'Two boys.'

'Wow. It's hard to imagine you with kids. I still think of you as that skinny little kid back at Camp Hill Christian.'

'What about you?'

'What *about* me?'

'Married? Kids?'

'No kids. I tried the marriage thing for a while but it didn't take.' She took her eyes off the road to look at him. 'It's good to see you, Tom. A head-spin, but a good one. You know, the whole reason I went to our twenty-year reunion was because I thought you might be there.'

Tom felt his cheeks flush. 'The whole reason I didn't go was because I assumed you wouldn't. Well, that, and I was worried Steve McDougal might give me a royal flush for old time's sake.'

'I could have arrested him.'

'I'd like to see that.'

'So, Tom, why the hell were you sneaking around a missing girl's house?'

Tom shook his head. 'Tracie was in my English lit class.'

'You're a teacher?'

'Yep.'

'Where do you teach?'

'You'll laugh.'

'Not Camp Hill Christian.'

'Guilty.'

She laughed.

'Told you,' Tom said. 'When Tracie went missing, I don't know. I guess I just wanted to help. Wild Place seemed like a good place to look. I didn't mean to frighten the mother. How's the investigation going?'

'There's not a whole lot to investigate,' Sharon said. 'She ran away from home. Her parents are getting divorced. That can be hard on a kid. Tracie will come home when she gets desperate enough.' Sharon hesitated. 'If she's still alive.'

'You think she could be dead?'

'The most common reason teenage girls run away from home is suicidal thoughts. You knew her. Did she seem like the type?'

'I don't know,' Tom said. 'How well can you ever know a teenager?' He trailed his arm out the window. The air was still and dry. The neighbourhood was quiet. 'So you don't think she was abducted by devil-worshippers?'

Sharon laughed. 'So Nancy showed you the necklace.'

'She did.'

'You have to give her a break for jumping at shadows,' Sharon said. 'She's living every parent's worst nightmare. Believe it or not, sometimes it's easier for someone to think their kid was taken, when the alternative is that they chose to leave. But there were empty coathangers in Tracie's wardrobe, a missing backpack, and she'd taken a bit of cash. All signs of a girl who couldn't hack it at home anymore. No signs point to Satan.'

Tom couldn't help but smile. Sharon had always been good at breaking balls. 'I'm just saying, some of these kids are into creepy things. Last year, someone left a pig's head outside the teachers' lounge.'

'Jesus.'

'I know. It had an inverted cross carved into the forehead.'

'Did you call the cops?'

'We did, but there wasn't much that could be done,' Tom said. 'Some of Camp Hill Christian's less academic students probably got the head from a butcher shop as part of muck-up day. It's left here.'

They turned onto Keel Street. Irene Borschmann was out walking her dogs again. She turned and watched Sharon's car roll by, waving before she even knew who was inside. Further up, Bill Davis was on his front lawn, dressed in a pair of loud Bermuda shorts and nothing else, watering his garden and smoking a cigarette.

Tom directed her to his house. Sharon pulled up outside but

left the engine running.

'Look at this place,' she said. 'Your own little patch of suburbia.'

'Embarrassing, right?'

'Not embarrassing. Surprising.' She smiled at him. 'Give me a call sometime, if you feel like taking a trip down memory lane.'

Heat rose someplace inside, and Tom got that warm, flirtatious, *what-if* feeling in his belly that married men get sometimes. Married women too, probably.

'How about dinner tonight, around seven?' he asked. 'You can meet my family. Then you'll know I'm not making them up. Unless you're busy?'

'I'll bring the wine,' she said.

He heard voices in the house. Keiran was home, along with his best friend Ricky, by the sound of it. There was something about their whispered, urgent tones that got Tom's parental antennae buzzing. It sounded like they were up to something.

Tom padded up the stairs to Keiran's door. He took hold of the handle and paused. He sniffed the air. It was thick with the sweet, beefy smell of male puberty. But there was something else too.

Smoke?

Tom threw open the door and charged into the room. Keiran and Ricky were crouched beneath the open window, a steel bucket between them, with a small fire inside.

'What the hell are you two doing?'

'Oh, hi, Mr Witter,' Ricky said. 'We didn't think you were home.'

Ricky was a big-boned boy from a line of big-boned adults. He was doing his best to look normal, but his cheeks were bright red and his eyes were like dinner plates.

'Ever hear of knocking?' Keiran snapped.

'Don't even,' Tom said. 'What are you burning?'

Keiran tried to shield the bucket with his arms but it was no use. Tom took three big strides across the room, picked up the bucket, and took it quickly across the hall into the bathtub. He doused it with cold water. It sizzled and fizzed. Smoke billowed out and got caught in the bathroom fan.

Wafting the smoke away with one hand, Tom looked inside. There were flecks of torn and charred black card. Letters and numbers were printed on it. Tom looked closer. He saw parts of the words *yes* and *no*. Then, in big gold letters, Tom saw the word, *Ouija*.

It was a spirit board.

'What have you boys been doing?' Tom asked.

Keiran stood in the doorway, shoulders hunched, staring at his feet. 'I didn't think you'd be home.'

'It bothers me that you're not answering the question.'

Keiran looked at Ricky. Ricky shook his head.

'Go home, Ricky,' Tom said.

He started off.

'And Ricky.'

'Yeah?'

'Don't cut through Wild Place on your way home. Take the long way.'

He nodded, and was gone.

Tom sat down on the lip of the tub.

'Don't make that face, Dad,' Keiran said.

'What face?'

'The face you make when you're getting ready to be angry.'

Tom exhaled.

'Fine,' Keiran said. 'We were messing around with the board,' he said. 'Then something sort of freaky happened. Or maybe it didn't happen. I don't know. It might be nothing. It probably *is* nothing. But we wanted to be sure. Just in case. We just wanted to get rid of it.'

'Start from the beginning,' Tom said.

Keiran closed the lid of the toilet seat and sat down. 'You're not gonna like it, Dad.'

'But you get points for honesty.'

Silence. Then a small reluctant nod.

'A few weeks ago, I snuck out,' he said.

Tom flinched but kept his calm. 'Where did you go?'

'Wild Place.'

'Why?'

'Ricky got the ouija board for his birthday and wanted to try it out. The rules say you have to find someplace quiet and dark and, well, spooky. Wild Place is all of those things. We found a creepy little clearing. It was a full moon that night. The plan was to contact some famous ghosts. Jim Morrison, Jimi Hendrix, Harold Holt.'

'Harold Holt?'

'That's the prime minister who drowned, right?'

'Yeah. I'm just surprised you knew that. What happened next?'

'Well, like I said, that was the plan. We tried reaching out but nobody answered. Nothing happened. The planchette didn't even move. So we tried something different.' He closed his mouth. A few seconds passed. 'We tried to summon the devil.'

For the record, Tom did not believe you could contact the other side with a glass and a piece of cardboard, and he certainly didn't believe you could summon Satan. But the fear etched on his son's face was real and deep. So, resisting the urge to joke and tease, Tom asked, 'Should I be worried about you?'

He shook his head. 'It wasn't even my idea.'

'Ricky put you up to it.'

'No,' he said. 'It wasn't his idea either.'

Tom leaned forward. 'Then whose was it?'

Silence.

'Keiran?'

'It was Sean's,' he said.

'Sean Fryman? From next door?'

He of black clothes and blacker tastes.

'Are you and Sean friends?' Tom asked.

'Sean doesn't have friends. But he was always nice to me, because of Marty. We asked him about the ouija board because we knew he was into all that stuff.'

'What stuff?'

'Witchcraft, séances, Aleister Crowley, the occult. Everyone knows it. In Camp Hill he's sort of ... what's that word that's like famous, but for something bad?'

'Infamous.'

'*In-famous*? That doesn't sound right.'

'Trust me. I'm an English teacher. What happened next?'

'It was just supposed to be a bit of fun. We lit candles, drew some symbols in the dirt, then we all got around the board. Satan didn't reveal himself. We didn't get dragged down to hell, obviously. The planchette didn't even move.' He looked Tom dead in the eye. 'But something did happen.'

Tom waited.

'Right in the middle of it all, Sean got a nosebleed. A bad one. And, yeah, people get nosebleeds all the time, but the timing really freaked us out. Then Sean started acting weird. He got really quiet, and started whispering to himself. Then he just left. He didn't even say goodbye or anything. He just disappeared off into Wild Place. It was almost like he was ...'

'What?'

'Possessed.'

Tom looked at his son and wondered – not for the first time – how healthy it was to raise a child within any given faith. Christian values were all well and good, but they came with a lot of baggage. To believe in God was to believe in Satan.

Gently, he said, 'Keiran, Sean was probably just trying to freak you out.'

'That's what me and Ricky thought too. We probably would have forgotten about the whole thing, but then you brought those posters home last night.'

'... Tracie's posters.'

'I went back and checked the date,' Keiran said. Tears welled in the kid's eyes. 'We summoned the devil on December eighth, Dad. The night Tracie Reed went missing.'

9

'I'm going to die, aren't I?' the man wheezed. He was stretched out and bleeding in the back of the ambulance, one arm slung over the side of the gurney, the other groping air. 'Please don't let me die.'

'I've had worse cuts shaving my legs,' Debbie Fryman told him.

The man did not smile and, honestly, who could blame him? Sixteen minutes earlier, he had been on his roof taking down the Christmas lights. Most people left them up well into January, but not this guy. He'd slipped, crashed through the ceiling of his garden shed and landed on an upturned pitchfork. Only two of the four prongs had penetrated the skin.

Small mercies, Debbie thought.

She slid an oxygen mask over Mr Winslow's face and monitored his heart rate: a rapid drumbeat. His eyes closed, then fluttered open. Blood pooled on the gurney. He kept talking, his voice muffled now behind the mask. It was a variation of what he'd been saying since they arrived on the scene to pick him up. A variation of what they all said, really. *Is it bad? Can you fix me? Am I going to die?*

'Mr Winslow, please don't take this the wrong way,' she said. 'But I need you to shut up.'

His eyes – already wide – widened even more. He said something else. Debbie drew an invisible zipper across her lips. He got the message. Debbie blocked one ear with her index finger and put the other close to the puncture wounds. As she'd feared, there was a hideous wheezing noise there.

Suck, hiss, suck, hiss.

Air entering the chest cavity.

Damn.

She slipped up front. Merri (real name: George Merrigold) was hunched over the wheel, eyes set on the road ahead, watching for breaks in the traffic. Red and blue lights danced across his face. He was a hulking man, with a round face and large nose. Debbie would never – *ever* – admit this to him, but he reminded her of a fairytale troll.

'Pull over,' Debbie said.

He turned. 'What is it?'

'Tension pneumothorax.'

'Shit.' He leaned forward, lifted himself off his seat to scan the road ahead. 'There's a service road coming up. Give me thirty seconds.'

Debbie returned to the man on the gurney.

'Please tell me what's happening,' he said.

At least, that's what it sounded like. It was hard to tell behind the oxygen mask. Either way, Debbie ignored him. She rifled through a nearby drawer until she found the fourteen-gauge catheter needle. It was wrapped in plastic. She tore it off with her teeth.

The man on the gurney grabbed her arm. 'Please!'

She removed his hand, but before she let it go, she gave it a squeeze. 'Your lung is collapsing, Mr Winslow. If we don't relieve the pressure you could go into cardiac arrest.'

He pulled off his oxygen mask and said, 'You mean ...' Pause. Gasp. 'Like a heart attack?'

The ambulance lurched to a sudden stop. Merri killed the engine. The sounds of passing traffic drifted in. Rumbling engines, honking horns, pop songs on radios.

'Why did we ...' Gasp. Wheeze. '... Stop?'

'The quickest way to relieve the pressure is to insert this' – Debbie showed him the needle – 'into the chest wall, and I'd rather not do that while we're moving.'

He tried to sit up. Debbie pinned him with a firm hand.

'I need you to relax, Mr Winslow.'

He looked at the needle and said, 'You're kidding, right?'

'Never show them the needle,' Merri said at the end of their shift, as they stepped out of Frankston Emergency into the warm afternoon air.

'He's stable,' she said. 'Scared is better than dead.'

'Your bedside manner could use some work.'

'Uh-huh.'

'Beers?'

'Not tonight.'

'Hot date?'

'I wish,' she said. 'No, this is the first time in four days I'm off work while the sun is still out. I might even be home by dinnertime. I plan on eating with my son.'

Debbie threw open the door of her lime-green Ford Orion. Hot, stale air rushed out. She braced herself and slipped inside. The steering wheel was almost too hot to touch. She'd have to hot-potato it for most of the drive home. She rolled down the window and gave Merri a weary wave.

'What I said about your lousy bedside manner, that's actually a compliment, by the way,' he said.

'How so?'

'You're bad at that stuff because you're a bad liar,' he said. 'That's not the worst thing in the world.'

He offered her a little smile and said, 'See you tomorrow for the graveyard shift.'

She drove via the Esplanade and looked down onto the beaches as she passed. Camp Hill was part of the Mornington Peninsula, flanked on three sides by water. There was Port Phillip Bay to the west, Western Port Bay to the east, and Bass Strait to the south. The beaches – on the Camp Hill side, at least – were packed. People sunbathed and splashed around in the shallows. Boats and jet skis cut clean white lines through the water. The sun was fat and full in a clear blue sky.

People were happy. *She* was happy, wasn't she? That didn't sound right, but with a rush of warm, salty sea air filling the car, everything was okay. Not perfect. Not great, even. But okay. And that was good enough. In fact, she'd gone the whole day without thinking once about Mike.

Damn. She just blew it. Forget it, that didn't count.

When Debbie thought about her life, she pictured a beaten-up old car. Her injuries weren't as obvious as those she treated, but they were there all the same. The word *damaged* came to mind. Damaged by a violent boyfriend (there she went again, thinking about Mike), then a surprise pregnancy, then a son who seemed determined to pull away from her. It was a life spent reaching and never quite grasping.

But lately there had been a shift. She might have been naïve, or it might have been the Christmas carols Merri had started playing in the ambulance back in November, but she felt a sharp, almost painful pang of hope.

It didn't last.

As Debbie pulled in to her driveway, Tom Witter walked across from his place to meet her. He'd been sitting in the shade of his veranda, watching the street, waiting for her, apparently.

'Everything all right, Tom?' she asked.

'Yeah, everything's fine. I was actually hoping to talk to Sean, but it felt a little wrong coming over when you weren't home.'

Debbie felt her pulse quicken. She wasn't sure why. It was just who she was. She lived her life like a rubber band stretched to breaking point.

'Did he do something wrong?'

Tom glanced at the street and said, 'Maybe we should talk inside.'

'Right. Yes. Of course. Come in.'

Debbie showed him in. The house was a mess. Last night's dinner plates were on the coffee table, alongside an overflowing ashtray.

'Do you want something to drink?' Debbie asked. 'Coffee? Shit, sorry, I just remembered the milk is past its use-by. You could take it black, or I could run out and get some.'

'No, thanks,' Tom said.

'Sean's probably in his room. I'll go get him.'

Debbie stepped into the hall and took a deep breath. After taking a beat to gather herself, she went to Sean's bedroom door and knocked. No answer. No surprise. She swung open the door. The curtains hadn't moved in months. The only light came from Herm's heat lamp. Herm was a carpet python, who lived in a large terrarium in Sean's room. Right now, he was coiled up beside a plastic rock, the tip of his tail resting in his little plastic lagoon.

As Debbie's eyes adjusted to the dark, the figure of a boy appeared on the bed. No. Sean wasn't a boy anymore. He was a man. Legally and biologically. He was looking more and more like his father each day: tall, broad, muscular. Formidable.

It wasn't just his father's build Sean had inherited, either. Around six months ago – or was it a year? – Sean turned moody and combative. Suddenly there were slammed doors, sullen looks, missed dinners, one-word answers, calls from teachers, arguments that went on and on while somehow going nowhere. Fights that didn't end until one of them walked away. Usually Debbie.

She flicked on the light. Her son blinked back at her. He was dressed in tight jeans and a black T-shirt with a barely readable band name printed in jagged letters on the front. He was wearing an enormous pair of headphones. The cord twisted all the way across the room, to his record player. The music was loud enough to hear from the doorway: thundering guitars, an ominous drumbeat, screaming vocals.

Earlier that year, Sean had bought his own personal stereo system. Debbie was impressed he'd managed to save up enough pocket money. Then he traded in all his old cassette tapes at the Frankston Record X-Change. Stuff like Starship and Prince. He came home with a handful of heavy metal records: Iron Maiden, Judas Priest, Black Sabbath. Since then, his collection had grown. Venom, Slayer, Onslaught, Mötley Crüe. Bands that screamed and thumped and raged.

Songs of anger, Debbie thought. That's what had changed most about her son. He never used to be angry, and nor should he have been. Debbie had busted her arse to get him into a good school in a good neighbourhood. She had no help from anyone and still managed to give him everything. What the hell did he have to be so angry about?

He whipped off the headphones.

'What do you want?'

'Get up,' she said.

'Why?'

'Tom Witter is here to see you.'

She waited for him to grimace or gasp or react in some way. He didn't. It was as if he'd been expecting this. Waiting for it. The thought terrified her. He rose slowly, as if he had all the time in the world.

'What's this about, Sean?' Debbie asked.

'Beats me,' he said.

10

Tom waited in the living room.

It was a cluttered space, with the faint smell of smoke and sweat in the air. But there was also a gentle, inviting energy to the place. The walls were busy with photos, and most of those photos were of Sean. Here he was from the time the Witters took him on a trip to Belport. Sean was just a kid in the photo, nine or ten. His face was tanned and bright and happy. Debbie probably hung so many pictures because they were photographic evidence her son was happy once.

Tom moved to a spread of heavy metal albums on the floor in front of the record player. He let his eyes wander over the album covers. He picked up Mötley Crüe's *Shout at the Devil*: red text on a field of solid black.

'Did you come over here to borrow some records, Mr Witter?'

Tom turned. A vampire had entered the room. This man-boy was an undead version of the original. His hair was long and black, and hung in a greasy tangle over his face.

It made Tom think of vines growing over the mouth of an ancient cave, filled with monsters.

Debbie trotted nervously into the room after him.

'I'm more of a sixties folk kind of guy,' Tom said.

Sean laughed – it hadn't been meant as a joke – and pointed to the record sleeve in Tom's hand. 'That album was originally going to be called Shout *with* the Devil. They got scared and changed it after one of the band members witnessed a knife and fork levitate off a table and stick into the ceiling. They were worried they'd tapped into something evil.' He paused. 'Cool, huh?'

'That's one word for it,' Tom said. 'Why do you like this sort of music?'

'No offence,' he said. 'But you wouldn't get it.'

'Sean,' Debbie warned.

'What? I said *no offence.*'

Sean slipped a cigarette from his pocket and lit it. Tom glanced at Debbie, waiting for her to scold him for smoking in the house. That's what he'd do if it were one of his boys. But she didn't. She just looked down at the floor, a flicker of shame on her face. It must have been hard for her, raising a kid like this on her own.

'You might be surprised about that,' Tom said. 'I was your age when the Manson Family went on their killing spree. I remember seeing it on the news. The way it felt. It was scary, of course, but it was also kind of exciting. Darkness is a break from the boredom.'

Sean scoffed. He was that special brand of teenager who

made you feel like everything was a joke you didn't get.

'Please, sit down, Tom,' Debbie said. She gnawed at her fingernails. 'What's this about?'

Tom leaned forward and put his hands on his knees.

'Keiran told me about the ritual,' he said.

Sean snorted. '*Ritual*? Is that what he called it?'

'What's he talking about, Sean?' Debbie said.

'Nothing,' he said. 'Keiran asked me how to use a spirit board and I showed him. It was harmless.'

'I'm sure it felt that way to you, but Keiran is an impressionable kid at an impressionable age.' Tom paused. 'That kid looks up to you, Sean. He always has. When you and Marty were friends, you were like a big brother to Keiran. But I can't have you filling his head with this sort of stuff. You're ...'

'A bad influence?' he offered.

'I was going to say *older*,' Tom said. 'I'm curious. What is it about the ouija board? Do you enjoy feeling scared?'

'I enjoy feeling something.'

That stopped Tom in his tracks. There was something desperate and sad about that, and, worse: something relatable.

'Whatever the reason, it's my job to protect my son,' Tom said. 'I'm sorry, Sean. In this case, that means protecting him from you.'

Debbie's smile disappeared.

'Don't you think that's a bit dramatic, Tom? I'm sure it's not as serious as all that. It sounds like kids being kids.'

'It's fine, Mum,' Sean said. 'He's right to be scared of me.'

'Sean ...'

'I'm not scared of you, Sean,' Tom said.

Sean stood up fast. For a moment, Tom thought he might come towards him. Shamefully, even though Sean was just eighteen, Tom felt the way he had in the shadow of Steve McDougal.

'Yes, you are,' he said. 'You all are.'

He started away.

'I'm sorry about him,' Debbie said. 'He's provocative. It's his way. I'll talk to him about Keiran.'

Tom said nothing.

'... Tom?'

He'd just noticed something on Sean's arm.

'That's an interesting tattoo,' Tom said.

Sean paused, turned around, and looked down at his arm. The ink was fresh. The tattoo was small – around the size of a fifty-cent piece – but striking: a five-pointed star within a solid black circle.

'That's a pentagram, isn't it?' Tom said.

'Yeah,' Sean said. 'So what?'

11

Pentagram ☆

A pentagram is a shape of a five-pointed star polygon, coming from the Greek pente ('five') and grammon ('line'). Used as symbology in ancient Greece and Babylonia, pentagrams are used today as a symbol of faith by Wiccans and in other belief systems. It has also been used within Freemasonry, Satanism, and has other magical associations.

He closed the encyclopaedia and sat back on the bed. Nearby, Connie was halfway through changing out of her third outfit and into her fourth.

'You should get dressed,' she said. 'It's nearly seven.'

He'd draped his good brown blazer over the back of the chair in the corner. He got up and put it on. Then, to his genuine horror, he realised it no longer buttoned across his belly.

'When did this happen?' he asked.

'I like it,' Connie said. 'There's a little more of you to love each year.'

'You're not helping.'

He returned the blazer to the walk-in and settled on a white linen shirt.

'Are we going to talk about Keiran?' he asked.

Connie moaned. 'Do we have to?'

'I'm thinking we ground him for sneaking out.'

'For how long?'

Tom sat down on the bed. 'Ten, twenty years. Just until he's married with kids of his own.'

Connie laughed. 'We can't protect him forever, Tom.'

It was a depressing thought. But she wasn't wrong. Keiran had stopped being a kid overnight. One second, he was dancing around the house with his underpants outside his trousers, pretending to be Superman, building forts with sofa cushions and begging for a puppy – Tom was allergic, so the answer was always no – and the next he was traipsing into the woods at midnight to summon the devil.

He looked out the window, over Wild Place. It would be dark soon, but the birds were still screaming. It sounded like the noisy miners were waging war against the ravens.

'Marty's leaving us, and now all this stuff with Keiran,' Tom said. 'Is there some way to stop them growing up?'

'Anti-growth hormones,' she suggested. 'Or a time machine.'

She joined him on the bed and slunk her arm around his. 'Honestly, I think we should go easy on Keiran. We've always said they get points for honesty.'

'You're too soft.'

'That's what she said.'

'Funny.'

'I thought so.'

'I'd be handling this a lot better if he snuck out to a party or for a secret rendezvous with some girl,' he said. 'But all this stuff with the ouija board and the devil is just so ... bizarre.'

'He's a kid,' Connie reminded him. 'Kids are weird. That's, like, page one of the parenting handbook.'

'I don't want him turning into Sean.'

She took hold of Tom's hand.

'Sean doesn't have you in his life, Tom. He doesn't have a father. And Debbie, I love her, but she's spent her whole life in the deep end. She's hardly ever there. We're present in Keiran's life. That's half the battle.'

'Are you telling me to relax?' he asked.

'I am.'

The doorbell rang.

'How do I look?' he asked.

'A little too fancy for an old high-school buddy. Should I be worried?'

'Don't worry. Sharon has much better taste in men than you.'

Sharon was an instant hit as a dinner guest. Being a police detective meant she was practically a celebrity to the boys, and Connie was always saying there weren't enough X chromosomes in the house. It didn't hurt that Sharon laughed a little louder at Connie's jokes, and complimented her spag bol at least three times. By the time dessert came – a Viennetta cut into big slices – the grown-ups at the table were suitably tipsy.

'We were on a school camp in Marysville,' Sharon explained. 'Ernie Taylor had snuck in a bottle of vodka he swiped from his parents' place.' She gave the boys a wink. 'Before this night, your father had never touched a drop of alcohol.'

'And I wouldn't again for years after,' Tom said.

Laughing, Sharon looked from Connie to Keiran to Marty, keeping them all engaged. 'Tom got so drunk that he scaled a fence into the town's water supply, unzipped his pants, and …'

'Ew, Dad,' Keiran said. 'You wanked into the water?'

Marty nearly choked on his Viennetta. 'He took a wee, Keiran. Jesus. Everything is wanking with you.'

'I'm shocked,' Keiran said. 'I always thought Dad was like this mega-dork in high school.'

'Oh, he was,' Sharon said. 'But he had his moments.'

As Connie topped up their wine glasses, she said, 'Okay, time to dish the dirt. Tell me about Tom's ex-girlfriends.'

'What ex-girlfriends?' Sharon said, laughing.

'What about Kate Kirino?' Tom said.

'Kate went out with you on a dare, Tom.'

'Still counts,' he said.

Connie gulped her wine, then leaned back in her chair with a sly smile. 'And you two really never …'

'We were just friends,' Sharon said, with a tight smile. 'Other people came and went, but mostly it was just us,' she said. 'I don't think either of us wanted to jeopardise that.'

Sharon fell silent for a moment. Then, 'We needed each other. The kids at that school were cruel. To both of us.'

Sharon hadn't technically answered the question, Tom noticed.

'Why were they mean to you?' Keiran asked.

'Well, your dad had his twitches and my mum was in prison. That was all the reason they needed to make our lives hell.'

Her face darkened.

'Do you ever talk to her?' Tom asked.

'She died,' she said. 'Lung cancer.'

'Sorry.'

'I'm not.' She looked around the table. 'Wow. I really killed the mood, didn't I?'

Tom cleared his throat and said, 'Sharon, do you mind if I raise a subject that my wife specifically asked me not to raise?'

Connie shook her head and topped up her wine.

'I'm intrigued,' Sharon said.

'Don't be,' Connie told her.

'It's about Tracie Reed,' Tom said.

'Why am I not surprised?'

'Tell him to shut up,' Connie said.

'No, it's fine.' Sharon leaned forward on her elbows. 'The main reason anyone becomes a cop is so they'll have good stories to tell at dinner parties. What about Tracie Reed?'

The boys fell silent and eager.

'I might have found a clue,' Tom said.

'Lay it on me, Columbo.'

'Well, as you know, Tracie's mum found a necklace in her

room, with a pentagram on the end. I saw that same symbol this afternoon, tattooed on one of the neighbours.'

'Which neighbour?' Keiran interrupted.

Tom turned to him. 'After we talked today—'

'Dad.'

'I had a talk with Sean.'

'You told him?'

'I had to.'

Keiran shot up from his place and did the old teenage storm-out. Colour rose on Connie's face. Sharon guzzled her wine.

Marty asked, 'What the hell just happened?'

Tom gave the abridged version: Wild Place, ouija board, demon possession.

'Who is this Sean kid?' Sharon asked when Tom had finished.

'The freak next door,' Marty said.

'Marty,' Connie said. 'He used to be your best friend.'

'What changed?' Sharon asked.

'He did. One day he was coming over and shooting hoops and reading comics, the next he was like this totally different person. It's like he got body-snatched.'

'Don't you mean *possessed*?' Sharon said.

She turned to Tom and grinned.

'I didn't say he was possessed,' Tom snapped. 'But that's a pretty big coincidence, right?'

'Not really. There's probably a hacky sack and a pair of parachute pants in his wardrobe too,' Sharon said.

'Meaning?'

'Meaning, that symbol is everywhere, Tom. Have you heard about the curse of the crying boy?'

He shook his head.

'A few months ago, while I was waiting to see the dentist, I picked up one of those awful tabloid papers. The kind with headlines like, *Cat Abducted by Aliens* and *Jesus Found on Piece of Toast*.'

'*Elvis Alive and Well, Seen Eating Whopper in Hungry Jack's*,' Connie added.

'Exactly,' Sharon said with a laugh. 'There was a story about a series of house fires in Britain. Every home had a specific painting of a crying kid and in every case, the painting was the only thing that remained untouched. Now, if you're like Tom, you'd probably think the painting is cursed, until you realise the thing is so mass-produced it's hanging in every living room in England, and the paint is treated with a fire retardant.'

'You'll have to forgive my husband,' Connie said. 'When he hears hoofbeats, he thinks—'

'Zebras?'

'I was going to say *serial killers*.'

They all laughed. At Tom.

'So you're just not going to do anything about it?' he asked.

'What would you suggest, Tom?' Sharon said. 'Call the Ghostbusters?'

Everyone at the table laughed again. Everyone but Tom.

'Is this how police investigations work?' Tom asked. 'You just decide what happened and ignore any evidence that contradicts it?'

Connie and Marty fell silent. Tom knew he'd overstepped the mark but he didn't care. He was sick of being ignored. Sick of being laughed at.

'Sharon's off-duty, Tom,' Connie said. 'How about we change the subject?'

Later, when Marty had gone up to his room and Connie was cleaning up the dinner dishes, Tom and Sharon took fresh drinks out onto the back patio. The outdoor setting overlooked Wild Place. The community forest was a deep black void, alive with the sounds of bats and insects.

'I like your family,' Sharon said. 'They're weird.'

'You noticed that too.'

'You've got the package, Tom. I don't quite know how Twitchy Witter managed it, but you've carved yourself out a perfect little life out here.'

'Yep,' he said. 'Perfect.'

She turned to him. Backlit by the house lights, she looked mysterious and beautiful.

In a low voice, Tom said, 'Hey, Sharon, I know it was a long time ago …'

'We don't have to do this, Tom.'

'I know. But I think I owe you an explanation.'

She made a strange gesture with her hands, as if holding an invisible jar with one hand and unscrewing the lid with the other.

'What are you doing?' Tom asked.

'Opening a can of worms.'

He laughed. 'I was young, and stupid, and impulsive. I should never have let it happen.'

'I don't regret that night, Tom. Honestly, I'm glad my first time was with you. I mean, don't get me wrong, the sex was terrible.'

'The worst.'

'But it was special, too. It felt right, you know. What happened afterwards, that's the part that hurt.'

'It's hard not to look at someone differently when you've seen them naked.'

'You didn't look at me at all, Tom.' There was a little ice in her tone now. 'It might be the copious amount of wine you've been pouring me since I got here, but I actually think I was in love with you.'

This should have felt like a revelation, but it didn't.

Sharon turned back to Wild Place. Her face was cast in shadow again.

'Why didn't you tell me?' he asked.

'I was too scared.'

'I didn't think you were scared of anything.'

'I was scared of everything, Tom.' She drank. Smiled. 'We both were. We just dealt with it differently. I'm the type of person to run towards the monsters. You're the type to run away from them.'

'It sounds like you're calling me a chicken.'

'If I was calling you a chicken, I would have made chicken sounds,' she said. 'But you did run away from me, Witter.'

'I ran away from Camp Hill,' Tom said.

He thought about Marty.

'Yet here you are,' Sharon said.

'I didn't plan to come back. It just happened.'

It might not have been a satisfying explanation, but it was the truth. Home was like a bungee cord. It didn't matter how far you went, it always pulled you back.

Sharon looked up at the house and said, 'Do you think this could have been us, in another life?'

'You'd go crazy living in suburbia,' he said.

'Yeah,' she said. 'Maybe.'

A possum, perched somewhere in the trees of Wild Place, hissed.

'I understand why you had your little spaz-out over dinner,' Sharon said.

'I wouldn't call it a spaz-out.'

'You're invested in this missing girl because you don't want to lose all this.' She spread her hands over Wild Place, the house, Camp Hill, Tom's world. 'This place is safe. Tracie Reed's disappearance threatens to change all that. But none of this is as exciting as you think it is. So leave it alone, okay? For me.'

Tom nodded.

'I have better things to do with my holidays anyway,' he said.

12

As he stood outside Sean Fryman's front door, working up the nerve to knock, Keiran thought about Robbie Knievel. In April of that year, Robbie Knievel had jumped his motorbike over the Caesars Palace fountains in Las Vegas. His father, Evel Knievel (*coolest name ever!*), had tried that same jump back in the 60s but crashed head-over-handlebars, so it was a big deal that Robbie landed it.

Keiran had watched the whole thing on TV with his dad. Before Robbie made the jump, he drove slowly to the end of the ramp and stared out over the fountains. He looked determined, but fearful.

'What's he doing, Dad?' Keiran had asked.

'Reconsidering his career choices, probably,' Tom had told him.

But that wasn't right. Robbie Knievel was psyching himself up because, as he stood at the end of that ramp and listened to the cheers of the crowd, and looked out at all the TV cameras, he knew there was no going back. He had to suck it up. Be a man. And jump. That was exactly – *exactly* – how Keiran felt right now.

He made a fist, lifted his hand, then lowered it. He unclenched, clenched again, lifted his hand, then—

'Hi, Keiran.'

He nearly leapt off the steps.

'Jesus, Mary and fuck,' he spat. It was Sean's mum. She was sitting on an overturned milk crate in the dark of the veranda, drinking something sweet-smelling. 'Shit, sorry for swearing. I didn't see you there.'

Debbie – she was okay with Keiran calling her that, which was good, because he wasn't sure if she was a *Miss* or *Mizz* – laughed. It was a lovely laugh. It made Keiran think of fluttering wings or bubbles in a glass of Coke.

'It's fine,' she said. 'I'm a big girl. I can take it.'

'What are you doing out here?' he asked.

'The house is like a sauna. It's not much better out here. How's this heat, huh?'

Debbie took her glass of whatever and put it against her forehead. As she lifted her arm, Keiran followed the shape of her breasts with his eyes, then quickly stared at his feet.

'Yeah,' Keiran said. 'It's hot.'

On *hot*, Keiran's voice decided to do that goddamn half-break thing it sometimes did. He felt his cheeks heat up. Debbie was, after all, gorgeous. That might sound like a strange thing to say about someone's mum, but it was undeniable. Looking at her now, mostly hidden in shadow, Keiran felt those funny, pleasant-but-not stirrings teenage boys sometimes feel.

'Is Sean home?' he asked.

Debbie sighed. 'Does your dad know you're here, mate?'

'No,' Keiran admitted. 'I'm sorry about him. He overreacts. About everything.'

She rose from the crate and came towards him. She was wearing denim cut-offs and no shoes. 'He's just worried about you. It's what dads do. The good ones, anyway. It probably doesn't always feel like it, but you're lucky to have someone like that watching your back.'

'If you say so,' Keiran said.

She laughed again, and again Keiran pictured fluttering wings.

'So does Sean think I'm, like, some total square now?' he asked.

Debbie's smile faded. 'You look up to him, don't you?'

Keiran shrugged.

'He's always been nice to me,' he said, although that wasn't strictly true. 'I just don't want him getting into trouble.'

'And all that darkness and death and angry music he's into doesn't bother you?'

Keiran shrugged again. At thirteen, a lot was communicated through shrugs. This one said, *maybe you're just looking at things the wrong way.*

'It's just different,' he said. 'Like olives.'

'Olives?'

'Yeah,' he said. 'Have you ever eaten an olive?'

'Many.'

'Right. The first time you try one it tastes likes arse, but then you have another one, and another one, and pretty soon you like the taste. It's just, you know, really salty and different.'

'An acquired taste,' Debbie offered. 'That's a lovely thought, Keiran, really. But not everyone thinks so. Can I be honest with you?'

Can I be honest with you? That seemed like a strange thing to say. Had she been lying to him so far?

'Okay,' he said.

'I worry about him sometimes. He scares people off. Maybe that's the point.' She looked down at her glass and wiggled it. The ice cubes inside chinked together. 'He scared your brother off.'

'Marty scared Sean off first.'

Debbie flinched at that. 'How do you mean?'

'I don't know.' Keiran shook his head. The truth was, he did know, but he wasn't sure how to put it into words. He thought about it. 'I guess what I'm saying is, my brother changed too. It was suddenly really important to him how he looked and what other people thought. He *grew up*.'

'Is that what growing up is?' Debbie asked.

Keiran thought about that, too, then said, 'Isn't it?'

She raised an eyebrow, opened her mouth, then closed it.

See, Keiran thought. *I have a point.*

He shrugged. This one translated to: *consider the following ...* 'Marty started hanging out with a new group of friends in his last year of high school. He got a new haircut – suddenly the Camp Hill Barber wasn't good enough for him anymore – and started shopping at *Myer*.' He stretched Myer out to make it sound fancy and la-di-da. *Myyyer.* 'Maybe Sean didn't fit into that world anymore. Maybe that's why he, you know, turned dark.'

'Did Sean tell you that?'

'Nah. It's just a feeling. I notice little things. And, I don't know, I guess I sort of know how he feels. Marty's moving out and …' He trailed off for a second, lost his path, then found it. 'It just sucks to feel left behind.'

She sipped her drink and watched him.

'So, can I go inside?' he asked.

'I don't think so, Keiran.'

'Why not?'

'Your dad was pretty clear about not wanting you two to see each other anymore.'

'But that's so dumb.'

'Maybe.'

'… But you agree with him.'

She did. Keiran could see it in her face. Where the hell did adults get off deciding which kids should talk to which?

'This might be hard for you to understand,' Debbie said. 'But what Marty did – how he *grew up* – is normal. It's healthy. But Sean is stuck. And, no offence, but maybe spending time with a kid isn't helping.'

Suddenly, Debbie didn't look as gorgeous as when Keiran had got here. Come to think of it, she was starting to look more and more like the rest of them.

'I'm not a kid,' Keiran said. 'I'm thirteen.'

Debbie waited.

'Can you just tell him I'm sorry?'

'Of course,' she said.

'Neville residence,' Ricky's mum chirped down the line.

Keiran twirled the banana phone's cord around his fingers, pacing the length of his bedroom and back again. He had to keep moving. If he stopped, he'd want to punch something. 'Hi, Mrs Neville. Is Ricky there?'

'It's pretty late, Keiran, is everything all right?'

'Yeah, sorry, everything's fine.'

'Oh, good,' she said. 'I get panicky whenever the phone rings this late.'

'Okay,' Keiran said. 'So, can I talk to Ricky?'

'Are you enjoying the holidays?'

He held the phone so tight he heard something crack. 'Yes, Mrs Neville.'

'Do your parents have any big plans for New Year's Eve?'

'No idea.'

'What about you?' she asked. 'Do you and Ricky have something special planned? You're welcome to join us at the beach for the fireworks, although you boys probably have better things to do than ring in the new year with an old lady like me, although—'

'Can you please just put him on the phone?!'

There was a long horrible silence on the other end of the line. 'Mrs Neville, I'm sorry, I'm just in a bit of a rush and …'

But she was gone. Keiran felt sick.

And the award for biggest wanker goes to …

Ricky came on the line and said, 'Hey, did you watch *Family Ties*? I'm officially in love with Justine Bateman. Do you think she'd marry a thirteen-year-old fat kid from Australia? Or if not marry, you know, just let me stick it in her?'

'He knows, Ricky.'

A pause, the sound of Ricky eating something crunchy, then, 'Who knows what?'

'Sean knows we told on him.'

Ricky choked. 'Oh, shit. Are you sure?'

'Dad went over to his house to tell him off.' Keiran slapped his head. 'I'm so embarrassed. Do you think he'll ever talk to me again?'

'*Embarrassed*? Forget *embarrassed*. You should be scared!'

Keiran stopped pacing. 'Why?'

'When I got home today I gave my cousin a call. She was in the same year as Sean and your brother. I caught her up with everything and guess what? Remember that pig's head someone left outside the teachers' lounge last year?'

'What about it?'

'Take a guess.'

'It was Sean?'

'That's the rumour.' Ricky paused to slurp and crunch some more on whatever it was he was eating. 'I'm just gonna say it: Sean killed her. He got juiced up talking to Satan and went off to look for someone to sacrifice.'

'I don't know,' Keiran said. 'I've known Sean since I was a little kid.'

'You've known the old Sean,' Ricky corrected. 'That guy you're living next door to is the bizarro version. You know what he's into, man. You've seen his room, you saw the way he was that night.'

Possessed, Keiran thought.

'If I were you, I'd lock the doors,' Ricky said. 'Because if Sean really did have something to do with what happened to Tracie, you're a potential witness. He might be coming for you next.'

'Shut up.'

Ricky kept eating. 'Look, I don't want to scare you. All I'm saying is, if you're not careful, you might turn up someplace with your throat slit, and when they ask Sean why he did it, you know what he'll tell the cops? *The devil made me do it!*'

There was a knock on the door. Keiran's dad wandered in, acting all casual, with his hands slung in his pockets.

'You know knocking only works if you wait for an answer,' Keiran told him.

Tom looked at the banana phone and said, 'Tell Ricky goodnight.'

Keiran made a big show of rolling his eyes, then told Ricky he'd call him back tomorrow. Tom picked up an issue of *Howling Commandos* from Keiran's desk and leafed through it.

'Dad,' Keiran said. 'What do you want?'

'Sharon left,' he said.

'And?'

'And you must have made an impression, running out like that without saying goodbye.'

'Wait. Are you mad at *me*? I'm mad at *you*.'

Tom sat down on the bed. 'I talked to Sean because I was worried about you, kid. That's my job.'

'But it's not your job to ruin my life.'

'That seems dramatic.'

'First you tell me I'm not allowed to go into Wild Place, which is, like, one of my favourite places on the planet. Then you go and make me look like a dobber in front of Sean.'

'Why do you care so much about what he thinks?'

It wasn't a terrible question, but, no, this is what adults did. They twisted the conversation until it led someplace they wanted it to go.

Case in point: 'You know, Keiran, Leonardo da Vinci said there were three types of people: those who see, those who see when they're shown, and those who do not see, and—'

'God, you can't resist, can you?'

'Resist what?'

'Teaching.'

'Was it the da Vinci quote?'

Keiran nodded.

'Let me try it another way. There's an old Greek proverb that says a society grows great when old men plant trees whose shade they know they will never sit—'

'You're doing it again.'

'How about: *don't cross the streams*.'

Keiran looked at him.

'It's from *Ghostbusters*.'

'This isn't funny, Dad.'

'You're right. I'm sorry. My point is, or was, that sometimes doing the right thing takes sacrifice.'

Keiran went to the window, peeled open the curtain and looked out. Wild Place was dark and alive. Things were supposed to feel smaller as you grew up, but tonight the forest looked endless.

'What if Sean comes for me next?' he asked.

For a moment, Tom said nothing. He just stared at Keiran like he'd asked him a question in Swahili. Then, slowly, Tom got it.

'I'm your father,' he said. 'I'd never let anyone hurt you.'

'What could you do to stop him?' Keiran asked. There was cold steel in his voice. He knew this next part would hurt his dad, but he went ahead and said it anyway. Maybe he wanted to hurt him, or maybe the truth just felt better out than in. 'You're soft, Dad, and old, and weak. So, I'll ask again: what could *you* do?'

13

Tom stepped back into the hall and closed the bedroom door behind him. He stood on the landing for a while, staring into the darkness of downstairs, listening to Keiran's words thump around in his head.

The worst thing about your kid thinking you were a soft, middle-aged suburbanite, an eighty-five-kilo weakling, a functionless old bastard – *feel free to stop me anytime* – was knowing he was probably right.

What could you do to stop him?

For now, he could have another drink.

He went down to the kitchen and got another beer. He drank half of it on the back patio, staring over the fence into the bush.

What could you do? Emphasis on the *you*.

Tom walked down to the back fence. He opened the gate that gave into the bush and stepped through it. There was just enough light from the houses to see. He scaled the embankment, reached the top of the ridge, then looked back.

His house was lit from the inside. Each window was like another screen, giving a glimpse into his world. The world which, until that morning, he'd assumed was private. He could see Connie in the upstairs window, reading in the glow of the bedside lamp. In the next window, Marty was reading an issue of *GQ* (the one with Michael J Fox on the cover). The curtains in Keiran's room were drawn.

Tom wandered the ridge, looking out for holes and loose soil. There were no lights on at the Fryman house, but the glow of their TV danced and wavered across the living room. He could see Debbie on the sofa, dressed in a pair of satin boxer shorts and a big pink T-shirt. It felt voyeuristic, watching her like this.

He searched the other windows for Sean, but couldn't find him. At a fallen gum he sat down. He stayed there like that, watching Debbie's house, far longer than he should have.

He was almost drifting off when a light in one of the windows blinked on. Tom heard the creak of the window opening, then the spark of a lighter. It was Sean. He was silhouetted, so Tom couldn't see his face, but he saw the red glow of a cigarette. Tom remained perfectly still. As long as he stayed in the dark of Wild Place and didn't make a noise, Sean wouldn't be able to see him.

Eventually, Sean finished his cigarette and flicked the butt out the window. It flew through the air and landed in the backyard in a splash of red sparks, then faded. The window closed. The light blinked off. Tom crept down the embankment. He reached the concrete channel, performed a less than graceful leap across it, and found himself face to face with the Frymans' back gate.

Tom kept low, moving in a half-crouch like a soldier, across the yard and into the shadow of the house. He put his back against the wall and scanned the lawn. Then he spotted it: Sean's cigarette butt.

He knelt in the grass and plucked the filter up with his thumb and forefinger. He angled it towards the moonlight so he could see.

Bingo.

There it was. A tiny pink *S*.

S for *Starling Red*.

14

Saturday

30 December 1989

The Camp Hill Library stood on the corner of Elm Street and the Esplanade, directly opposite the Old Mariner, an all-you-can-eat seafood place whose bottomless dessert bar was the stuff of legend.

The library was open between nine and midday on Saturdays over the school holidays. Tom was there by quarter past. As he pressed through the big old double doors, a rush of musty, old-book smell wafted out, and set off a nostalgia bomb in his head. He'd spent a good chunk of his teenage years in this old stone building. It had been a haven. He would laze in the stale armchairs by the window during his Greek mythology phase, getting lost in stories about gods and monsters. Sometimes he'd sit cross-legged between stacks reading *Stranger in a Strange Land*, *Catch-22* and, when he was a little older, *In Cold Blood*.

The place hadn't changed: domed ceiling, towering stacks, dimly lit corners. It was another scorcher outside but in here the air was cool. Almost too cold. Tom had forgotten how cold this place could get. It didn't matter what the weather was like outside – the library followed its own rules.

He made his way over to the circulation desk and saw that not everything was the same after all.

'Excuse me,' he asked. 'Does Mrs Houlton still work here?'

The librarian today was a youngish man with frizzy corn-coloured hair and a grey and tan blazer. He made a clicking sound while he considered the question. *'Mrs Houlton. The name rings a bell. I think she retired before I started.'*

'That makes sense,' Tom said. 'Still, it threw me a little seeing someone else behind the desk. Mrs Houlton was an institution back in the day.'

'Can *I* help you find anything?' the librarian asked.

'No. That's okay. I remember my way around.'

Tom walked straight to the back wall. That was where they kept the philosophy and religion books. He ran a finger along the spines. He wasn't sure exactly where to start, so he cast a wide net. Going broad and basic, he pulled down *Art and Imagery of Witchcraft*, *The Hidden Symbolism of Alchemy, Paganism and More*, and *The Big Book of Masonic and Occult Symbols*.

He took them over to one of the circular tables and spread out, starting with *The Big Book of Masonic and Occult Symbols*, because a starburst on the cover declared, *New edition with over 500 illustrations!* He wondered what Mrs Houlton might think if she still worked here, if she wandered over and saw him poring over ancient hieroglyphs, Wiccan sigils, magical codes and mystical alphabets. Actually, he was pretty sure he knew exactly what she'd say: *'You haven't changed one bit, Mr Witter.'*

Sad. But true.

Tom paused on an illustration of a pentagram. According to the small caption, the five points of the star were said to represent the five wounds Christ received during the crucifixion. Later it was used as a protective symbol by witches. Nowadays, the pentagram was most commonly used by Satanists.

He turned the page to find an illustration of a striking creature labelled *Baphomet*. With the head of a goat and the body of a woman, this *demon* – there was no other way to describe it – had large wings, horns and an inverted pentagram on its forehead. Its forearms bore the words, *Solve* and *Coagula*, which apparently translated to *separate* and *join together*.

Tom stared at the image. A chill crept through him.

He went back over to the shelves and revised his search for anything to do with the Church of Satan, Satanism or devil worshipping. He was surprised – *shocked* might be more accurate – to discover dozens and dozens of books on the subject.

He pulled down *Hidden Monsters: Satanic Ritual Abuse*, *Secret Truths About the Devil*, *The Cult of Satan* and something called *MEMORIES OF MARY: The True Story of Satanic Ritual Abuse and a Child's Escape from Evil*. When he got back to the table, that's the one he started with.

The cover was striking: a frightened teenage girl kneeling in a ring of candles. Above her, a horned demon, jaws held wide, ready to consume her. Splashed across the top in big blood-red letters was, *You'll never forget what Mary remembers!*

He only intended to leaf through a few pages and maybe scan the blurb, but the first paragraph captured him.

Mary was just fifteen years old when she was lured away from her home, with the promise of love and power.

He spent the next few hours devouring the book. It was a harrowing read, but an educational one. It told the real-life story of Mary Smith (not her actual name). Born in 1951 and raised in Portland, Maine, Mary moved to Oceanside, California. She had a miscarriage in her mid-twenties, which led to a bout of depression so bad she was briefly committed to a private psychiatric hospital. There she met psychiatrist, and author of the book, Jean Elizabeth Lentz.

As part of Mary's therapy, she underwent hypnotic regression and recovered repressed memories of ritual abuse at the hands of a Satanic cult. Doctor Lentz recorded over four hundred hours of sessions. The highlights were transcribed and included in the book. They told a grim story: at sixteen, Mary was lured away by a group of older kids she met in a gaming arcade. They held her captive and forced her to witness – and later, take part in – a series of bizarre, devil-worshipping rituals.

It wasn't easy reading. Mary described being tortured, locked in a cage, forced to drink animal blood, and, in one particularly gruesome entry, being sewn into the cavity of a disembowelled cow. Mary claimed her captors were acting on behalf of Satan.

Tom wondered how credible the whole thing was. Mary's accounts pushed the boundaries of believability, and he'd heard about hypnotic regression before. It was how all those people uncovered memories of being abducted by UFOs. Then again, he worked with teenagers every day. In most ways, they were a different species.

'Just a little light reading?'

Tom spun around. The librarian was standing a few feet away.

'Something like that,' Tom said.

'What's all this research for? Are you writing a horror novel or something?'

'Something like that,' Tom said again.

The librarian glanced around, then dropped his voice to a whisper. 'That's good, man. Not enough people know how dangerous Satanism is.'

Tom looked up at the guy. 'But you do?'

'I saw a show about it a few weeks back. It had Ozzy Osbourne in it and everything. We've probably got it in our video section if you missed it.'

'You have a video section?'

Now *that* was new.

The librarian showed him into a long narrow room. On the left were several desks, each equipped with a small television, headphones and VCR. On the right were shelves, stacked floor to ceiling, with videos. There were Hollywood movies, black-and-white classics, nature programs, and news segments.

'You can't take any of the tapes home,' the librarian said. 'It's a dumb policy. They're worried people would make copies. But you can watch anything you find in here.'

Tom stood before the wall of selections.

'I'm not sure where to start,' he said.

'Crime documentaries. Back shelf. That's where we keep all the shows about serial killers, cults and crazy schizoids. They keep it up high so kids can't get to it. Stuff like that would give them nightmares. Come to think of it, stuff like that might give *me* nightmares.' The librarian dug around for a while, then brought down a video. It was in a nondescript plastic case. 'Here's the devil worship one.'

He handed the tape to Tom. A machine-printed label on the spine read: *The Devil Inside: Exposing Secret Satanists.*

'Anything else I can help you with?' the librarian asked.

'No, that's it, thanks,' Tom said.

He sat down behind one of the small TVs and put on the chunky headphones. He slipped the tape into the VCR and, without hesitation, pressed the play button.

The opening titles rolled over ominous music and images of Satanic symbols and spirit boards, of teenagers standing in line for a rock concert and a shot from *The Exorcist* – the one where Regan's head turns all the way around. When the credits faded, a grand, ancient forest loomed into view. It looked to be somewhere in middle America. The camera zoomed in to find a shock of red spray paint on the trunk of an oak tree – a pentagram.

Tom sat forward.

A man stepped into frame. His mop of black hair and wide, bushy moustache were instantly recognisable. It was Geraldo Rivera. Eyeballing the camera, he said: 'The existence of Satan is a matter of belief, but the existence of Satanism is undeniable.

Darkness lurks behind the lyrics of your child's favourite song, on the shelves of your local video store, in the homes, schools and parks of every small town across the country. In tonight's Special Look, we'll be diving deep into the dangerous and troubling world of devil worship. It's an epidemic and spreading fast. Nobody is safe. Especially not your children …'

Tom got home around lunchtime. His mind was buzzing. He'd gone to the library to learn if he should be worried or not – about Keiran, about Tracie, about Sean – and returned with a loud, resounding *yes*. As he carried the armful of borrowed books across his driveway, he wondered what exactly he was going to do about it. The answer came from an unlikely place.

'Good afternoon, Tom.'

It was Lydia Chow. She was wearing tennis shorts and a green visor. For anyone else, this might have meant she was on her way to or from a tennis match. But Lydia just liked the way it looked. Tom doubted those whites had ever seen a real court.

'Hi, Lydia,' he said.

'Tom, dish.'

'About what?'

'I have it on good authority that the detective in charge of Tracie Reed's disappearance spent the evening at your place last night.'

'Good authority, huh?'

'I was spying through my kitchen window when she arrived,' Lydia admitted. 'I'm not ashamed. A person should know what's going on in their street.' She looked at the books in Tom's arms. 'Speaking of, is this something I should be worried about?'

'I probably shouldn't talk about it, Lydia,' Tom said.

'Oh, come on, Tom, I'll show you mine if you show me yours.'

Tom put the books down on his front step, then shielded his eyes against the hot sun to look at Lydia. 'You know something about what happened?'

Lydia grinned.

'My place or yours?' she asked.

Five minutes later, Tom sat down with a cup of tea in Lydia's parlour. Yes, she had one of those. Floor-to-ceiling windows looked out over her garden. It was perfect. The grass was cut and the garden beds freshly mulched. There was not a weed in sight. Even the birds that were frolicking in the birdbath seemed storybook happy.

There were, however, flies. Scores of them. In the cooler months, Tom forgot all about them, only to be surprised every time summer rolled around and the flies hatched and swarmed. He guessed it was some sort of defence mechanism on his part, something like burying trauma.

'I've got the place to myself for a few days,' Lydia said, adding a sugar cube – yes, she had *those* too – to her tea. 'The girls are staying with their father for the school holidays, and Rob is away on a fishing trip. I'm sure that's code for something, but I haven't quite figured out what yet.'

'Well, if anyone can get to the bottom of that mystery, it's you.'

She laughed, then leaned back in her chair. Her smile didn't slip for their entire conversation. 'Speaking of mysteries, I've already worked out that Sean is a suspect in Tracie Reed's disappearance. That part is obvious. But it's the *why* I'm still struggling with. My guess?'

She did her best impression of bedsprings squeaking.

'Charming,' Tom said.

'The cliché about the allure of the bad boy is true. The whole reason I got together with my first husband was because he rode a motorbike. Of course, I forbade him from riding it after we got married. Those things are death-machines. So, am I right?'

'You go first.'

She narrowed her eyes. 'Fine. A woman in my aerobics class, Betty Garland, went to school with Debbie Fryman's cousin.'

'Okay.'

'She didn't have a whole lot to say about Debbie, aside from the fact she used to have a lot of boyfriends and, really, I could have told you that just by looking at her. But she had a lot to say about Debbie's ex.'

'Sean's father?'

'He was a drunk, apparently, and when he'd had too much, he got violent.'

'He was abusive?'

Lydia nodded and, strangely, smiled. 'He put Debbie in the hospital twice. One of those times the bastard had broken her arm. Debbie lied to the doctors about how she got it. She lied to her family too. But everyone knew better. But another true cliché is that you can't help someone unless they want to be helped.'

'What happened?'

'The way Betty tells it is that one cold and windy night, Debbie turned up at her aunt's house, distraught. She was covered in blood, sobbing uncontrollably. Ranting about Sean.'

'Where was he?' Tom asked.

'Debbie had left him at home with his dad,' Lydia shook her head and made a *tsk* sound. 'The only way she could escape was if she left him there. Eventually she went back with family and got the boy out. By then, I suppose she had the strength to leave the husband and he had heart enough to leave her the fuck alone. But what must Sean have witnessed, Tom? A thing like that, well, that's how serial killers are made.'

Sean had spent countless hours over at Tom's house and never once mentioned his father, at least not that Tom could remember.

'Violence is inherited, you know,' Lydia said. 'And abuse is cyclical. If Sean's daddy liked to hurt women, maybe he does too.'

'That's a disturbing thought.'

'Tom,' she said. 'What aren't you telling me?'

He sighed. 'It'll sound crazy.'

'I'm waiting.'

Tom sipped his tea, then, as casually as he could muster, asked, 'How much do you know about devil worship?'

'An emergency neighbourhood watch meeting?' Connie removed her Camp Hill Savings & Loans name tag and set it down in the bowl on the dresser. 'Seriously, that woman is getting more and more deranged. One meeting a fortnight isn't enough for her anymore. She gets off on this nonsense, I swear.'

'Strictly speaking, it wasn't *just* Lydia's idea,' Tom said.

Connie stopped what she was doing and stared at him. 'You?'

'You know what people in this street are like. They notice things. They notice everything. Why not use that to our advantage? We could help solve the case.'

'Darling, please don't take this the wrong way, but Lydia should mind her own business and so should you.'

'How could I possibly take that the wrong way?'

'You're jumping to conclusions about Sean.'

'There's something off about him, Con.'

'That's one way to look at it,' she said. 'The other is that he's the victim of his circumstances. You had a bizarrely normal childhood, Tom, so you don't understand how hard it is when your mum and dad split up. For kids, there's nothing worse than a broken home.'

'You turned out all right,' he said.

'Did I?'

Tom smiled. 'Yeah, Connie, you did.'

She pointed to the bed, where Tom had spread out his research. 'And anyway, you don't actually believe all this, do you, Tom? Blood sacrifices, secret tunnels, Satanic rituals?'

Tom opened his mouth to reply but, really, what was the point? Instead, he lay back on the bed and watched the ceiling fan.

'Why are you so fixated on this, Tom?'

'I'm not fixated. I just care.'

'No, *I* care. You're obsessed.'

'If there's something sinister going on in our neighbourhood, we have a responsibility to do something about it before it harms our kids.'

'*We*? Tom, you're a high school English teacher.'

'I'm getting pretty sick of people telling me what I can't do.'

'If there's something "sinister" going on' – she made air quotes around the word *sinister* – 'then the police will do something about it.'

'They haven't yet,' he said. 'What if one of our kids is next?'

Connie joined him, touched his arm gently, offered him a truce-smile. 'The best thing we can do for the kids is to be there for them, together. Just promise me you'll be careful.'

'Careful?'

'When you tip over the first domino,' she said. 'You can't always control how the rest fall.'

15

'Welcome, members of the Keel Street Neighbourhood Watch,' Lydia Chow told the room. 'Thank you all for coming at such late notice. If you're here, it's because you care about our community and keeping it safe.'

Once again, Lydia had transformed her house to accommodate them. The furniture had been pushed back against the walls and the plastic chairs had been dragged back in from her garage and arranged in rows. Tom sat up front. While Lydia got started, he swivelled in his seat to get a look at who had turned up.

Most of the houses on Keel were represented, with a few noticeable exceptions. Donnie and Clara Hines gave what Lydia described as *a pissant excuse*: Donnie's sister was visiting for the long weekend and blah blah blah. The Knapp family had already left for their holiday place in Belport, and Gary Henskee, apparently, had hidden quietly inside his house until Lydia gave up and went away. Still, considering how fast Lydia had pulled the meeting together, the turnout was respectable.

'While we wait for our special guest to arrive, let's get started,' Lydia said. 'The date is December thirtieth, 1989. Ellie has graciously agreed to take minutes again, mostly because none of you other lazy bastards would step up.'

A murmur of laughter. Ellie, who was sitting to Tom's left, jotted down Lydia's joke word for word on a Spirax notepad. Tom leaned across to her and asked, 'Who's the special guest?'

'She wants it to be a surprise,' Ellie whispered.

Perfect. Lydia had gone rogue.

Up front, she paced and said, 'We've called you all here today because there's been a development in the case of the local missing girl. Tracie Reed.' She paused melodramatically and cast her eyes around the room. 'It may shock some of you to know that a suspect in the case lives on our street.'

Tom was quick to interject. 'We're not here to accuse anybody of anything, Lydia.' Then, to the group, 'We're just trying to establish a few facts. On the night Tracie went missing, some sort of ritual was performed in Wild Place.'

A murmur. Eager silence. Betsy Keneally, a heavy-set brunette who lived in the small house at number seventeen, jumped in, 'I bet it's that kid who dresses like he's out of the Addams Family. Sean Fryman.'

Tom cleared his throat and stood. He thought about Connie's warning, but he'd come this far. So: 'Yes,' he said. 'There's reason to believe Sean Fryman was involved.'

Another wave of excitement swept through the room. There were whispers and tsks and a quiet 'I always knew there was something off about that kid.'

'A Satanic ritual,' Lydia clarified. 'A necklace was found in Tracie Reed's bedroom with a pentagram on the end. That same symbol is tattooed on Sean's arm. Tom has the inside scoop on all of this because he used to date the detective who's running the case.'

'We never dated,' Tom said. 'She's just a friend from high school. That's it.'

'I bet those handcuffs came in handy,' Bill Davis called from the back row, then looked around to make sure everyone had heard him. He'd come dressed in Bermuda shorts and a linen shirt, top three buttons open, and was rocking back on the legs of his fold-out chair.

Ingrid Peck, the desperately lonely divorcee from number fifteen, asked, 'So are we saying this kid sacrificed her to the devil?'

'Nobody's saying that,' Tom said.

'Nobody's not saying it, either,' Lydia said.

'If this is all true, why haven't the cops arrested him?' Betsy asked.

'There's not enough evidence,' Tom explained. 'That's why we need your help. The purpose of this meeting is to gather as much intel as possible. We'll then give that over to the police.'

'What sort of intel?' This time it was Irene Borschmann, from number sixteen.

Lydia answered, 'Suspicious behaviour, unusual habits, mysterious visitors. Someone in this room might know something that will help get a monster off our street. Has anyone seen or heard anything about Sean that's out of the ordinary?'

'Aside from the fact he dresses like a vampire?' Bill asked.

'I don't know how I feel about this.' Irene from sixteen again. 'It's not right to talk about someone when they're not here to defend themselves. I'm not saying I like the guy. I don't even really know Sean or Debbie.'

'None of us do,' Lydia said. 'That's the point.'

'Debbie's a good woman,' Tom said. 'Being a single parent can't be easy, and we can't always control the path our kids choose to take.'

Lydia looked off over all their heads, then lit up like a Christmas tree. Tom turned to the back of the room. A stranger was hovering in the doorway. A particularly huge stranger. He was dressed in slacks, long-sleeved shirt and tie. Lydia left her post at the front of the room and practically lunged at the guy. She took his right hand in both of hers and shook it violently.

'I'm Lydia Chow, chairwoman and host of the Keel Street Neighbourhood Watch group. We spoke on the phone.' She turned to the group. 'I'd like you all to meet Owen Reed. Tracie's father.'

There were gasps and eager looks. A sorta-kinda celebrity had just entered the room. Then, in a gesture that seemed absurdly intimate under the circumstances, Lydia scooped Owen's arm into her own and led him to an open seat at the front. During all this, he said nothing. He just glanced around the room, red-faced.

Lydia addressed the group again. 'I invited Owen here because I wanted him to see how much the neighbourhood cares. To remind him he is not alone. The true value of community is that, for better or worse, we watch each other's backs.'

She looked at Owen, expectantly. He looked around. His red face turned redder.

'Would you like to say a few words, Mr Reed?' Lydia prompted.

'No, thanks,' he said.

For a moment, Lydia just stared at him. Then she shook off whatever trance she'd fallen under and said, 'Where were we, Tom?'

Ingrid Peck answered: 'Our neighbour the Satanist.'

Owen furrowed his brow.

Tom offered Tracie's dad a stumbling, stilted explanation. 'We're all worried. About your daughter. There's a kid on our street. A teenager. And—'

'Lydia filled me in,' Owen said.

'I know it sounds far-fetched,' Tom said. 'But there are dozens of cases of kids being lured away to be abused, or to become abusers. I spent all morning reading about it at the library. These things are happening.'

'Yeah, in America,' Irene said. 'Everything's bigger and louder and freakier over there.'

Lydia said, 'I'm sorry, Irene, but if you think Australia is immune to stuff like this, then you haven't been paying attention. Hello, Milperra massacre? Russell Street bombing?'

'That's different.'

'How?'

'Come on, Lydia. Devil worshippers? Secret symbols? Stuff

like that doesn't happen in Australia and it sure as heck doesn't happen in Camp Hill.'

Tom was frustrated. He shook his head. 'What about Kylie Maybury?'

'Who?' Irene asked.

He stood, turned to face her. 'She was kidnapped and strangled to death in '84, in Melbourne. An hour's drive from here. She was six.' Then, to everyone in the room: 'Then there's David and Catherine Birnie in Perth. They went on a killing spree in '86, abducting, raping and murdering. Just a few months ago, in Brisbane, a woman stabbed a man to death before drinking his blood. There's an active serial killer on the loose right now in Sydney, killing old women.'

He felt Owen's eyes burning into him.

'I'm not saying anything like that has happened to Tracie,' Tom said. 'My point is, bad things happen everywhere.'

For a moment, everyone just stared at him. Then James Fellers, one of the Keel Street elders, said, 'Was only a matter of time, if you ask me.' James was in his eighties. He'd lived in Camp Hill longer than Tom had been alive. His voice had a gravelly, seen-it-all-before edge.

'Ever since women stopped being housewives, kids are being left home unsupervised for hours on end. Nobody's around to keep an eye on them anymore. Not only that, but divorce rates are up. No offence, Ingrid.'

Ingrid Peck said, 'That was the right thing for my marriage, James.'

James waved a dismissive hand. 'All I'm saying is back in my day, we didn't have custody disputes and trial separations and AIDS and missing kids on posters.'

'He's not wrong.' It was Karina Alvarez, who lived in the big white house on the corner. 'My Michael has spent the holidays in his room with the blinds drawn, playing *Dungeons & Dragons* with friends. He's so pale you can just about see his heart beating through his skin.'

Bill Davis clucked his tongue. 'Kids are different now. When I was my Kirsty's age, I went to see *The Exorcist* and was too scared to sleep for a week. Now every kid wants a ouija board for Christmas.'

Tom clenched his jaw at the mention of the ouija board.

'We're here to do something about it,' Lydia said. 'We need to take back control of our kids, of our neighbourhoods, of our homes. It's not enough to sit back and complain. It's always someone else's kid, right before it's your own.'

Karina said, 'Well, I haven't seen Sean Fryman dancing naked around a campfire in his backyard or sacrificing animals or anything, but his mother comes and goes at all hours of the night. He's left unsupervised a lot. He could be doing anything over there.'

Alyssa Lindley from number seven chimed in. 'He buys dead mice.'

'Wait, what?' Bill asked.

'I've been working at Pets 'n' Pieces this summer, to earn a little extra money. We sell dead mice, whole and frozen. Sean came in before Christmas to stock up.'

'That's it, I'm moving,' Bill said.

'He has a pet snake,' Tom said.

'Honestly, that's even creepier,' Alyssa said. 'Who keeps a snake in their house? Satan was a snake in the Garden of Eden, wasn't he? Maybe there's a connection there.'

'I'm not sure this is helping,' Tom said. 'Does anyone know anything that could actually help?'

Silence then, as not a single, lonely hand rose.

Owen Reed stood, shook his head, and looked Tom dead in the eyes.

'I think you have your answer,' he said.

Tom walked home slowly after the meeting, which, he supposed, was officially a bust. The air was summer-cool, perfect T-shirt weather. Moths battered the streetlamps. The lights in the houses were starting to blink off. The night sky was brilliant and clear. Keel Street was quiet. Camp Hill was quiet. His mind was not.

There was a yellow convertible parked on Keel Street, a few doors down from Tom's place. The engine was off and the top was down. Owen Reed was behind the wheel. Tom noticed three full beer cans on the passenger side, two empties on the floor, and one in Owen's hand.

'We haven't officially met,' he said. 'I'm Tom Witter. I was one of Tracie's teachers at Camp Hill College.'

Owen looked up at him. 'You want a drink?'

'... Sure.'

Owen cleared off the passenger seat. Tom walked around

the car and got in. He cracked one of the cans and drank. The beer was warm. It didn't matter.

'I'm sorry tonight wasn't more productive,' Tom said.

'I'm not sure what you expected.'

Tom shrugged. 'For what it's worth, I hope I'm wrong. About everything.'

Owen chugged his beer, then turned to look at Tom.

'Why do you care about all this, Tom? I know you taught Tracie, but you must have taught hundreds of kids over the years.'

'My youngest, Keiran, was in Wild Place the night Tracie went missing. He was with our neighbour's boy, Sean.'

Owen took a slow swig. 'The kid with the snake?'

'Yeah.'

Owen waited.

'They were messing around with a ouija board, performing some sort of séance or ritual. I'd like to believe it's kids' stuff, but denial will only get you so far, you know.' He took a deep breath. 'The short answer to your question: I don't want what happened to your kid to happen to mine.'

Owen drank, then nodded slowly.

'Well,' he said. 'Thanks.'

'What for?'

'For giving a shit. I haven't felt like I have a lot of allies lately.'

'What about your wife?'

'Things are weird there. Even before Tracie, we were going through this huge thing with our marriage, and now, I don't know.' He drank. 'I keep thinking – hoping – that my daughter ran away to bring Nancy and me back together. Tragedy is supposed to bond people. But if that was her plan, it backfired.'

'What do you mean?'

'All the bad stuff between Nancy and me is still there. But before, at least we were talking about it. Working through it, for better or worse. Now …'

'It's the elephant in the room.'

Owen nodded.

'Can I ask …'

'What happened between us?'

'If that's too personal …'

'No, it's fine.' Owen drew his lips tightly together. 'There was someone else.'

He left it at that. Tom didn't ask him to elaborate but, playing the averages, it was safe to assume Owen had stepped out on his wife.

In the dull yellow glow of the streetlamp, Owen looked pale and disconnected, like a ghost still clinging to the body. 'Which one is Sean's house?'

Tom hesitated.

Owen looked at him with a weary, wild face. 'I'm not going to drag the kid into the street and beat him, Tom.'

'It's that one, over there.'

He pointed to the Fryman house. It was still. The veranda light was off, but a sliver of yellow fell out through the curtains. In the distance, a summer storm was rolling in.

'How well do you know him?' Owen asked.

Tom thought about it. 'He used to be close with my son. Marty. But then he changed.' But that wasn't quite right, so he added: 'Something changed him.'

'What about his parents?'

'He lives with his mother. His father hasn't been in the picture for a long time. There are rumours about him.'

'Rumours?'

'That he was abusive.'

Two doors down, Lydia Chow's front door opened, and Ellie Sipple came out, holding a clipboard to her chest. She stared at the footpath as she walked home, but right before turning up her driveway she looked at the street. She spotted Owen's convertible, leaned forward and squinted, trying to get a look at them. She held Tom's eyes a moment, then went inside.

'Tracie was being stalked,' Owen said.

Tom perched forward on the seat. 'What?'

'She told Nancy about it the night she disappeared. She felt like someone was watching her. Following her.'

Tom sat back and looked out the window. Wheels turned in his head. They might have been loud enough for Owen to hear, because he said, 'What is it?'

'I'm not sure if Nancy told you or not, but the other day—'

'You snooped around my house.'

'I wasn't *snooping*, exactly, I just …'

He waved a dismissive hand. 'You don't have to explain. My wife is reactive – Tracie's the same way – and I know you were just trying to help.'

'I appreciate that,' Tom said. 'Anyway, when I was in Wild Place, behind your house, I found a pile of cigarette butts. Then, last night, I found out Sean smokes the same brand. I'm not saying it's proof of anything, but …'

Owen turned to him. 'Do you think Sean could have hurt her?'

'It's not my place to say.'

Owen waited.

'But yes,' Tom said. 'He could have hurt her.'

Owen drained his can of beer, crushed it with his hand, then flipped it into the back seat. 'It occurs to me that as we sit here and speculate, the answers to all our questions are right there. Why don't we just go over there and ask him.'

He pointed to the Fryman house. His jaw clenched, as if he was chewing and swallowing a thought. Then, suddenly – at least, it felt sudden to Tom – Owen threw open the door and climbed out.

'Well,' he said to Tom. 'Are you coming or not?'

16

As they approached the house, Tom felt a wave of nerves so strong that it just about knocked him off balance. Something hot and wild and thrilling coursed through him. The storm was almost here. The sky was rumbling.

He scanned the street. There was nobody around, but there were a lot of windows, and on Keel Street someone was always watching. *Let them watch*, Tom thought.

When they reached Debbie's house, Owen didn't hesitate. He blazed up and over the veranda, pulled up just short of the door, and knocked. Hard. Tom fell in behind him. Heavy metal music was blaring. Owen knocked again. There were shuffling footsteps inside, followed by a heavy *click* – Debbie must have managed to install the deadlock – and then the door cracked open.

Sean peered out.

'Mr Witter?' His voice was rough. His eyes shifted from Tom to the giant guy with him.

'Hi, Sean,' Tom said. 'This is Owen Reed.'

'... Reed?'

'Tracie's dad,' Owen said.

Sean licked his lips and looked down at his feet.

'Is your mum home?' Tom asked.

'She's at work.'

'Good,' Owen said. 'We're not here to talk to her.'

Without another word, almost as if Sean had been expecting them, he stepped back. Owen strode quickly inside. Tom cast a lingering look over his shoulder first, to Keel Street, then followed them into the house.

The living room smelled of cigarettes – there was an overflowing glass ashtray on the coffee table – and the music was loud enough to make the floor vibrate. Pounding drums, too-loud guitars, screaming vocals. It just sounded like noise to Tom. Sean killed the music, and a sudden silence fell over the room.

A selection of Sean's records was spread out on the floor. Now that Tom looked – now that he *really* looked – the pentagram was, well, everywhere. Here it was in gold, on the cover of Venom's *Welcome to Hell*. Inside the symbol was what looked like a goat's head. There it was again on the cover of Slayer's *Show No Mercy* album, this time entangled with four swords and the band name. The cover of Onslaught's *Power from Hell* depicted a smoke demon rising from the middle of a five-pointed star. The pentagram even featured on the Mötley Crüe record he'd held in his hand just yesterday. Now, in the right light, at the right angle, there it was. Large and black against a field of more black. Hidden in plain sight. How had he not seen it before?

A tight, cold knot grew in Tom's gut.

'Take a seat, Sean,' he said.

'You're in my house,' Sean said. 'Shouldn't I be the one saying that?' He paused. 'Or not saying it.'

Owen glared.

Sean shrank and dropped down onto the sofa. Owen sat down opposite. Tom remained standing. To be more accurate, he remained *pacing*. He paused to look through the window. Wild Place seemed darker tonight. There was no moon in the sky and the lights from the houses seemed to stop abruptly at the back fence, as if an invisible barrier existed between suburbia and the wild. Between Tom's world and whatever lay beyond. Whatever was coming.

Owen glared at Sean and asked, 'Do you know why we're here?'

'... No.'

'There was a neighbourhood watch meeting tonight,' Owen said. 'Right across the street. Your name came up more than once.'

'... Me?'

'My daughter's missing, Sean. There's a rumour going around that you had something to do with it.'

Sean slouched lower on the sofa.

'We're not here to intimidate or scare you. We just want to know the truth. A lot of people are talking about you. I wanted to talk to you. You understand?'

Sean looked at Tom, and for a moment he was that sweet young kid who'd practically grown up in his house. The boy who pitched a tent in Tom's backyard and spent the whole night giggling with Marty. The sun-kissed, freckled child who never missed Atari Sundays or Meatball Mondays or Ice-cream Fridays at the Witter house. Tom could just about hear Debbie's voice, calling over the fence at sundown for Sean to come home for dinner.

His gut began to ache.

'I had nothing to do with what happened,' he said.

'Why do people think you did?' Owen asked.

'Isn't it obvious? I dress differently and listen to different music and I don't pretend I'm happy all the time. But I don't even know your daughter.'

'You went to the same school.'

'I know who she is, but I don't *know* her.'

'You weren't friends?' Owen said.

'No.'

'You weren't more than that?'

'I'm not really into blondes.' He forced a little smile. 'People like Tracie don't go for guys like me.'

'People like Tracie?'

Sean hesitated. 'She's a snow-glober.'

'Is that slang?' Tom asked.

He picked up a lot of slang in the classroom but had never heard that one before.

'Camp Hill's like a snow globe,' Sean explained. 'It's like this perfect little glass bubble. Most people are happy to live inside it. It makes them feel safe. I call those people snow-globers.'

'What does that make you?' Owen asked.

Sean raised a smile, but it was humourless. It made Tom picture a small dog with its hackles up. He'd read somewhere they do that to make themselves appear bigger. It was a defence mechanism.

'I'm the guy who shakes it,' Sean said.

Owen and Tom exchanged a glance.

'Is that what the tattoo is about?' Owen asked.

Sean looked down at the fresh black pentagram on his arm. He shook his head slowly. 'No.'

'Isn't that some sort of devil worship thing?' Owen said.

Sean scoffed.

'Is that funny?'

'Kind of. Yeah.' He looked at Tom. 'I don't worship anything.'

'Could have fooled me,' Owen said. He gestured to the heavy metal albums on the floor. 'We'll get out of your hair in a sec. I just have one more question. But I want you to look at me while I ask it.'

Reluctantly, Sean did as he was asked.

'Do you know where my daughter is?' Owen asked.

'... No.'

They were all silent for a beat. The sound of screaming cicadas drifted in from the other direction, from Wild Place.

'Let me tell you what I do for a living, Sean,' Owen said. 'I'm a claims investigator for an insurance company. Do you know what that means?'

Sean shook his head.

'It means I investigate suspicious insurance claims. Fires, accidental deaths, stuff like that. My job is to determine if the claims are fraudulent or not. It's mostly paperwork, but occasionally I'm required to go into the field and interview the client.'

Tom took a small step closer.

'I'm good at my job for two reasons,' Owen went on. 'One, I'm big. You probably noticed that. People are less likely to lie to a big guy. Two, I'm an expert on body language. Everyone has a tell. Most people have more than one. Reluctance to make eye contact, a pursing of the lips, profuse sweating, change in complexion, tics and twitches …'

Tom scratched hard at his chin, then wondered what Owen might make of that.

'Everyone thinks they're a good liar but, nine times out of ten, your body language will give you away. Your subconscious has a cheeky way of sneaking up and ruining your day.' Owen leaned forward and stitched his fingers together. 'When I came here, I didn't expect you to tell the truth, Sean. I just needed to see your face when I asked the question.'

The muscles in Sean's neck tensed once.

'… And?' he asked.

'You've been lying to us from the second we arrived.'

Sean looked at Tom.

'My mum will be home soon,' he said.

'There's another lie,' Owen said.

He put his hands on his knees, clenching his fists so tight his knuckles turned white.

Tom pictured falling dominoes.

'I think it's time to go,' he said.

'So go.' Owen shot him a quick glare, then turned his attention back to Sean. 'Where is my daughter?'

'I don't know.'

'Did you see her on the night she disappeared?'

'No.'

'What happened that night?'

'I told you, I don't know.' Sean looked over at Tom. 'Mr Witter, can you do something?'

'Did you hurt her, Sean?'

'No.'

'What did you do to her, Sean?'

'Nothing.'

'Owen,' Tom said. 'Let's go. Now.'

Owen rose from the sofa, like some leviathan rising from the sea. He was a giant. A monolith. Towering over the boy – *why does Sean look more like a boy now?* – on the sofa.

'Men crave,' Owen said. 'They want what they can't have. What they can't touch. And if they can't get it, they take it. Is that what happened, Sean? Did you *take* my daughter?'

'Owen,' Tom spat. 'Please. Let's just leave.'

Tom put a hand on Owen's shoulder. For a second he thought Owen might break it off. But slowly – *slowly* – he drifted out of his rage-filled trance and nodded. Without another word, he started for the door.

Tom took three steps after him, then froze. He turned around slowly.

'How did you know Tracie was blonde?' he asked.

Sean didn't say anything.

'You said you weren't into blondes, but Tracie only dyed her hair the night she went missing.'

Owen exhaled. Sean lunged off the sofa. The coffee table reared on two legs then slammed back down. The glass ashtray flew through the air and landed once with a heavy thud against the carpet. A cloud of ash and cigarette butts filled the room. He took two quick steps towards the back door.

Tom was in his way. Sean shoved hard against him. Tom stumbled backwards, arms flailing. His sense of balance abandoned him. On his way to the floor he reached out blindly, grabbed a handful of Sean's black T-shirt, and dragged him down with him.

He felt a sharp jab against his liver, felt an arm slam against his neck. The air was sucked suddenly and violently from his lungs. Sean was on top of him, thrashing out blindly, grunting and crying and shouting. Owen was somewhere behind them now, rushing forward, a blur of colours and shapes.

Later, Tom would only remember bits and pieces. His brain was too busy dealing with the *now* to store much for *later*. But he'd remember the pain, and the fear. He'd remember his right hand closing tight around the fallen ashtray, and the sound it made against the side of Sean's head.

17

The force of the blow had knocked Sean's head to one side. It stayed that way for the few seconds he remained conscious. There was something almost comical about it – face locked at a forty-five-degree angle. It made him look curious. It wasn't until Sean's eyes flickered shut and his body slumped onto the floor that Tom got it. The full picture rushed to the front of his mind, blinking like a neon sign.

This was real. This was happening.

'I didn't mean to …'

'Get up,' Owen said.

'Owen, I …'

'Get. Up.'

Tom looked at the ashtray, chipped and blood-spattered, still clutched in a hand that didn't feel like his. He dropped it. What little ash was left inside sprayed out in a faint grey puff.

'We need to call an ambulance,' Tom said. 'Wait. We can't do that. His mother's an ambo.'

'Tom,' Owen hissed. 'We can't call an ambulance, full stop.'

Tom was three steps behind. 'But if we don't, he'll—'

'No, he won't.'

Owen felt Sean's pulse.

'Is he …'

'He's alive.'

'I didn't mean to do that. You need to believe me, I didn't—'

'Come on, help me with him.'

Owen rolled Sean onto his back and took hold of his legs.

'What are you doing?'

'We have to get him out of here,' he said. 'And hope like hell his mum's working the night shift.'

Tom opened his mouth to speak, but no words came. His throat was dry and tight. He was having some sort of physical reaction to the situation. The colours in the room dipped and faded. He felt a strange and sudden urge to pee. A numb, tingling sensation crept over him. Sweat began to fall in drenching sheets, even though he wasn't hot. In fact, this house, which moments ago had been stuffy and warm, felt cold. Ice-cold.

Tom closed his eyes. His life felt gone. He prayed to the god he wasn't even sure he believed in anymore, for reality to change. For what had been done to be undone. But when he opened his eyes again, he saw the narrow gash on Sean's face, leaking slick and oily blood in rhythmic gushes. Glug, still, glug, still, glug, still, in time with his heartbeat.

'What was that?' Owen asked.

His voice cut through Tom's trance.

Then Tom heard it too. A car outside. He pictured Debbie walking in to find two men standing over her unconscious, bleeding son. What then? Would she call the cops? Would Tom be arrested?

He shifted the nearest curtain in time to see Gary Henskee's Scorpion roll by. Tom exhaled. 'It's not her.'

'Stay away from the windows,' Owen snapped.

But Tom didn't move. He couldn't. He stared out over Keel Street and thought of all the people who might have seen them come over here. He'd spent the meeting ranting about Sean to the neighbourhood, then Ellie Sipple had seen him in Owen's car and—

Two big hands grabbed him by the shoulders and pulled him back into the room. Owen whipped the curtain shut.

'Get it together,' Owen said. He was talking at a low volume, but his words had a sharp edge. His voice was tight with panic. 'Here are the facts: we came into this boy's house when his mother wasn't home and you attacked him.'

'But I didn't mean to—'

'It doesn't matter. You have two choices, Tom. You can wait for the police to show up or you can help me make the best of a bad situation. You heard the kid. He knew she'd dyed her hair. He must have seen Tracie that night. We can make him tell us where she is. If we do that, then this isn't for nothing.'

'*Make him?*' Tom asked.

'Get his legs.'

Then they were carrying him.

Sean Fryman might not have been dead, but he was dead weight. Tom waddled backwards down the hallway, straining, Sean's feet tucked under his arms. Owen was on the other end, his big arms through the teen's armpits. The torso, Tom supposed, was the heavy end, but Owen didn't appear to be struggling. In fact, he was calm. It put Tom on edge.

Their plan – if you could call it that – was broken into two stages. Stage one: get Sean to a safe place. Stage two: figure out what the hell to do next.

'We'll take him out through Wild Place,' Owen said. 'There's a lane that cuts between the houses onto Novak Street.'

Between strains and grunts, Tom managed, 'Then what?'

'What kind of car do you drive?'

'No.'

'You'd rather try to fit him in the convertible?'

Tom's sneakers hit the back door. Without letting Sean go, he felt behind for the handle, turned it, and pressed with his back. The air outside was cool and fresh. A gust of wind whipped through Wild Place and across the garden. The sky had turned grey. The air was electric. The storm was close.

To one side, Dwayne and Libby Knapp's house stood blissfully dark and empty. The Knapps were holidaying in Belport. But, to the other side, the windows of Tom's house loomed. The curtains in Marty's room were drawn, but the light was on. If he chanced a look through the window, this was over.

'We need somewhere to take him,' Owen whispered. 'Someplace quiet and out of the way.'

'I have an idea about that,' Tom said.

Sean was out cold. Before moving him, Tom had wrapped his head with a blue tea towel. It was purple now, after soaking up so much blood.

Thunder rolled overhead. Rain began to fall. It didn't bother spitting. It came down in fat, cold drops.

When they reached the back gate, Owen said, 'Put him down a second.'

They lowered Sean to the soft grass. He rocked to his left, pulled his arms up, but didn't wake.

Owen creaked open the gate and looked out. 'It's clear. Ready?'

Tom grabbed Sean's feet. 'One, two, three.'

On three, they lifted. Tom felt something in his lower back pop out of place. They carried Sean out through the rear gate. Wild Place was waiting on the other side, ready to swallow them.

'The embankment is too steep,' Tom said.

Owen lowered Sean's head and joined Tom at the feet. They each took a leg and dragged him up and into the trees. It was a little drier beneath the canopy and branches. They set Sean down while Tom caught his breath.

'I'll take him the rest of the way,' Owen said.

'By yourself?'

'I'll manage. Meet me at the stormwater drain on Novak Street. Do you know it?'

'Yes.'

'Park as close as you can.'

Tom checked his watch. It was twenty past nine.

'What am I going to tell my wife? She'll think it's weird I'm going out after dark.'

Owen just shook his head. On his list of problems, Tom

guessed that wasn't a big one. 'Tell her anything but the truth.'

Tom nodded, then started away.

'Tom.'

He turned back.

'Can I trust you?'

'I've got more to lose than you,' Tom said.

He couldn't make out Owen's features in the dark of Wild Place, but he took his silence to mark the end of the conversation. He scrambled back down the embankment and out into the rain. When he reached his back gate, he looked back. Owen and Sean were gone.

Tom paused halfway across his back lawn to look up at the house. He could lose all this, he thought. He could lose them all. Connie, Marty, Keiran. If they knew what he was doing … what he'd done …

Focus.

He reached the back door and stepped under cover. He was soaked. He stepped out of his shoes and went in, leaving a trail of wet footprints down the hall. *Family Ties* was playing on TV in the living room. Michael J Fox must have said something funny, because Tom heard Connie laugh.

How the hell was he going to explain this to her?

Maybe he wouldn't have to. Not right away, at least. The garage door was at the end of the short hallway. The living room door was open, but Tom slipped past it. He glanced in. Connie was facing away from him, watching the TV. Marty sat next to her, one leg over the arm of the sofa. Keiran was on the floor, half-watching, half-reading an X-Men comic book.

Tom was tempted to sit down with his family and watch the rest of the episode. Then he'd take a shower, polish off the Christmas leftovers, and make love to his wife. But the image of the ashtray against Sean's skull played on a loop in his head. This was real, he reminded himself. This was happening.

He kept moving. He slipped into the garage and closed the door gently behind him. Stepping into a pair of old sneakers, he hit the switch by the door. Fluorescent tubes blinked on overhead, revealing a standard two-car garage, complete with boxes of miscellaneous stuff and the mandatory exercise bike, used once then left to gather dust and cobwebs and regret.

The rain pounding against the corrugated roof made it hard to think.

Moving fast, Tom opened the rear door of his station wagon and folded down the back seat. The last time he'd done this was a summer ago, on the Witters' trip to the Dromana Drive-in. The back was big enough for the whole family, so there was sure to be enough room to fit one skinny teenager. But Tom would need something to cover him.

He looked around, clocked a grey tarp in the corner, folded into thirds. They used it to cover the barbeque in winter, so it smelled like smoke. He tossed it into the back of the car. He was halfway around to the driver's side when—

'I thought I heard you creeping around in here.'

Connie stood in the doorway, draped in her tattered pink dressing-gown, a big glass of white wine in her hand.

'You're soaked,' she said.

18

Tom was staring at his wet clothes as if he'd only just noticed he was drenched.

'I got caught in the rain,' he told Connie. 'How about this storm, huh?'

'How was the meeting?' she asked.

The neighbourhood watch meeting seemed like a hundred years ago, in another time and place.

'Pretty much a bust,' he said. He tried to act calm and light and breezy, but he felt as though the truth was written on his forehead, waiting for Connie to read. He looked at his shitty brown Sigma. 'I'm going to run to the shops. You need anything?'

'Now?'

Stay calm. Breathe. Act casual.

'We need milk for the morning,' he said. 'It was on my list, but the day sort of got away from me.'

'Is everything all right, Tom?'

'Everything's fine.' He forced a smile. 'Why do you ask?'

Connie cocked her head at a curious angle.

'What's with the look?' Tom asked.

'Where have you been, Tom?'

'Lydia's place.'

'The meeting ended an hour ago.' She stared at him. 'And you're soaked.'

'I got caught talking to Bill after the meeting,' he said.

'Ah. That'll do it.'

She didn't buy it. That didn't matter right now. There were more important things to worry about. He pictured Owen dragging Sean through Wild Place, saw him crouching by the mouth of the lane that gave onto Novak Street, getting poured on.

'Back soon,' he said.

'Tom.'

He paused. '… Yeah?'

'Get me a Cornetto.'

He nearly burst into tears and told her everything right there in the garage. She turned, stepped through the garage door, and closed the door behind her. Tom got in the car and hit the clicker on the dash. The garage door rolled open to reveal a gloomy, rain-streaked Keel Street.

Tom drove out into it.

Rain filled the windscreen of the Sigma. Tom hit the wipers, saw who was standing on the other side, and slammed on the brakes.

It was Bill Davis, standing beneath an umbrella. It was the kind used on the golf course, comically huge and multicoloured.

He came towards the Sigma, knocked on the driver's side window and shouted, 'Hey, Tom.'

He considered pressing his foot down on the accelerator but that wouldn't exactly be normal behaviour from The Brainiest Man on Keel Street. Tom edged open the window. As he wound the handle, he saw blood on his hands. He tucked one under his leg, hid the other behind the wheel and said, 'Hi, Bill.'

'You might want to take it easy, mate. You were tearing out of your driveway like Ayrton Senna.'

'I don't know who that is, Bill, and listen, I'm in kind of a hurry so—'

'You don't know who Ayrton Senna is?'

'Bill ...'

'My point is, if you'd run me over Lydia would probably petition the council to put a speed bump on your driveway.'

'Is there something you need, Bill?'

He shifted nervously from one foot to the other, looked up at the storm. 'How's this weather, huh?'

'*Bill.*'

'Right. Sorry.' He moved the umbrella from one hand to the other. 'I need to talk to you about something. It's kind of ... sensitive.' Bill took a breath. Held it for an unbearable amount of time. Exhaled. 'It's kind of awkward to talk about and, well, come to think of it, maybe I shouldn't bother.'

'Okay. Well, see ya.'

Bill put his hand on the car. 'My New Year's Eve party is tomorrow night and, not to sound like a broken record or anything, we still haven't got your RSVP. And, look, you know me: I'm cool either way, but Vicky wants to get an idea of numbers, so she knows how many sausage rolls to put on, so, what do you say, Tom, can we count on you and Connie to—'

'We're not coming to your fucking party, Bill,' Tom blurted.

He planted his foot and pulled sharply onto Keel. In the rear-view, Bill walked into the street and watched him go, his umbrella a blur of colour against the gloom, like some sad, middle-aged clown.

Novak Street connected Bright and Keel. There was a big stormwater drain there, at the end of a grassy laneway. It was one of the few ways to get in and out of Wild Place without crossing someone's yard. Owen was standing on the footpath outside the laneway, hunched against the rain, his big hands plunged into his pockets.

Tom pulled up beside him and got out. 'Where is he?'

Owen pointed into the forest. The drain, which must have been still for the past few weeks, was now noisy with churning water. Tom started down the lane. Owen scanned the street for witnesses, then followed. Fences rose on either side. They reached the drain and moved around it. Then they were in the full black of the forest. Rain trickled through the canopy of branches.

'He's over here,' Owen said.

Sean had been propped against the trunk of a paperbark tree. Seeing him triggered a new surge of horror in Tom. He swallowed it. They had a job to do. Without another word, the two men went to Sean, assumed their positions, and lifted him.

It mustn't have been longer than forty seconds between Wild Place and the Sigma, but it felt like hours. Foot over foot, out of the forest, past the rushing stormwater drain and onto the damp grass. Through the dark and the wet.

When they finally reached the car, they rolled Sean into the back. Tom shook open the tarp to cover him. He paused, looked down, saw dozens of tiny black shapes moving quickly across the grey. Then they were on his arms. Tom recoiled, took three big steps back into the rain, and started sweeping them off his skin.

'What is it?' Owen asked.

'Spiders,' Tom said. 'They must have nested in the tarp.'

'Keep your voice down,' Owen hissed.

Tom tried to keep calm, *but there were spiders crawling on his skin!*

He flailed his arms, trying to shake off the feel of them all over his flesh.

'Tom, pull yourself together.'

Owen yanked the tarp out into the rain and shook it off. Countless spiders were cast out onto the road. They hit the hot, soaked bitumen and struggled off in different directions. Tom tiptoed around them and helped Owen cover Sean with the tarp.

'You'll have to take it from here,' Owen said.

'You're not coming with me?'

'I shouldn't leave my car parked in your street.'

He was right, of course. It would look suspicious if he left his convertible – top down – parked outside the Fryman house, filling up with rain. But the idea of driving Sean on his own filled Tom with a nasty brand of fear. What if Sean woke up halfway there? What if someone saw them?

'Where are we meeting?' Owen asked.

It was late, and wet, but there was plenty of holiday traffic around. The foreshore was packed with full wagons and campervans. The line for the drive-thru bottle shop – they stayed open late during the summer – snaked all the way out to the street.

Tom drove past it all, checking and re-checking the rear-view mirror. The tarp in the back remained still, but he expected it to rise at any moment. Sean would lurch at him and drive them off the road or scream out the window for help. Then it would all be over.

He pushed the thought away and kept his mind on the road. He did not need to draw any attention to himself. He stuck to the speed limit. He indicated and gave way and stopped at all the right places.

The tarp didn't move.

When he stopped at a red light at the intersection of Druitt and Lett streets, a police car slid up behind him. The driver was a cop in his fifties. Heavy-set. A stern, seen-it-all-before expression on his face. Tom locked eyes with him through the mirror. The windscreen wipers thumped back and forth.

Something brushed Tom's elbow. He lifted his arm into the light. A baby spider was perched there. He took a deep breath, rolled up his index finger, and flicked it across the car.

Honk!

Tom jolted, looked forward. The light had turned green. He pulled off at a respectable speed. The cop followed him for a few blocks, then turned off. Tom could breathe again. But what should have been a quick ten-minute drive was turning into a tension-filled road trip. He wanted this to be over.

Up ahead, he saw the sign for Camp Hill Christian College, checked that he wasn't being followed, then turned in.

It was a mid-sized school with all the facilities you'd expect. It consisted of two large single-storey buildings, connected via a breezeway. Classrooms and the canteen were to one side, gymnasium, indoor pool and the Janet David-Holt hall/theatre to the other. The staff car park was on that side, hidden from the main road, so that's where Tom parked the Sigma.

He killed the engine, unclipped his seatbelt, and swivelled around to look into the back. The tarp shifted gently, up and down, up and down. It reminded Tom of sneaking into his kids' room after dark, checking on them while they slept, making sure they were breathing. He did that well into their teens. Nobody knew that, not even Connie. There was a lot they didn't know.

He tugged back the tarp cautiously. Sean was still out to it. A small, plump spider crawled across his left cheek and disappeared into the darkness of the car. Tom would need to get the Sigma fumigated.

Minutes dragged by, feeling like hours.

Eventually, headlights burst into view, illuminating the back of Tom's car and temporarily blinding him. Owen was here. He parked alongside the Sigma and got out, bracing himself against the rain. Tom got out to greet him.

'Any change?' Owen asked.

Tom shook his head.

Owen looked up at the school towering over and around them. Then he threw open the rear door of the Sigma. He took hold of the tarp with both hands and tugged it off. Sean lay quietly beneath it. He was still alive. Tom stared at him, trying to digest the horror of what had happened.

'Let's go,' Owen said.

They'd parked close to a big set of double doors. Tom hurried over and sifted through the keys on his key ring. Principal Burch had entrusted him with a copy of the master because he always arrived at school before anyone else. It took him a second to find it because his hands were trembling.

He slid it into the lock and pushed the double doors open. A short corridor lay beyond. To the left was a glass door that led to the pool. To the right, stacked lockers, a graffitied drinking fountain, and a trophy case that was almost completely empty. There was something dreamlike about being back here in a familiar world.

He turned back. Owen was waiting by the Sigma.

Moving Sean got a little easier with practice. They got him out of the wagon, through the double doors and into the school. They carted him to the end of the hall and through the door marked SICK BAY. It was a small, narrow room with no windows, stacked with shelves and cupboards, filled with first-aid supplies. A hospital-style bed ran along the nearest wall. Tom stepped back as Owen removed his belt to bind Sean's hand to the side of the bed.

It was sickening.

Tom and Owen eased Sean onto it, then pulled away.

Glancing around, Owen said, 'This was a good idea, Tom. This place.'

None of this felt like a good idea to him. 'What now?'

'Go home,' Owen said. 'Your wife will be wondering where you are.'

'What about you?'

'Nobody's waiting for me at the motor inn.'

'What are we going to do, Owen?'

'What happens next is up to him,' Owen said. 'If he tells me where to find Tracie, things will go easy for him.'

'And if he doesn't?'

Sean moaned. Groggily, he lifted his head and blinked. One eye didn't open all the way.

'... Mr Witter?' he muttered. He looked confused. Maybe he didn't remember what or who had hit him. He tugged weakly at his restraints. 'Mr Witter, please ...' He collapsed back down and closed his eyes. 'Please ... help me ...'

Then he was out again.

Owen gestured for them to step into the hall. Tom dropped onto a wooden bench while Owen took a sip from the drinking fountain. He wiped his mouth with the back of his hand, then stood over Tom, hands on hips.

Tom said, 'If he leads you to Tracie, then what? The second we let him go he'll go straight to the cops.'

Owen lowered his voice. 'Who said anything about letting him go?'

'Jesus.'

'Go home, Tom. Try to forget about what happened. You did a good thing. You maybe helped bring her back. But I can take it from here.' He took a step closer. 'But Tom …'

'You don't have to say it.'

'Say what?'

'I'm not going to tell anyone.'

'Not even your wife?'

Tom shook his head.

Owen pointed to Tom's hands and said, 'You should clean yourself up first.'

Tom looked down. His hands were still stained with blood.

'Shit,' he said.

'What is it?'

'I told Connie I'd get her a Cornetto.'

Minutes later, he unlocked the door to the teachers' lounge and went inside. He opened the fridge. Someone – probably Jim Tanner, the PE teacher, although Tom would never be able to prove it – had left a Tupperware container of leftover pasta on the top shelf. To be more accurate, it used to be pasta. Now it was a bulging, growing green mass.

Tom flipped open the freezer door and rummaged around inside. It was in dire need of defrosting. The walls were thick with white ice. There were frozen meals inside, an unfilled icetray, and an unopened packet of Zooper Doopers. No Cornetto. It had been a long shot anyway, but Tom had a vague memory of Jen Stupin keeping chocolate Drumsticks in here, which weren't exactly the same as Cornettos, but they might be close enough to …

'What the hell am I doing?' Tom said aloud.

He went back into the hall and into the bathrooms. He snapped on all the light switches with the heel of his hand. It was a typical, budget-deprived high school bathroom. One of the taps was leaking, and two of the mirrors had chips in them. The stall doors were busy with graffiti.

Tom went to the nearest sink – the one with the leak – and fumbled for the hot tap. He turned his hands over beneath the water, scrubbing them with a little white bar of soap. Scrubbing until they were raw. He felt like Lady Macbeth, whose hands might appear clean but would never truly be free of the blood.

He wanted to cry, but no tears came. God, when was the last time he'd allowed himself a good cry? There was such power in it, but men weren't supposed to. They were supposed to carry their shit around with them, the load getting heavier and heavier with each year that passed, until they keeled over with crooked spines.

The weight of the night's events pressed down on his shoulders. They played on a flickering loop in his head. The trip to Camp Hill Library, Geraldo Rivera, Owen's burning glare at the neighbourhood watch meeting, the ashtray: first in his hand, then slamming against the side of Sean's face.

He closed his eyes, then opened them. A strange new face stared back at him from the mirror. His hair had dried wild and frizzy, and there was a smudge of ash on his forehead, but that wasn't it. The eyes were different. They'd now seen further than the walls of suburbia, and it showed.

Tom was dimly aware that beyond the shock and fear and desperation he felt, there was something else. Something had been making noise inside his head. For years. Since high school. A high-pitched air-raid siren. It had always been there, but had been dulled by the silence of suburbia, by middle age, by a wife and kids. Over the past few days, he'd begun to hear it, and today, for better or worse, he'd let it out. Today, he'd acted like a man.

19

After padding quietly down the upstairs hallway, Tom stripped naked in the bathroom and slipped into the shower. He eased down onto the shower floor and tried to stop himself trembling. An excess of adrenalin was surging through his system, and now it felt as though his skin was vibrating.

He reached up and cranked the heat. It didn't help. Instead, it made him think about washing away sin. Would God – if there really was a God – forgive him for what he'd done tonight? The answer, he supposed, was complicated. If his actions led to finding Tracie, then he was pretty sure the Big Guy would understand. After all, He sent bears to maul forty-two children to death after they made fun of Eliseus for being bald.

But if they were wrong about Sean—

No.

Tom snapped the thought in two like a dry branch. They had to be right about Sean. Because if they weren't—

Stop.

The bathroom door slid open. Connie hadn't bothered knocking. She appeared on the other side of the frosted shower screen, looking ghostly and angelic.

'I was waiting up for you to get home,' she said.

'Sorry,' Tom whispered. 'Go to bed. I'll meet you in there.'

She was quiet for a moment, then put her hand on the frosted glass. 'Everything all right in there? My wifey-sense is tingling.'

Tom turned his head to face the stream of hot water.

'I'm fine,' he said.

'Is there room in there for one more?'

'What about the kids?'

'How do you think we made them in the first place?' she said. 'Besides, it might be our last chance to have sex before 1990. Come to think of it, given your age and the way your knee clicks out of place when you walk, it might be the last chance to have sex in the shower, full stop.'

'Can I take a raincheck?'

'Ah, now I know something's wrong. That was a test. In all our years of marriage, you've turned me down for sex exactly zero times. Are you jerking your gherkin in there?'

'Jesus, Connie. Is it too much to ask for some privacy?'

He tried to apologise, but the words wouldn't leave his mouth.

Connie's hand disappeared from the glass.

'You forgot my Cornetto.'

Tom closed his eyes. 'They were out.'

'And the milk?'

'They were out of that, too.'

She drifted away for a moment. Tom thought she might leave – he really did need the privacy – but she sat down on the lip of the tub instead.

'If you're going to feed me bullshit, Tom, at least have the courtesy to shovel it.'

'Connie.'

'Lauren thinks you're having an affair.'

'I wish you wouldn't talk to your sister about our marriage.'

Connie wanted something from him – reassurance, probably – but his mind felt stretched out and filled to bursting point. Under normal circumstances, he would have known all the best and sweetest untruths to whisper, but there were bigger things to worry about. When this was all over, he'd spend time mending fences. But, for now, this conversation felt about as important as the items on her holiday to-do list: *fix leak in bathroom, paint sewing room, repair marriage.*

'No offence, Con, but I'm not sure you should be taking relationship advice from someone on their second marriage.'

'Just saying *no offence* at the start of a sentence doesn't let you off the hook for being an arsehole. And that's exactly why we should be listening to her. Lauren's first marriage failed because she and Rod didn't talk. As the years went past, more and more got swept under the rug, until, to stretch my sister's metaphor even further, their house collapsed. Or burnt down. Or got washed away in a flood of metaphorical tears. The point is, there's value in communication. Nowadays, Lauren and Dave practise something called emotional spring-cleaning.'

'Seriously?'

'I'm sure she got it out of a magazine, but it makes sense. If a marriage is like a house, every once in a while you need to fling open the doors and air the place out.'

'Are you getting anywhere near a point, honey, because we don't have endless hot water.'

'The point, husband, is that when you're ready to talk, I'm ready to listen.' There was no venom in her voice. 'Just don't wait too long, because the window won't stay open forever.'

After his shower, Tom poured himself a glass of straight bourbon and parked himself in front of the kitchen window to drink it. It gave the best view of the Fryman house. The driveway was empty, but it was only a matter of time before Debbie got home. Then what? She would go inside, discover a mess of ash on the living room floor and – blood? Had they left blood? – notice her son was missing. Then she'd be dialling triple zero.

Then again, maybe not. Sean was Marty's age. They were adults, if only by a technicality. If Tom came home and found Marty missing, he'd probably assume he'd gone out, spent the night at a friend's place and forgot to tell him. He'd worry. He might even start calling friends. But he wouldn't necessarily call in the cavalry right away. But how long would he wait?

In the meantime, what the heck were they going to do about Sean?

Best-case scenario: Sean would confess to having some part in Tracie's kidnapping. She'd be rescued. Tom might convince a judge to give him community service. The community would call him a hero. Worst-case scenario …

Nope. Not yet.

They got the wrong guy. They went into an innocent kid's home, beat him, then dragged him off to hold hostage for—

No.

Sean might succumb to his head injury overnight and die. That's what happened to Bobbie Brown at Camp Hill Christian. He took a boot in the head playing football at lunch and was dead by fourth period. Tom could be charged with murder and be sent to South Hallston for the rest of his—

Enough!

'Read it again in a decade or so,' Tom had told Tracie, the last time they spoke. 'You'll figure it out.'

Dusty afternoon light fell over her face as she turned to look out the window. Outside, the car park was empty aside from Tom's Sigma. Most of the students were gone, but a few hovered around. The dedicated ones were on their way home from the library, the less dedicated were leaving detention.

Their conversation had come to a natural end, yet Tracie lingered.

'Is everything all right, Tracie?' he asked.

She turned back. 'Not exactly.'

'You want to talk about it?' Tom asked. 'There's no such thing as teacher–student confidentiality, but I promise whatever is said in this room will stay between us.'

She frowned. 'My parents are getting a divorce.'

'I'm sorry. What happened?'

She shook her head. 'I don't know. They're both being super secretive about it. They keep using words like *mutual* and *amicable*, and I keep using words like *bullshit*.' She pressed down on her lip with her index finger. 'Am I allowed to swear in front of you now, too, Tom?'

'Shit, yeah,' he said.

She smiled for a second. Then the smile slipped away.

Tom said, 'You know, Tracie, it might feel like your parents are giving up, but being happier apart beats being miserable together.'

'Mum and Dad tried that one on me already. It didn't help.'

'I'm sure their decision had nothing to do with you.'

'They used that one too.'

Tom smiled. 'How about: life sucks sometimes.'

'Wow, did you come up with that all by yourself, Mr Witter?'

'Funny,' he said. 'And it's *Tom*, now, remember.'

'So, what's the secret recipe for a perfect marriage, Tom? Maybe I can pass it along to my mum for next time.'

'There is none. Marriage is like building a house or running a marathon or sailing across a rough ocean. Pick your metaphor. It takes a lot of hard work. And, even then, sometimes it's just not enough.'

'What about love?' Tracie asked.

'It takes a lot of that, too.'

'I'm not sure my parents were ever really in love,' she said. She chewed her lip and stared off out the window again. She looked beautiful in the afternoon light. It made Tom picture the Virgin Mary. 'From my very limited experience on the subject, when you love someone, you don't let anything get in the way.'

Headlights spilled in through the window, piercing the memory. A lime-green Ford Orion had just pulled into the Fryman driveway. Debbie was home.

20

It was the end of a perfectly average graveyard shift. Of course, in Debbie's line of work, perfectly average meant a stroke and two cardiac arrests (although the second one turned out to be heartburn). Whatever the case, Debbie wanted bed. No, she *needed* bed. Longed for it. Had thought of little else for the past hour.

She parked at the top of the driveway and, moving like a zombie, walked towards the front door. The air was hot and damp. The rain had come and gone. It might have put a dent in the heatwave, but it hadn't broken it. The pathway between car and front door was like an oven, and it wasn't much better inside.

The house was quiet. The lights were on. The air smelled like cigarettes. She felt an all-too-familiar brand of disappointment, which turned quickly to anger when she stepped into the living room. The place was a mess. Records were splayed out on the carpet, but that was only half of it. There was a trail of ash and cigarette butts halfway across the room. This was beyond disrespectful.

Who did Sean expect would clean this up? He was behaving like a rock star. No. He was behaving like his father. He was getting more and more like Mike each day. The moodiness, the attitude, the lack of respect. The rage. When exactly had that change started? She looked down at the heavy metal albums and thought: *that's when*. It was the music. It turned him cold and dark because it was cold and dark. What was it about that noise that her son found so appealing?

She thought about leaving the mess for tomorrow. She thought about marching into Sean's room, dragging him out by the ear and making him clean it himself. But, really, who was she kidding? She'd be the one to clean up sooner or later, so it may as well be sooner.

Just as her disappointment had shifted to anger, now it turned into guilt. Welcome to the Debbie Fryman emotional merry-go-round, folks. First, she'd get mad at Sean, then she'd get mad at herself.

She should have taken him away from his father sooner. She left it too long, long enough for him to get his hooks in. Yes, she should have pulled him away from that man sooner, then found him another one. A kind, easy-going, no-fuss sort of stepdad. Someone who was maybe a little blah and vanilla, but who could have taught Sean how to be a man. Someone like Tom Witter. He'd done a good job with Marty. How could two kids the same age end up on such divergent paths? Simple. Look at who their parents were.

See, now that she'd twisted and spun it just right, the mess in the living room was her fault, at least in an indirect way. So she cleaned. She used a dustpan and brush to collect the ash. She could have used the vacuum but – how pathetic was this? – she didn't want to wake up Sean. She wiped the coffee table down with a sponge, collected Sean's empty bottles and gathered his records into a stack.

When she was done, she carried the records down to his room. She knocked gently, but there was no answer. Juggling the records in one hand, Debbie used the other to turn the handle. The door opened with a slow creak. Her plan was to slip in quietly, leave his records on the dresser, and finally, blissfully, it would be her bedtime. It didn't work out that way.

The gooseneck lamp on his side table was on. It cast a dull orange light across a messy – and empty – bed. She flicked on the overhead light. The bedcover was tangled and unwashed. Dirty laundry sat in three loose piles on the carpet. Herm the carpet python lazed beneath the heat lamp in his terrarium, digesting a mouse.

Where was her son? He never went out. If he was any other kid, he might have been off seeing *Karate Kid Part III* or even drinking Fruity Lexia at the beach. But Sean was a loner. He didn't have any friends to sneak off with.

She dumped the records onto his bed. Should she be worried? He was eighteen, and surely disappearing in the middle of the night was the natural progression of things. First, he'd dyed his hair, then he'd started smoking, then he'd got that tattoo, and now this …

She slumped to the floor, landing so hard her back thumped against the wall. The impact made the needle on Sean's record player drop, shriek and crackle through the speakers. She stood, lifted the needle, then hesitated. She took one of the albums off the bed – Mötley Crüe's *Shout at the Devil* – and put the record on the turntable. She lowered the needle and closed her eyes, as a low rumble filled her ears. The sound grew more unsettling. It was like traffic in a tunnel, but less familiar. Then, a muffled voice. Spoken word. Descriptions of fallen cities and evil, of hatred and hell. Then, suddenly: thundering guitars, an ominous drumbeat and powerful vocals. Yes, that was the right word for it: *powerful*. It was dark, and unsettling, and strange and sinister, but it was powerful too. It lured you in. Held you down. Is that what drew Sean to music like this? Had he come looking for this darkness, or had it found him?

She looked at the album cover. If you angled it to the light just right, a pentagram could be seen. Her eyes shifted to a shoebox poking out from beneath Sean's bed. It was marked with a matching pentagram, this one scribbled in Texta. It looked hidden. But it also seemed to have been waiting for her. As if her parental instincts had led her here.

It might have been his porn collection. From what she understood, all men had nudie mags stashed someplace. If that were the case, Pandora could keep it. She didn't need to know what her kid was *into*. Still, she didn't walk away.

With Mötley Crüe still blaring, she stooped and drew the shoebox out. She took a beat to steel herself, then, without hesitation or ceremony, pulled off the lid. She looked inside and felt a sudden and violent rush of vertigo.

'... The hell?'

21

Sunday

31 December 1989

Irene Borschmann let her dogs out at six. She didn't usually let them run in Wild Place, but Lola the rottweiler had snatched some salami from the coffee table the night before, and Irene knew that whatever came out the other end would not be pretty. She did not want Lola emptying out on Patti Devlin's agapanthus or – god forbid – Lydia Chow's front lawn, so Wild Place it was.

Dude the chihuahua was first up the embankment. Lola was next, moving with a sort of graceful waddle that never failed to crack Irene up. Irene was a spritely woman in her fifties, with taut skin, tanned brown after too long in the garden. She went up the embankment after them, scrambling like a crab, taking care not to step in the stream of muddy water that ran behind the fence line.

Once they were up on the ridge, she let her dogs pick the trail and followed them. The pathway weaved and wound through the bush. Branches creaked, leaves rustled in the light breeze. Birds rooted around in the underbrush. Insects chirped.

It was another humid day, but the air was always a few degrees cooler in here beneath the trees.

Dude and Lola sniffed and barked and did their business. Dude just about gave her a heart attack when he stuck his head in some tall yellow grass and came out with what Irene thought was a snake. It turned out to be a used condom, which, considering the alternative, was preferable.

'Kids nowadays,' Irene said, shaking her head.

She fished the condom away from her chihuahua with a stick, flicked it into the bushes, and kept walking. The condom in the grass was all set to be the most exciting part of her walk, but then it happened.

First, Dude caught a phantom scent on the trail. He froze, tail out, nose up. Irene read the dog's body language.

'Don't even think about it, Dude,' she said. '... Dude?'

Dude wasn't listening. The scent must have been too good to ignore, because he skipped off the trail and into the long grass, tail wagging. And where Dude went Lola followed. The rottweiler bounded off before Irene could grab her collar. She crashed through the underbrush and disappeared.

'Lola,' Irene shouted. 'You dogs, you get back here right now. I know you can hear me.'

Beyond the tree line, branches crashed, and Dude yapped. Irene looked one way up the path, then the other. Damn. She was wearing shorts and sandals: not exactly good bushwhacking attire. But if the dogs found something stinky enough or dead enough, they'd roll in it, and then Irene would have to spend the better part of her morning bathing them. Dude could fit in the kitchen sink, but Lola would get the hose, and when Lola got the hose, she stared at Irene for hours with deep and genuine hurt in her eyes. So, what choice did Irene have?

She followed her dogs off the path and into the long grass. It was almost waist high. She kept half an eye out for snakes and tried to keep in the wide path Lola had forged. When she reached the tree line, she ducked into it. A low-hanging branch clocked her on the head. Something small and sharp – the thorn of a blackberry bush, probably – grabbed hold of her left upper thigh. She winced and yanked the skin free, drawing blood.

She trod on something soft and wet, and felt her balance give.

'Fucker,' she said, and hit the ground.

Luckily – or unluckily, depending on how you looked at it – she pitched forward into a small clearing. The grass was soft and damp. It broke her fall. Well, sort of.

She rolled onto her back, then her backside. She caught her breath and looked around. Her dogs were both here. Dude was yapping and spinning in place. Lola was digging at a mound of loose soil.

22

Tom woke and rubbed his sore, crooked neck, then gazed around. He was slumped in the chair he'd dragged over to the kitchen window. The empty bottle of bourbon was open on the counter. Had he slept here the whole night? Come to think of it, had he slept at all? He must have dipped once or twice into foggy, drunken unconsciousness, but all he remembered was watching the street and waiting for the police to arrive, running through what-ifs and should-have-dones.

Tom stood up too quickly, wavered, then steadied himself on the counter. He reached for the kettle to make coffee, but it was already hot. He checked the clock on the wall. Somehow, he'd managed to sleep until eight. He wandered out into the hall. The front door was wide open.

Connie and the kids were outside, loading up both cars with Marty's packing boxes. Damn. Connie's gardening gear had been removed from Lil' Red and unceremoniously dumped off the driveway. It was moving day. All Tom wanted was to drive over to Camp Hill Christian to check in, but he'd be stuck all morning carting boxes back and forth to Frankston.

Keiran was talking at Marty: 'Do you realise that in ten years and one day, it'll be the year 2000!' His tone was bright and unburdened, but when he spotted Tom, he tightened. 'Oh, hey, Dad.'

They'd hardly spoken since Keiran called him soft and old and weak. In a twisted sort of way, Tom wished he could take him aside and tell him what went down last night: make the kid eat his words. Instead, he tousled his hair – he couldn't remember the last time he'd done that – and said, 'Morning, Keiran.'

Tom shielded his eyes against the morning sun peeking over the houses on the opposite side of the street. He watched Marty jam a large, misshapen packing box into the back of the Sigma. It took him two tries to close the hatch. He wasn't taking much to his new flat, yet they'd somehow managed to fill the backs of both cars.

'Where'd this tarp come from?' Marty asked.

He dragged the tarp out of the wagon and into the light. Tom couldn't see any spiders on it, but there was a patch of dull red against the grey. Sean's dried blood. Tom lunged forward and snatched the tarp. 'Give me that. It's nothing. I was going to throw it away. It's got a hole.'

Smooth.

Marty raised an eyebrow, then returned to the packing. Tom hurried over to the bins and shoved the tarp inside. He felt something small and fast crawl up the sleeve of his T-shirt, but he was 99 per cent sure it was his imagination. When he turned back, Connie was watching him. She was dressed in denim overalls, a cup of instant coffee in her hand.

'You know,' she said. 'When most couples fight, the man sleeps on the couch, not in a chair by the window.'

'Are we fighting?' Tom asked.

'Honestly, I was hoping you could tell me.'

He glanced next door. Debbie's Orion was still in the driveway, and there were no police sirens screaming this way. It was only a matter of time, though.

Marty dusted his hands and came up the driveway to meet him.

'Well, this is it,' he said.

'When did you get taller than me?' Tom asked.

'Three years ago,' Marty said. 'I'm surprised you don't have a few words prepared.'

'I do,' Tom said. 'Is it too late to get out of your lease agreement?'

Marty surprised him then, by giving his old man a hug. Tom held him firm, looked once at Keiran – he'd flung himself in front of the Sigma and was modelling the new pair of Bollés he got for Christmas – then at Connie, who watched them with a sad, nostalgic smile.

You're risking this, Tom realised suddenly. *You're risking them.*

Marty stepped back, looked to their left, and said, 'Hi, Miss Fryman.'

Debbie was standing on her side of the property line, arms crossed, hunched and ragged. Her eyes were bloodshot and swollen. She was dressed in her ambo uniform. There was a pink stain on her left shirtsleeve, which could only be blood.

'Hi, Marty,' she said. 'You haven't heard from Sean, have you?'

Marty frowned. 'Not for a while. Why?'

'Keiran?'

Keiran shook his head.

She looked at them all. From her side of the fence, the Witters must have looked like a perfect family – a tableau of the suburban dream.

'He went out last night and he hasn't come home yet,' she said.

'He probably just stayed over at a friend's place,' Tom offered.

'Yeah,' Debbie said. 'Maybe.'

'It's a kid's job to make their mother worry,' Connie said. 'I'm sure he'll wander home soon with a rubbish excuse.'

She managed a limp, desperate little smile.

Tom felt Connie's gaze on the periphery of his vision. He turned to her and said, 'Why don't you go ahead with the first load? Take the kids. I'll be right behind you.'

She hesitated, glanced from Tom to Debbie, then back again.

'I'll have to drive the Sigma. All the seats are full in Lil' Red.'

'No worries.'

'The clutch is still sticky, even after the service.'

'Con, it's fine.'

Reluctantly, Connie crammed the two boys into the one passenger seat of the Sigma and left. Debbie watched after them.

'I'm sorry, I didn't mean to interrupt.'

'You didn't,' Tom said. Then, feeling maniacal, he added: 'You look like you need to talk. Want to come inside for a coffee?'

She tilted her head. 'Thanks, but no. I want to be near the phone, in case he calls.'

'Of course.'

He shut Connie's hatchback.

'I'm worried about him, Tom,' she said. 'With everything that's been going on around here, I'm wondering if I should call the police.'

A little too quickly, Tom blurted, 'No.'

Debbie glared at him. Or maybe it just felt that way.

'It's probably a little too early for that,' he said. 'Connie's right. I'm sure he'll be home any minute.'

'You're probably right. I must sound crazy.'

Tom put on a big, confident, it's-all-in-your-head smile. 'You sound like a parent. We all get a little crazy.'

She offered a strange little wave, then ambled home. Tom watched her. He felt rotten. But he also felt, well, relieved.

Across the street and a few doors down, Betsy Keneally from number seventeen was out on the footpath with her husband Albert. They were laughing and pointing at something Tom couldn't see. Their scruffy kid – his name was Ritchie or Rocky or something stupid like that – was circling them on his BMX. He bunny-hopped onto the road, slammed on his brakes, and said, 'Whoa! That's one of the coolest things I've ever seen!'

Albert turned to his wife. 'See, this is why we need to start bringing the video camera with us everywhere.'

'Oh, please, you can hardly lift that thing,' she said.

'This would get on *Funniest Home Videos*. Guaranteed!'

Tom stepped out onto the street to see what they were talking about. Irene Borschmann was walking towards them with her two dogs. She moved with a slight limp, and was covered in a tangle of dirt, leaves and twigs. Was that what Tom's neighbours were laughing at? That seemed cruel. But then he saw it.

Dude the chihuahua was carrying a pair of headphones in his mouth. The way they were positioned on his head, with the ear pads facing up and over its ears, made it look like he was listening to music. The dog's little prance only added to the picture. It looked like he was dancing.

Despite everything, Tom allowed himself a smile.

'What's he listening to?' Betsy called to Irene. 'The Flea Gees?'

Albert burst out laughing.

Irene's frown didn't budge.

'Or maybe The Rolling Bones.' Another zinger from Betsy.

That one just about bowled Albert over. He put his hands on his knees and howled.

Their kid said, 'I don't get it.'

'Airedalesmith!' Albert began to sing, *'Janie's got a boooone!'*

'Please don't encourage her,' Irene said. 'I just got through scolding this little mutt.'

The rottweiler pulled up to piss on Patti Devlin's agapanthus. What was it about that spot?

On any other day, Tom would have joined in with a pun of his own. He was confident he could at least come up with something better than Airedalesmith, but he'd have to move fast if he was going to catch up with Connie and the others.

He got behind the wheel of Lil' Red. The car was packed and ready to go. Then that damn chihuahua crossed his rear-view, wagging its tail, the headphone cord trailing behind. A flash of red caught Tom's eye. He stared at it dumbly for a second, and swivelled in his chair to get a better look. Then it hit him. Hard. He flashed back to three days earlier, sitting in Lydia's living room, looking down at Tracie Reed's missing-person poster for the first time.

Then he was out of the car and running across the street towards Irene and her dogs. He left the driver's side door slung open.

'Irene,' he called.

Both dogs turned in unison.

'Morning, Tom,' she said. 'Come to see the show?'

He knelt beside the chihuahua and wrestled the headphones from its tiny jaws. 'Where did you find this, Irene?'

She shrugged. 'This little bastard dug it up in Wild Place.'

'Where?' Tom said.

'I just told you.'

'Where *exactly*?'

'What's going on, Tom?'

He examined the small strip of red tape holding one of the ear pads in place. 'I think these were Tracie's.'

23

The phone rang. Sharon got up to answer it too fast, then discovered a jackhammer in her head. She'd had a little too much wine before bed, and not enough water. Come to think of it, she hadn't had any water. Now her body – and whoever was calling this early – was punishing her. She forced herself up and began a slow zombie-walk into the kitchen.

Sharon lived in a ground-level flat right around the corner from the station. It had come furnished, so it never really felt like hers. Everything was a generic, inoffensive shade – soft greys, soft whites, soft beiges. A few small paintings decorated the walls. Her landlord would probably describe them as abstracts, but Sharon suspected they were meaningless. It was the sort of place you stayed at on your way to somewhere else. Sharon had lived here for seven years and counting.

The word *stuck* came to mind.

She answered the phone just to stop the noise. 'Hello?'

'Whoa, you sound awful, Shaz. Are you sick?'

It was Constable Daniel Bradley-Shore, he of the bulky

build and Lego-man haircut.

She groaned. 'What have I told you about calling me that?'

He didn't laugh. There was no banter. He took a slow, deep breath. 'Are you sitting down?'

She wasn't. The phone cord didn't reach the nearest chair. 'What is it, Danny?' she asked.

Sharon parked in Novak Street, which intersected with Bright Street, where Tracie Reed lived. A police car was parked outside a laneway that cut between houses. It gave the best access into the community forest beyond.

A constable was cordoning off the entrance of the laneway with blue-and-white-checked police tape. Sharon was sure they'd met before but she couldn't remember his name off the top of her head. She'd have to fish her eyeglasses out of the glove compartment if she had any hope of reading his name tag, and who had time for that?

'Hi, mate,' she said.

He pointed into the laneway. 'If you go to the left of that storm drain, you'll see my partner ... or I can show you the way, if you want.'

He seemed reluctant, and Sharon was pretty sure she knew why. Judging by the dark yellow stain on the front of his shirt and the smell of vomit on his breath, he had seen something terrible in that bush and had had, well, a normal reaction.

'A CSI team will be right behind me,' she said. 'Send them in when they get here, and don't let any of *them* get close.'

She pointed across the street. A crowd was growing. A half-dozen locals were out on the footpath. Some were watching Sharon and the constable, others were staring through the gaps between the houses, shielding their eyes against the sun, trying to get a look into the forest. There were more little groups huddled on stoops, verandas and front lawns, all the way up the street.

The constable lifted the tape for Sharon to duck under. At the end of the laneway, Sharon did as she was told and took a left around the drain. She paused at the top of a small grassy slope. She looked left and right. A concrete channel ran along the back fences, feeding into the stormwater drain via big steel-covered drains. Three doors up, a man was standing outside his back gate. Further down, a woman with a baby stood at the top of a sloped lawn. They were both watching.

Sharon ignored them. In front of her was a wall of bushland. A light breeze shifted through it. Branches creaked and whispered. She could see why people called it Wild Place.

Senior Constable Sue Lee stepped out of the tree line to greet her. Lee was a lean and muscular woman, somewhere in her thirties. Her brow was stiff, but there was a hint of a smile on her lips.

'Hey, Guff,' Lee said.

Guff. Well, at least it was better than *Shaz*.

'Where is it?' Sharon asked.

'Follow me.'

They moved a short distance along a trail, then Lee stepped off and started through the underbrush, ducking beneath a branch. They passed by the remnants of an old campfire littered with broken bottles. Sharon stuck close, keeping her eyes on the long grass, watching out for snakes.

While they walked, Lee talked. 'A woman was walking her dog in here this morning and found this.' She handed Sharon a brown paper bag. There was a pair of dirty, discarded headphones inside. 'The missing girl's mother found a Walkman a couple weeks back. We had a look around but we weren't even sure it was hers. A neighbour recognised the headphones from a poster of the missing girl. We had the dog-walker lady lead us to the spot. I kicked around in the dirt for a bit and, well, she wasn't hard to find.'

Lee lingered. Sharon stepped forward into a small clearing. There were two more uniformed officers, both with their backs to Sharon, both staring at the ground. Radio static cut through the silence. The officers turned to her slowly, then each took a step back to give her a clear view.

And there she was, half-buried in the dirt before her. Slivers of sunlight fell in through the canopy of trees, flashing on a pair of dead eyes, sunken cheeks, a wide-open mouth packed with dirt, a black mess of dried blood in tangled, bleached-blonde hair.

'It's her, right?' Lee asked. 'The missing girl.'

Sharon's heart hurt. She'd seen dead bodies before, but never one so young. A word swam up from someplace. 'Wasted.'

'What's that, Guff?' Lee asked.

'Cordon off the site. Twenty metres in both directions.'

'That's a lot of tape.'

'Get more uniforms down here. Every inch of this place needs to be searched. Not trampled. Searched. I want every house with a fence that backs onto the forest doorknocked.'

'Got it,' Lee said. 'What else?'

'Stop right there, mate!'

Sharon looked up. One of the officers was looking over Sharon's shoulder. Tom Witter was barrelling towards them. Before Sharon could say anything, Lee had spun on one foot and shouted, 'This is a crime scene! Freeze!'

But Tom kept coming. His eyes were fixed on the grave. Lee tackled him. He went down hard. The other officers surged forward to assist. Tom's face, shocked and bewildered, got lost in a game of stacks on.

'Stand down,' Sharon called. 'Let him up.'

One by one, the officers climbed to their feet. Lee was the last one up.

'This guy's harmless,' Sharon told them. 'He's a dopey bastard for charging into a crime scene, but he's harmless.'

Sharon walked Tom back to his yard, then made sure they were safely behind a closed gate before she spoke. 'Tom, there's no right way to ask someone this, so I'm just going to come out with it: have you gone mental?'

'I'm sorry, Sharon,' he said.

'You're lucky you weren't shot.'

'It's her, isn't it? It's Tracie?'

She sighed. Nodded.

'How was she killed?'

Tom's neck and shoulders tensed and twisted as he spoke. Sharon could see his muscles working overtime to subdue his Tourette's.

'We won't know that for a while.' She put her hand over his. 'I'm sorry. I know you taught her.'

People had started to gather on the ridge that ran behind Tom's house, wanting to get a look at what was going on. It was only a matter of time before the news got out.

Damn you, Rambaldini, Sharon thought. Quite a time he'd picked to go on holiday.

'I have to go, Tom,' she said. 'Are you going to be all right? You want me to call Connie?'

He slipped his hand from hers, then shook his head.

Sharon started away.

'Were there any markings?' he called after her.

She stopped. 'Markings?'

'Around the grave. Were there symbols? Like the one they found on the necklace in Tracie's room.' He looked next door. 'And the one tattooed on Sean Fryman's arm.'

Sharon looked at him, baffled. 'No. There were no symbols. Tom, are you okay?'

'I'm fine,' he said.

There was ice in his tone.

'I have to go,' Sharon told him. 'I have the privilege of telling a woman her seventeen-year-old daughter is dead.'

Sharon pulled up outside Nancy Reed's house and told herself not to cry. This was their tragedy, not hers. Their grief, not hers. Her job was to tell the parents what she knew, be sympathetic, apologetic, and get out. It was cold to look at it that way but part of the job. It was the same reason welders wore masks and surgeons wore gowns. The same reason that, in the unlikely event of a midair catastrophe, you were supposed to affix your own oxygen mask before helping someone else.

It was never easy, but this one was going to be a real doozy. Before she stepped out of the car, Sharon took a deep breath and pictured where she would be later that night: in the tub back home with a glass of Jim's Johnnie Walker. She'd have a soak, a drink, and then, if she needed to, she'd cry it all out.

As she approached the front door, Sharon saw that all the neighbours were out, watching and talking and shaking their heads. One guy had even brought his Polaroid camera out. It hung around his neck on a strap. He lifted it, locked eyes with Sharon, then lowered it. She nodded her thanks, then she knocked on the front door.

The ghost of Nancy Reed answered. She didn't seem to be living anymore. She moved, existed, functioned, but she looked dead behind the eyes.

'Hello, Mrs Reed,' Sharon said. 'Mind if I come in?'

'There's news, isn't there?'

Sharon nodded. Nancy let her in. The house was dark. All the curtains and blinds were drawn, but it wasn't just the light. The place *felt* dark. Heavy. Haunted.

They sat in the living room. A single yellow lamp was on.

The shade was a stained-glass landscape of a desert, complete with oasis and wandering camels. There was a half-drunk glass of red wine on the coffee table between them. Nancy picked it up and threw back what was left.

'She's dead, isn't she?'

Sharon's mouth turned dry. 'A little after six this morning, a dog walker stumbled on some loose soil in the community forest behind your house. It was later discovered to be a grave.'

'How long?'

'Excuse me?'

'How long has she been out there?' Nancy asked.

'It's too early to say for sure, but judging by the' – Sharon took a breath – 'decomposition, I'd say she was put in the ground right around the time she went missing.'

'How?'

'We don't know yet. We'll know more when we—'

'Get her on the table and cut her up.'

Sharon flinched. 'After the medical examination. Yes.'

'Where's Detective Rambaldini?'

'Unavailable.'

Nancy glared at her. 'Still?'

'He's on holiday,' Sharon said. 'With his family.'

Nancy stood suddenly. Instincts kicked in. Sharon went for her side-arm but relaxed when the woman strode past her and into the kitchen. There was the sound of banging pantry doors, then Nancy came back into the room with a fresh bottle of red. She splashed some into her glass from a height, then guzzled it.

'Would you like me to call Mr Reed?' Sharon asked.

'You could try, but my ex-husband seems to have gone MIA.'

'What do you mean?'

'I tried calling him last night at the motor inn, and again this morning. He didn't answer and he didn't call me back. If you do manage to get a hold of him, will you give him a message for me?'

'Of course.'

'Tell him: they believe us now.'

'... Mrs Reed?'

Another two big swigs of red, then: 'When I filed a missing person's report for our daughter, we were told she was a runaway. When I insisted she was kidnapped, we were as good as told she wasn't *really* being looked for. But now they send you, a woman, to my house. You're here, speaking in soft little funeral-director tones, with the taste of crow in your mouth. So I assume I'm right in thinking you believe us now.'

Sharon looked at her hands. She could have told Nancy it wasn't her fault. Technically, she was just babysitting her daughter's case. But that would only make things worse. She could have said everything was done to find Tracie, but simply, tragically, that just wasn't true. It also didn't matter. The damage was done. Nancy Reed would never un-feel this. She would never un-remember. In most ways – all the ways that counted – this moment marked the end of her life.

What can you say to someone like that?

So Sharon kept it simple.

'Yes, Mrs Reed,' she said. 'We believe you now.'

24

Tom drove fast. He wasn't used to driving Connie's little red hatchback. Even packed full of Marty's belongings, it had some heft to it. He crept up to the limit, then over it, weaving in and out of tourist traffic. He kept a close eye on the rear-view. He didn't really think anyone would be following him, but it was better to play it safe.

He was only dimly aware that it was New Year's Eve, even though every second car he passed seemed to be blasting Prince's '1999'. This was not how he'd envisioned spending the last day of the 80s, seized by grief, grappling with a new, terrifying reality.

He pulled into the school and rolled past the main buildings, following the road around until he reached the staff parking bay. The car park was empty. Owen's convertible was gone.

Tom jerked on the handbrake and bustled out. He moved briskly to the double doors that led into the school. He shoved against them. They were locked. He fished his keys from his pocket and froze. He had Connie's set. The school master was with her.

He banged on the doors. There was no answer. He banged again. Damn. Where was Owen? Was Sean with him? He paced. Knocked again. Nothing. He started back to the car, made it halfway before—

'Tom.'

He turned. Owen poked his head out from the doors, scanned the car park, then gestured for him to come inside. Tom hurried in. When the doors were closed and locked safely behind him, Owen blurted, 'Did anyone follow you?'

'No,' Tom said.

'Are you sure?'

'Pretty sure.'

'*Pretty sure?*'

'Nobody followed me,' Tom said firmly.

'What about the police? Has his mother called them?'

'Not yet,' Tom said. 'Where's your car?'

'I parked it around the corner. I doubt anyone would see it from the road, but I didn't want to take any chances.'

'And Sean?'

Owen looked terrible. His hair was wild, his skin red and dry. His shirt was soaked with what Tom assumed was sweat. 'There are too many exits in here, so I moved him too.'

'Is he …?'

'Alive,' Owen said. 'And awake. Come on. I'll show you.'

Tom tried to tell him there and then about Tracie, but the words refused to leave his mouth. The big man started away from him down the corridor. Tom had to trot to catch up.

They trudged down the hallway and around the corner, pulling up outside a door with POOL stencilled over a frosted glass panel. Owen moved to open the door but Tom grabbed his arm.

'Wait,' Tom said. 'Let me talk to him. You should go home.'

'… Home?'

'Go be with your wife.'

Owen stiffened. His shoulders flung back; his chest inflated. 'Has something happened?'

Tom hesitated. 'It's Tracie.'

'Is she …?'

'I'm sorry, Owen.'

He fought the news at first. He shook his head firmly. That couldn't be right. His daughter couldn't be dead. She was missing. In danger, maybe. But not *that*. Then, Tom watched as the horror dawned on his face.

He held Tom's gaze a moment more, then his eyes shifted to the closed door behind him. Tom blocked his path.

'Go home,' Tom said again. 'Nancy will need you.'

Owen took two short steps backwards, turned and ran. His big footfalls echoed against the empty corridor. Tom watched him, feeling heavy and rotten and ashamed.

As he stepped through the doors, the thick, overwhelming smell of chlorine drifted out. It triggered a series of memories from Tom's youth: backyard pools, swimming lessons, diving headfirst into the deep end of the Medford Park Public Baths. Now, he supposed, it would remind him of Sean, of Tracie, of the summer of 1989 when everything – *everything* – went so horribly wrong.

The pool was 25 metres long, separated into six lanes with bright yellow rope. The water was still beneath the high ceiling. Coloured streamers hung from the rafters, bright reds and blues and greens. A huge bank of windows ran the length of the far wall. It looked out onto a steep grass hill and, beyond that, empty fields that had been sold off and were waiting for subdivision. They were hidden from view.

Sean was in a heap on the ledge at the top end of the pool. Owen must have found a bike lock in one of the open lockers or in the lost and found box in the teachers' lounge, because he'd used it to chain Sean in place. One end was attached to the bottom step of the diving board, the other was around Sean's neck.

Tom recoiled, then eased a little closer. Sean raised his head. He was in bad shape. The gash left by the ashtray was covered with a sopping brown bandage. There were flakes of dried blood tangled in his hair, along with a smattering of cigarette ash, like bad stage make-up.

'Hello, Sean,' he said.

Sean cowered.

'How are you feeling?'

Sean sat up and sank forward against the chain. He ran his fingers between his throat and the lock, making some room to breathe, then said, 'How do you think?'

'Do you need anything?'

'... Water.'

'Wait here,' Tom said.

Wait here? Slick, Tom.

Tom went over to the lifesaver's station, which was more of a storage closet: a narrow, windowless space filled with racks and shelves. It was bursting with cleaning materials, life-preservers, kickboards, foam noodles, fresh towels, fold-out chairs, and one long yellow lane rope that hung in a coil like a giant anaconda.

At the back of the room was a sink. A couple of dirty mugs were inside. One had *SWIM HARD, DREAM BIG* printed on the side, the other, *I PUT THE 'P' IN POOLS*. He grabbed the 'P' one, rinsed it out using hot water and two fingers, then filled it from the tap.

On his way out, he pulled down one of the fold-out chairs. He put the mug in front of Sean, then scrambled quickly backwards. He needn't have bothered. Sean hardly moved. He took the water and guzzled it, while Tom set up the plastic chair and sat down.

'Mum would have called the cops by now,' Sean said. 'They'll be looking for me. And you. How many people saw you two come to the house last night? How many people saw you come here?'

Tom replied with a question of his own. 'What happened to you, Sean?'

The prisoner – and that's what Sean was now – manoeuvred the chain around his neck again, this time so he could sit up straight against the steps of the diving board. 'I could ask you the same. You used to be one of the good ones.'

He wasn't surprised Sean was trying to get under his skin, but he was surprised it was working.

'If you're wondering about Tracie, I locked her in a dungeon without food or water,' Sean said. 'If you don't let me go, she'll starve to death.'

'Did that work on Owen?'

He shook his head and offered a strange little smile.

Tom felt sick.

'So, what happens now?' Sean asked. 'You torture a confession out of me?'

'Nobody's going to torture you.'

'What about Tracie's dad?'

Tom said nothing.

'He might kill me, you know,' Sean said. 'He's so sad. And so angry. Men like that don't think. They just act.'

'Men like your dad?' Tom asked.

Sean flinched. 'You don't know anything about him.'

'I know he hurt you, and your mum. And I know violence is like a language. If you learn it at a young age, it gets easier and easier to use.'

Silence.

'Tracie's dead, Sean,' Tom said. 'It's time to start telling the truth.'

There was more silence then, but this time it was of the stunned variety. But was he stunned because Tracie was dead or because Tom knew about it?

'Her body was found this morning,' Tom told him.

Sean bit his lip. 'Are you telling me the truth?'

'Yes.'

'This isn't some tactic to get me to talk?'

'I wish it was,' Tom said, and meant it. 'Owen's distraught. He's gone home to be with his family. I'm worried what he'll do when he gets back if we don't have something to tell him.'

Sean furrowed his brow at that, and looked, to Tom at least, genuinely confused.

'I guess it didn't work,' he said.

Tom got to his feet. 'What didn't work?'

Sean took a deep breath, repositioned the chain around his neck, and rolled up his T-shirt sleeve to expose his tattoo.

'This,' he said.

'What are you talking about?'

'Mum had me when she was sixteen. Did you know that?'

Tom shook his head. He knew Debbie was a young mum, but he had never done the maths.

'That's two years younger than I am now. I mean, that's just crazy, right? I have a hard enough time looking after myself. I can't even imagine having an extra little mouth to feed and an extra arse to wipe. She must have been scared out of her mind.' He sat forward. 'I think that's why she stayed with my dad for so long.'

'What's this got to do with Tracie?'

'He never hit me,' Sean said, as if he hadn't even heard Tom. 'Mum was a different story. He threatened me, but he never did it. At least, not that I can remember. It's ironic, I guess. You used to be like the father I never had. If someone said you'd be the one to hit me instead of him ...'

Tom considered pleading self-defence, but now seemed like the time for honesty.

'I'm sorry,' he said. 'I lost control.'

Sean grunted but didn't look up. 'Dad used that line, too. After going to town on my mum.' Tears came then. 'I was too little to do anything about it.' If this was all an act, it was a good one. 'I still feel too little, sometimes. That probably sounds stupid to you.'

'Actually, it doesn't sound stupid at all,' Tom said.

He thought about all the bullies in his life. That feeling of being too weak, too inconsequential – *too little* – had never gone away.

'It was on one of those bad nights I first saw this symbol,' Sean said. He stared down at the pentagram on his arm. 'Dad had just lost his job. I must have been, I don't know, seven or eight. He went to the pub after his final shift and came home shit-faced. I got good at seeing the signs, so I went to hide in my room. That's what I'd do, like a stupid fucking baby. Hide in my room, under the bed.' He gave a little shrug. 'When it was over, and the house was quiet again, Mum came into my room. She was banged up. Bad. She had to drive over to the hospital to get stitches, and told me I needed to stay with my dad. I begged to go with her. I was scared. So she gave me something. For protection. A necklace.'

'With a pentagram on the end.'

Sean nodded. 'Before heavy metal bands used it, and before

Satanists or whoever got their hands on it, it was a protection symbol. A Wiccan thing. Mum didn't believe in that stuff, but she made out like she did, for me. Mum didn't come back for six days. From what I pieced together later by talking to relatives, she never went to the hospital that night. She ran away. She left me with him.' He wiped his tears with the back of his hand. 'The most fucked-up part about it is I don't even blame her. I get it. She had no idea where she was going to go, how she was going to survive. It was kinder to leave me there.'

'But then she came back.'

'I guess she couldn't live with her decision. Anyway, we both got out, eventually, and I wore that symbol around my neck for years. I even took it in the shower with me. When I was eighteen, I made it permanent.' He rolled down the sleeve of his T-shirt. 'After that, I didn't need the necklace anymore.'

'How did it end up in Tracie Reed's bedroom?'

'I gave it to her.'

'When?'

Sean was quiet for a moment. Then: 'The night she went missing.'

Just like that.

'You went to her house,' Tom offered.

'No,' Sean said. 'She came to mine. She was waiting outside my back gate when I got back.'

'Back from messing around with the ouija board?'

He nodded. 'I got a nosebleed so I had to head home early. I get them sometimes when the weather's warm.'

'Keiran thought you'd been possessed by the devil.'

'Yeah.' He almost smiled. 'When Tracie saw me, she freaked out. She thought I'd been in a fight or something. Mum wasn't home, so Tracie came inside to help patch me up. Mum usually treats my nosebleeds with a tampon, but I wasn't about to do that in front of Tracie.'

'Why was she there so late?' Tom asked. 'Was Tracie your girlfriend?'

'It wasn't like that. I told you. She'd been out that night with her friend, Cassie. She was supposed to stay over at her place, but they had a fight.'

'What was the fight about?'

'I didn't ask,' Sean said. 'But if I had to guess, I'd say it had something to do with Tracie's hair. It was blonde. Well, it was supposed to be blonde. It looked more like margarine. If it was any other night, I might have told her it was a wonderful shade of bimbo. Something like that. But there was something different about her that night. I got the sense that if I'd made fun of her, she might have just burst into tears.'

Tom sat down again and asked, 'What makes you say that?'

'Just a feeling,' he said. 'Usually Tracie is – was – light.'

'Light?'

'Yeah. You know. Some people are heavy, some people are light. Maybe *light* isn't the right word. Maybe *ethereal* works better. But that night, she was …'

'Heavy.'

Sean thought about that for a second. 'She wasn't herself, that's all I know.'

'Did you ask her about it?'

'I did.'

'And?'

'She asked me if I ever got the feeling I was being watched. I told her I did. When you dress like I do in a place like Camp Hill, everyone stares. But that's not what she meant. I was talking about being *noticed*. Tracie was talking about being *watched*. Stalked.' Sean looked up, twisting his lips as he read something on Tom's face. 'Oh. You already knew that part.'

'I found a stash of Starling Red cigarettes outside her house.'

'Starling Red is a popular brand,' Sean said. 'I wasn't the one who was following her.'

'Then who?' Tom asked.

'She didn't say. I don't think she knew. But if someone really was following her, it probably had something to do with her snooping.'

'Snooping?'

'I don't know what else you'd call it. She wanted to be an investigative journalist, so as part of her training she'd sneak around, listen in on people's conversations, that sort of thing. She was the kind of person who'd ask to use the toilet just so she could sneak a look at your medicine cabinet. Know what I mean?'

'Actually,' Tom said. 'I have no idea what that means.'

'Tracie has a TCM-100B.'

'Pretend I don't know what that is.'

'It's a Walkman,' Sean said. 'But it has a voice-record function. She makes secret little recordings of people. She played one for me that night. A conversation between some random old couple she sat next to at the bus stop. They were bickering over something. One of them thought that whoever sits in the middle seat of a plane should automatically get both arm rests. The other one disagreed.'

'I'm not following,' Tom said. 'Why did she record them?'

'She'd probably call it journalism practice,' Sean said. 'But to me, it seemed more like she was collecting little moments. Preserving them before they were gone.'

'What's this got to do with her being followed?'

Sean shrugged. 'Maybe she listened in on the wrong conversation. Heard something she wasn't supposed to.'

Tom thought about it. 'Or maybe you're making this whole thing up.'

'Yeah,' Sean replied. 'Maybe.'

The sharp, chlorine smell wafted off the pool. It made it hard to think.

'Is that why you gave her the necklace?' Tom asked. 'Because she was scared?'

'It sounded like she needed it,' Sean told him. 'I thought it might make her feel safer, at least. It worked that way for me.'

'What happened next?'

'Nothing,' Sean said. 'She took her bag and left.'

'Through Wild Place?'

'Out the front door,' Sean said.

'Did she say where she was going?'

'Yeah. She was on her way to her dad's place.'

Tom stood again, and paced. 'Something still isn't adding

up. You still haven't told me why she was there that night. If it was so innocent, why didn't you tell me? Why didn't you tell the police?'

Sean smirked. He *actually* smirked.

'Is something funny?' Tom asked.

'No. Everything's pretty fucking un-funny, Mr Witter. See, none of this has anything to do with devil worship or demonic possession. It's not as complicated or as deep as you're trying to make it. Tracie was there to buy a little pot.'

'Pot?'

'I'm not a devil worshipper, Mr Witter,' he said. 'I'm a drug dealer.'

25

The house on Bright Street would always be home, but Owen would never be welcome here again. It would never be *his* again. It was an odd feeling. He stood before the front door, wondering if he was supposed to knock. If not, if he was still allowed to stroll right in, when would that privilege be revoked? When the divorce was finalised?

Owen split the difference. He knocked, then opened the door. The house was dark and stuffy. That seemed about right. It was a place of grief and mourning. Owen wasn't a particularly religious or superstitious man, but he knew those things had a way of spilling over and seeping into the furniture, the carpets, the walls. In that sense, maybe it was good he didn't live here anymore. Maybe he should take a match to the place and burn it down.

He checked the living room for Nancy. There was an empty glass on the coffee table, a tangled knitted blanket on the armchair, and Tracie's baby album. Seeing it filled him with white-hot rage.

Nancy wasn't in the bedroom either. He turned on the light and went to the wardrobe. He felt around on the top shelf and found the brown leather case. He took the case down, set it on the bed and unzipped it. He ran his hands slowly, almost religiously, over the butt of the hunting rifle. He checked for shells in the inside pouch of the case. There was one. That was all he needed.

He zipped up the case, slung it over his shoulder, and started out. On his way back down the hallway he paused outside Tracie's room. Nancy was curled up on the floor with a bottle of wine, foetal and almost catatonic. He didn't step into the room. He just stared at her. She stared back. They were in a place beyond words now. They had become members of a raw, brutal and exclusive club: parents who outlive their children.

Nancy's red-rimmed gaze shifted to the rifle. She seemed to regard it with dark wonder. Her expression hardened. Then she nodded.

Owen nodded back.

26

As far as Sharon could tell, Sean Fryman had little to no connection to Tracie Reed. Sean and Tracie went to the same high school, but so did hundreds of other kids. The same symbol found in Tracie's room was tattooed on Sean's arm but, as she'd pointed out to Tom over dinner, that symbol was everywhere.

So why was she knocking on Sean's front door? It might have been the tongue-lashing she'd just got from Nancy about not listening to civilians. Or maybe – just maybe – she was starting to hear the same hoofbeats Tom had heard.

The door opened.

Sean's mother was younger than Sharon expected, and prettier, too. Her eyes were a piercing shade of blue. Her milky skin was lightly freckled in that approachable, girl-next-door way. Sharon hated her for it. It was also possible that Sharon was having a very shitty day and was looking for someone to take it out on.

'Are you Deborah Fryman?' Sharon asked.

'Debbie, yeah,' she said.

'And is your son Sean Fryman?'

Debbie leaned against her screen door and squinted at her. 'What's this about?'

'I'm Detective Guffey.' Sharon flashed her ID. 'I have a few questions for your son.'

Debbie stood there a moment, not moving.

Sharon prompted her: 'Maybe we should talk inside.'

She gestured to the street. Neighbours were crowding the footpaths. Some of them looked sombre, others were smiling and laughing. One particularly chubby genius had dragged a banana lounge and mini-Esky out onto his front lawn and was watching the show in style. She couldn't blame them. Things like this weren't supposed to happen in places like Camp Hill, land of bright green lawns and little rainbows that glimmered in sprinkler showers. It was a spectacle, and people love spectacles – so long as whatever happened didn't happen to them.

Sharon prompted her again.

'Debbie?'

'Right,' she said. 'Come inside.'

Debbie led her into a cluttered, well-lived-in family home. Sharon wasn't offered a place to sit. Debbie planted her feet in the middle of the living room and waited.

'Where's Sean?' Sharon asked.

'First, what's this about?' Debbie said.

Ah. So this was how it was going to be.

'Did you hear about the girl who went missing on the other side of Wild Place? Her name was Tracie Reed.'

'Was?'

'She's dead.'

Debbie flinched. She put her hands into the pockets of her denim cut-offs and chewed her lip. This woman was hiding something. 'What's that got to do with Sean?'

'I just have a few questions for him,' Sharon said. 'I only came here to talk.'

'Well, you can't.'

Sharon took a beat. She could push or back off. She really wasn't in the mood to back off. 'Fine. You're welcome to come down and have a formal chat at the station instead.'

A deep crease appeared on Debbie's forehead.

'No,' she said. 'I mean, you can't talk to him because he isn't here.'

'Where is he?' Sharon asked.

'I don't know. He didn't come home last night.'

Debbie took her hands out of her pockets and flopped backwards onto the sofa.

'I have this awful feeling,' she said. 'I just keep thinking something horrible has happened to him. That whoever kidnapped the Reed girl – whoever *killed* her – took Sean too.'

The window over the TV gave a view of Tom's house. Sharon wondered what it must be like in there on a Saturday morning: cartoons on the TV, laughs around the breakfast table, everyone still in their pyjamas. She couldn't help but contrast Tom's life to Debbie Fryman's.

'There is another possible scenario,' Sharon told her. 'Tracie Reed's body was found today. If Sean got wind of that, he might not have wanted to stick around for the aftermath. He might have run.'

Debbie's gaze darkened.

'Why would that make him run?'

Sharon said nothing.

Debbie said, 'You're not here to talk to my son, are you, detective? You're here to accuse him of something.'

Sharon shook her head. 'I heard a rumour.'

'About Sean.'

'Yes.'

'Who from?'

'It doesn't matter.' Sharon let the silence linger, then sat down across from her. 'People are saying he had something to do with what happened to Tracie. You'd have to admit, him disappearing like this doesn't exactly make him look innocent.'

Sharon braced herself for attack. Not a physical one – although that wasn't entirely out of the realm of possibility – but a desperate lashing out.

It didn't happen that way. Instead, Debbie began to cry.

Situations like these were tricky to navigate, not just as a cop, but as a woman. Should Sharon hug this woman or pat her arm or tell her everything was going to be okay? Or should she drive the dagger in deeper?

'In your opinion, is Sean capable of hurting someone?' she asked.

The tears spilled down Debbie's face.

'Has he given you any indication he might have committed a crime?'

Debbie didn't move to wipe them.

'Has Sean ever demonstrated a proclivity for violence?'

Nothing.

'Ms Fryman?'

More crying.

'Debbie?'

'I don't know!' Debbie blurted. 'And I don't know what this says about me as a mother, or the way I raised him.' She looked Sharon dead in the eyes. 'But I know he didn't run.'

'How?'

Debbie fell silent.

Sharon leaned back in her chair. The fabric smelled strongly of ash.

'I thought Tracie Reed ran away,' Sharon said. 'Right up until I saw her body this morning. Her mother told us she didn't. She told us until she was blue in the face, actually. We ignored her.' She tried to hold Debbie's gaze, but it wasn't easy. 'A mother knows. I'd forgotten that. Maybe because I'm not a mother myself. Maybe because my own mother was shithouse. But I won't make that mistake again. If you tell me Sean didn't run, I want to believe you, Debbie. But you need to be honest with me. You need to tell me everything.'

Debbie's tears dried up.

Whoa, Sharon thought, when Debbie turned on the light. Sean's bedroom looked like the lair of a serial killer. There were heavy metal records and posters, weird wood carvings, a dead toad in a jar and a live snake in a tank. There were too many details to take in, but Sharon felt drawn to, of all things, a grand old chess set on the dresser.

Its theme appeared to be Heaven vs Hell. God vs Satan. The light side was made up of angels with golden locks and outstretched wings. Their queen was the Virgin Mary. The dark side was the colour of burnt skin, with cloven-footed, demonic beasts. Their queen was a scowling woman with fiery red hair, dressed in a black cloak.

'It's Lilith,' Debbie said.

The game was set and ready to play except for one piece. The light side's king (God?) was toppled, lying half off the board. It didn't look like an accident. It looked like a statement. If this whole thing went the way Sharon thought, and ended in Sean's arrest, all the jury would need to convict was a look at this bedroom.

Debbie drew her attention to a shoebox on Sean's bed. A pentagram had been drawn on the top.

'When I got home last night and Sean wasn't here, I guess I went snooping,' Debbie said. 'I found this.'

She opened the shoebox.

It was stuffed with cash.

'It's nearly eight thousand,' Debbie said. 'I counted.'

'Where did he get this kind of money?'

Debbie shook her head. 'No idea. But if you were a kid Sean's age and you decided to run away, do you think you'd leave this behind?' She didn't give Sharon time to answer. 'You said you wanted to know everything?'

Sharon nodded.

'Last night, when I got home from work, the living room had been trashed,' Debbie said. 'There was ash all over the carpet. I assumed Sean did it, so I cleaned up. Begrudgingly. But now I'm wondering if it was, you know, signs of a struggle.'

Her eyes were wide and terrified.

Sharon asked, 'Can you think of anyone who might want to hurt him?'

'No.'

'Does Sean have any enemies?'

She shook her head.

'Did you notice anything else when you got home last night?'

'Like what?'

'Anything strange?' Sharon suggested. 'Anything out of the ordinary?'

Debbie shook her head again. But then, abruptly, she stopped shaking it. 'I'm not sure if this qualifies as strange, but I worked the graveyard shift last night, which means I leave the house around seven. On my way out, I noticed half the street heading over to Lydia Chow's place.'

'Was there some kind of party?'

'It was our regular neighbourhood watch meeting,' Lydia Chow said.

She sat in an antique armchair in her parlour, hands flat on her thighs, back straight. Lydia was, in a word, impeccable. Her skin was smooth and faultless. Her outfit managed to be both conservative and sexy. Her home matched. The walls were clean and white, the floors spotless. The temperature was perfect. Even the air smelled sweet.

A lot of people got nervous talking to the cops, even if they knew they'd done nothing wrong. It was human instinct. Lydia, on the other hand, seemed thrilled to be talking to Sharon.

'We usually only have one meeting a fortnight,' she said. 'But with everything that's been going on, and as chairwoman of the Keel Street Neighbourhood Watch group, I thought it wise to get everyone together and pool our info.'

When she was finished with Lydia, Sharon went next door and asked similar questions of Norma Spurr-Smith. All along the street, she repeated the process. Digging for the truth was a lot like digging for anything: it meant doing the same thing over and over. Most real police work was like this. An exercise in persistence.

'Tracie Reed's father was there,' Norma Spurr-Smith said, standing in her front doorway. Sharon looked over the woman's shoulder. This house was a stark contrast to Lydia's. It was cluttered and noisy and lived-in, but, unlike the Chow residence, this one had a soul. 'He was like a special guest or something.'

'Owen Reed was at the meeting?' Sharon asked.

'Yep, he was there,' said Ingrid Peck, in the house across the way. 'He was sort of a strong, silent type. Although I don't know what else I expected. Poor guy.'

'How many people were at the meeting?' Sharon asked.

'All the regulars. Well, almost everyone. Gary Henskee was a no-show. I nearly sat it out myself. I mean, two meetings in one week seems sort of excessive, no? Anyway, in the end I'm glad I went. I had no idea about all that Satanic stuff.'

'Satanic stuff?' Sharon asked. 'That's what the meeting was about?'

'Well, sort of.'

'Sort of?'

'It was really about Sean Fryman,' Betsy Keneally told her.

James Fellers said, 'It was about that weird kid who lives down the street.'

Alyssa Lindley: 'He buys dead mice!'

'I hate to admit it, but I sort of pooh-poohed the whole thing at the time,' Irene Borschmann told Sharon. 'I didn't like the idea of talking about someone behind their back. That sort of thing happens too much in this town. But now, after that poor girl turned up dead, I don't know …'

Karina Alvarez said, 'I had no idea that sort of thing went on, and right under our noses.'

Mrs Alvarez lived in a big house on the corner of the street. It had a white picket fence and everything.

'After the meeting I went right home and had a long talk with my son,' Karina said. 'I warned him to stay away from Sean, but my Michael didn't need to be told. He already knew Sean was bad news.'

'How do you mean?' Sharon asked.

'Apparently Sean grows marijuana.' She stretched out each syllable of the word. 'Well, Michael didn't actually say he *grew* the stuff, but he certainly sells it. Not that my son would ever buy it. I made him swear that on the Bible.'

Sharon thought about the shoebox under Sean's bed.

'Drugs on my own street.' Karina shook her head. 'I feel like I've been living with my head in the sand. I think we all felt that way. Everyone except for Tom.'

'Tom Witter?' Sharon asked.

'Yep. He made what I guess you'd call a speech, but it was more like a warning. I went right home after and banned my Michael from playing *Dungeons & Dragons*.'

'What else did he say?'

'I don't mean to sound rude,' Bill Davis said, 'but is this going to take much longer? The wife and I are hosting a little New Year's Eve soiree tonight and we need to start setting up. You're welcome to come if you don't have plans.'

'No, thanks.'

'What's this about, anyway?'

'Sean Fryman is missing,' Sharon said.

Cheree Gifford gasped and put a hand to her chest. 'Missing?'

'He didn't come home last night,' Sharon said. 'His mother is very worried.'

'I would be too.' The woman paused, then arched an eyebrow. 'Have you talked to Ellie Sipple yet?'

'Not yet. Why?'

'I saw something last night,' Ellie Sipple said.

She was a gangly woman with a short perm and tortoiseshell eyeglasses. It was approximately a million degrees in her kitchen, but this woman was wearing a heavy knitted jumper. Stranger still, she didn't appear to be sweating.

'What did you see?' Sharon asked.

'On the way home from the meeting I noticed Tom Witter and Owen Reed. They were sitting in Owen's car. It looked like they were drinking.' She frowned. 'I suppose I must have been curious, because I kept an eye on them. The window above the kitchen sink gives a good view of the street. It's not like I'm a spy or anything. But when I'm doing the dishes I … notice things.'

Uh-huh.

'What did you notice last night?' Sharon asked.

Ellie cleared her throat. 'They went and knocked on Sean Fryman's front door.'

'Both of them?'

'Yes.'

'Are you sure?'

'Positive.'

Sharon's throat turned dry. 'What happened next, Miss Sipple?'

27

Bang-bang!

Tom leapt to his feet and spun towards the sound. He waited.

Bang!

'… Tom?'

Tom exhaled. It was Owen, knocking on the double doors at the end of the corridor. Tom stepped away from the pool and went down to open them. Owen shoved past him and marched inside. The doors slammed shut behind them as Tom hurried after him. There was a brown leather case slung over Owen's shoulder, but it took Tom a second to identify it.

'Is that a gun?'

Owen didn't respond. He just went on marching. The overhead lights were off but every few metres a small square window let in light. They created a strobe effect. Owen disappeared and reappeared over and over.

'What are you doing with that, Owen?' Tom asked.

Owen looked at him with an expression that said: *Isn't it obvious?* But it wasn't. Did he intend to use the gun to scare

Sean, or shoot him? Tom might have asked, but he wasn't sure he wanted the answer.

They arrived at the pool. Owen moved to the door, but Tom blocked his path.

'Get out of my way, Tom.'

'Wait.'

'Out of my way.'

'Just stop for a second,' Tom said. 'Sean and I talked.'

'And?'

Tom told Owen about the pot, the necklace and Tracie's alleged stalker. Owen listened with a stony expression: eyes narrow, lips drawn tightly together.

'He's lying,' Owen said. 'Tracie would never do drugs.'

'It's not heroin,' Tom told him. 'A lot of kids her age have tried it.'

'What about your kids?'

Tom rushed to answer *no*, then pulled back. 'Tracie and Cassie Clarke had an argument the night she disappeared. Did you know that?'

Owen shook his head, then shrugged.

'The police talked to Cassie,' he said. 'I don't remember her mentioning a fight.' His nostrils flared. 'He's lying.'

'But what if he's not?' Tom said. 'Don't you want to be sure? Let me talk to Cassie. I can dig out her address from the files in the office. She might know something. I can be there and back in an hour. Two, tops.'

Owen turned back to the door. Tom could almost hear the cogs turning in his brain.

'Do you want the truth, Owen? Or are you just looking for someone to take it out on?'

As much as Tom didn't want to think about Sean being innocent, he couldn't ignore it, either. Compartmentalisation only got you so far.

Owen clenched his jaw and said nothing. Tom waited. For what, he wasn't sure. For Owen to nod silently and agree? For Owen to jam Tom into one of the lockers, like Steve McDougal used to do? To shove past him, put the hunting rifle against Sean's head and pull the trigger?

When Tom couldn't stand the silence anymore, he said, 'Let me try.'

'A few hours,' Owen said. 'After that, we do it my way.'

Tom started away.

'Tom.'

He pulled up. 'What?'

'If you come back here with the police—'

'I won't.'

'I'll kill him before I let them get to me,' he said.

Tom believed him. A man was never so dangerous as when he had nothing left to lose.

Tom pressed back through the double doors and out into the warm air. The sound of people eager to start their New Year's Eve house parties drifted in from multiple directions: dance songs and power ballads, whoops and cheers.

He reached Connie's Lil' Red, saw the back seat full of

packing boxes, and remembered it was moving day. Tom had told Connie and the boys he'd be right behind them. That was an hour ago. He jumped into the driver's seat, backed quickly out of his spot, and blazed out onto the highway. The road was busy with very loud and very happy people. He peeled between and around the traffic, eyes fixed on the road ahead, hands tightly gripping the wheel. The sun baked down.

You used to be one of the good ones, Sean had told him.

He thought about the bears that God sent to maul forty-two children when they made fun of Eliseus. Was he one of the bears? Was it time to repent?

Tom thought about praying. It had been a while since he'd prayed, officially, anyway. There had been plenty of whispered goodbye prayers and the occasional amen at funerals, but they were routine. Chore-prayers. Now he thought about it, he couldn't remember the last time he hit his knees and talked to the big man upstairs.

Lately, when Tom thought about God, it was to wonder whether such a being could even exist. God was the only 'truth' he took on faith, and the only one that required the rejection of logic. Now, though, he felt a stirring in his heart. God had to be real. Otherwise, he was going through this alone. Didn't they say there were no atheists in foxholes?

He came up too fast on the intersection of Carlyle and Goldin, then pressed down too hard on the brake. He wasn't used to how responsive Lil' Red was. The wheels locked, spitting out smoke. The hatch came to a screaming rest inches from the car in front. One of Marty's packing boxes slung forward with the force and tipped over, spilling a random collection of stuff out onto the passenger-side floor: a clock radio, a postcard-sized picture of Cindy Crawford in a white, form-fitting tank top (cut from a magazine), the Christmas card Tom and Connie had given him that year.

'Shit,' he muttered.

The light changed. He stalled. This damn car. The clutch was fucked. Connie had taken it to the mechanic a few weeks before Christmas and, apparently, they hadn't done a thing. He should go over there right now and give them a piece of his mind. And if they didn't listen—

Stop.

He had to relax. Breathe.

He restarted the car and drove on.

A few seconds later, a black four-wheel drive pulled in close behind him. A few seconds after that, red and blue lights began to flash. Tom's heart sank to the floor. He glanced in the rear-view to look at the driver. It was Sharon Guffey. In the second or two it took common sense to catch up, Tom considered planting his foot down on the accelerator and taking off. But how far would he get?

He pulled off into a service lane and parked in the shade of a spotted gum. Sharon pulled in behind him. He watched her in the rear-view. She climbed down from her four-wheel drive, hiked up her pants, and strolled towards him. He slung his elbow out the window and mustered a smile. 'Was I speeding, officer?'

'You know, Witter, most guys your age go for a red convertible, but the hatchback suits you.'

'It's Connie's,' Tom said. 'She's got the Sigma. We're helping Marty move today. But, seriously, was I speeding?'

She shook her head. 'I doubt it. You always struck me as a hands-at-ten-and-two sort of guy. Anyway it wouldn't have mattered if you were. I'm a detective, Witter. Not a traffic cop. I've been looking for you, so when I saw you I thought, hey, why not abuse my police powers and pull you over?'

She crossed her arms and parked her feet on the gravel, like she was set to stay a while.

Tom felt restless. 'You said you were looking for me?'

Sharon swept a hand through her hair and took a breath.

'I need to ask you about the neighbourhood watch meeting last night.'

'What about it?'

'My first question is an obvious one: did you learn nothing from Mrs Hastings when she taught us about the Salem witch trials?'

'It wasn't a witch-hunt. We were just trying to narrow down our suspects.'

'My second question is: what the actual hell are you thinking? Do you have any idea how dangerous it is to turn a group of people against an individual? You're skirting pretty close to vigilantism.'

'Guess all I need now is the cape and mask,' Tom offered.

He got doughnuts.

'Look,' he said. 'You've seen my neighbours. They notice stuff. I thought someone might know something that could help. If I found anything, I would have come to you with it.'

Sharon was quiet for a moment, then she frowned.

'Tell me about Owen Reed.'

'What about him?'

'For starters, why do you react when I say his name?'

'You know about my tics.'

'I know they get worse when you're stressed out or anxious about something,' she said. She tilted her head. She might have been moving away from the glare of the sun, or she might have been gauging Tom's reaction. 'I'm looking for him. I went by his motel but he wasn't in. A moon-faced kid on reception told me he never came home last night. Do you have any idea where he might have gone?'

'Why would I?'

'Because it's like you said, Witter, your neighbours notice stuff.'

His pulse quickened. Fear squirmed in the pit of his stomach.

'Owen Reed was at the meeting last night, wasn't he?'

'Yes.'

'And he left in an agitated state.'

'I suppose you could say that.'

'What happened then?' Sharon asked.

'When?'

'After the meeting.'

'After the meeting?'

'Is there an echo?'

He smiled, big and bright and phony. 'After the meeting I went home.'

'Straight home?'

'Yep.'

'You didn't sit in Owen's car and talk for a while.'

The pit in his stomach grew. He took a deep breath and tried to clear his head. 'Look, after the meeting, I went over to Owen to introduce myself. He was understandably disappointed about what happened at the meeting. I was too. We talked, as parents, as dads, as men.'

'What happened next?'

'Nothing.'

'Are you sure? Because the same neighbour who saw you sinking beers in Owen's convertible, also saw you two walk over to Sean Fryman's place.'

Damn. Was it all over? His heart slammed against his chest. He wanted to throw up. He wanted to plant his foot down on the pedal and drive. 'What are you asking me, Sharon?'

'Tom, you stood up in front of the whole street last night and accused Sean Fryman of kidnapping Tracie Reed and sacrificing her to the devil.'

'That's not exactly what I—'

'And today Sean Fryman is missing.'

There it was. She knew. Tom had mentally prepared himself for this — as much as anyone could prepare for something like that — but Sharon's words still landed hard. He tried to keep his face neutral.

'What happened last night, Tom?'

'Nothing.'

'So you didn't go to Sean's house?'

'Owen and I had some unanswered questions.'

'About Sean?'

'Yes.'

'So?'

'So,' Tom said. 'We went over there. To talk.'

'And what happened?'

'We talked.'

'About?'

'Tracie.'

'And?'

'And what?'

'What did he have to say?'

'Nothing,' Tom said. 'He denied knowing her. We could see we weren't going to get anywhere with him, so we left.'

'Your neighbour saw you go in,' Sharon said. 'She didn't see you leave.'

Ellie Sipple. It had to be. The big nark.

'I don't know what to tell you. We were at the Fryman house all of five minutes. Then I went home, watched some TV and went to bed. Look, if you're wondering where Sean is, maybe we spooked him. He probably ran off because he knew it was only a matter of time before you caught him.'

'Will Connie vouch for your whereabouts last night?' she asked.

Panic seized him. He tried hard to keep it from his face. Before he could answer, Sharon made a fist and slammed it down against the car door. If Tom wasn't buckled in, he might have jumped out of this seat.

'Sorry,' Sharon said. 'I saw a spider.'

'Yes,' Tom said. 'Connie will vouch for me.'

Something sad came to Sharon's face. 'Can I talk to you for a second as one of your oldest friends, Tom, and not as a cop?'

'It's kind of hard when you have a gun on your hip.'

An attempt at levity. Swing and a miss.

'Sometimes good people do bad things, Tom,' she said. 'I've seen it happen. If this is one of those times, and there's something you're not telling me, now is the time.'

Tom took a breath. His heart was pounding. His lungs wanted to constrict. Sweat poured off him. His muscles seized. Somewhere behind the eyes, tears were starting to well. Then, somehow, he dived deep and summoned a smile.

'Happy New Year, Sharon,' he said.

She stared at him.

'Happy New Year, Witter.'

28

Cassie Clarke lived in the next suburb over from Camp Hill, in a lower socio-economic neighbourhood lined with small brick commission houses set back behind wire fences.

It was hot. Tom's skin prickled with sweat as he climbed the few steps to Cassie's front door. The security screen was shut, but the front door behind it was open, giving a clear view into the house. There were big work boots by the front door, plastic toys strewn about on the floor, and a tacky replica of Ned Kelly's helmet on a side table which, by the look of it, doubled as a bottle opener. Curiously, classical music was also playing.

Tom knocked. A short stocky man with a handlebar moustache appeared. He glared at Tom through the security door and snapped, 'What?'

'Hi, my name is Tom Witter and—'

'We don't want any.'

Tom forced a smile. 'I'm not here to sell you anything. I'm a teacher at Cassie's school and was hoping I could talk to her.'

'Why?'

A small voice rose behind him.

'Mr Witter?'

Cassie was a slim, gangly thing with red hair and a chalky complexion. She pushed past the man Tom assumed was her father, unlocked the security door and nudged it open.

'What are you doing here?' she asked.

'I'm here about Tracie,' Tom said. 'I'm helping the people who are trying to figure out what happened to her.'

It was sort of the truth.

'I know what happened to her,' Cassie said.

'You do?'

'She went north. Sydney, probably. Maybe Queensland. She always wanted to see Byron Bay. I told the cops the same thing.'

Tom winced. Cassie didn't know her friend was dead.

'Mind if I come in?' he asked.

She held the door open for him.

Tom waited for the girl's father to protest or at least question why his daughter's teacher was visiting the house on the holidays, but he didn't. If he was concerned – or even curious – he didn't show it. He just shuffled back to the record player, where Bach and a cold beer were waiting for him.

Cassie showed Tom into the kitchen. Two small windows above the sink gave a view into the backyard. It was small, with yellow grass and a dilapidated caravan. Cassie helped herself to a beer from the fridge. It was busy with magnets. Most of them held overdue bills.

'You want one?' she asked.

'No,' Tom said. 'Your dad doesn't mind you drinking?'

'Dave's not my dad. He's my mum's boyfriend. It won't last. And anyway I'm practically legal.'

She chugged the beer. It seemed strange to Tom that this was Tracie's best friend. But, then again, he really didn't know Tracie at all. An innocent, idealised concept of her lived in his head, but it wasn't the real thing. Maybe not even close.

'It's kind of weird seeing you in my house,' she said. 'I mean, I know teachers have their own lives and everything, but I was never quite sure you existed outside of school.'

Tom tried to smile. Cassie drank.

'I already told the police everything I know,' she said. 'Tracie and I hung out that night. The night she went "missing".' She made air quotes around the word. 'She was here for a couple of hours. I helped bleach her hair. Dave got pissed off because we stained the bathmat. But, you know, fuck him.' Even though there was a wall dividing them, she gave Dave the finger. 'After that, we went to the movies. Everyone's acting like I'm keeping this big secret about where she went, but she didn't tell me anything.'

'She was meant to stay over here, is that right?'

She shrugged. 'Can't remember.'

'You can't remember?'

'I mean, fine, yeah, she was going to stay over.'

'What changed her mind?'

Cassie practically inhaled the beer, then put her hand over her mouth to burp. Charming. 'It's a woman's prerogative, isn't that what they say?'

'You two didn't have an argument?'

She flinched, then shook her head.

'I don't know what you're talking about,' she said.

Tom looked her in the eye. He liked to think he had a relaxed teaching style. He tried not to lose his temper. He tried to remain unflappable. Students liked him because he went easy on them. So, on those rare occasions when he talked firmly, they listened.

'You're not being honest with me, young lady,' he said.

The *young lady* part was too much. But it just slipped out.

'Ah, no offence, Mr Witter, you're a little outside your jurisdiction.'

But there was a tremble in her voice. Tom held her gaze. She looked away first. She lowered her beer, then her head.

'What was the fight about, Cassie?' he asked.

She picked up her beer again and turned it slowly in her hands, staring into the opening. 'Tracie's always banging on about her parents getting a divorce, you know. And I get it, it's fresh and the pain is still raw, but look around.' She gestured to her world of dirty dishes and long yellow grass. 'Does this look like a happy home to you?'

'I thought you and Tracie were friends.'

'We are,' Cassie said. 'Real friends are honest with each other, which is why I told her she wasn't special. That if there was a competition to see who had the shittier life, I would win in a landslide. That her parents split because her dad couldn't keep his dick in his pants.'

This wasn't news to Tom. Owen had told him there was someone else.

'How did you know Tracie's dad cheated?' he asked.

'Because it's what men do, Mr Witter. It's what my dad did.' Again, she pointed to the wall keeping them from her mum's boyfriend. 'Old mate in there's probably got someone on the side. You people are like cavemen.'

'Not all men are like that, Cassie.'

She glared at him and drank.

'So, Tracie didn't take too kindly to you trashing her dad. Is that it?'

'She told me I was being insensitive. I told her to fuck off.'

For a young girl whose best friend was missing, Cassie didn't seem to be losing any sleep about it.

'What do you think happened to her?' Tom asked.

'I told you: Byron Bay, probably. This whole thing is just a stunt to get back at her dad. She's punishing him. Maybe her mum, too. I don't know. She knows the longer she waits before coming home, the bigger the fanfare will be.'

'Did she ever talk about being scared?' Tom asked.

'Scared?' Cassie smiled. 'All the time. There was always someone stalking her or following her or turning up in weird places. She answered the phone once and there was nobody on the other end, so she assumed it was a rapist, calling to see if she was home.'

'So she was paranoid.'

Cassie burped again. She didn't bother covering her mouth this time. 'That's part of it, I guess. But Tracie didn't have brothers or sisters growing up. She was an only child. They need more attention than us regular middle-kids. They exaggerate and embezzle and make up little stories to make themselves seem more interesting.'

'I think you mean *embellish*,' Tom said. 'And that's no way to talk about your best friend.'

'I'm not telling you anything I wouldn't say to her face. That's what real friends do. They call each other on their bullshit.'

He had to tell her.

'Cassie,' he said. 'Tracie is dead.'

'What?'

'Her body was found this morning.'

'That isn't funny, Mr Witter.'

'I'm sorry.'

Her eyes welled up with tears. Her mouth opened and closed like a fish.

'Should I get Dave?' Tom asked. 'Where's your mum? Can I call her for you?'

Cassie shook her head and went on shaking it.

'This is my fault,' she said.

'No, Cassie, it's not. Of course it's not.'

'I said I didn't believe her,' Cassie stammered. Tears spilled down her cheeks. 'This is my fault. This is all my fault.'

'It's all right.'

'I didn't know.'

'It's okay.'

She looked at him with desperate, pleading eyes. 'I didn't actually think he'd do anything.'

Tom froze.

'Who are you talking about, Cassie?'

29

Tom parked Lil' Red outside a block of brick flats in Frankston. He locked the doors, then double-checked he'd locked the doors. His son's new neighbourhood was, to put it as diplomatically as he could, sketchy.

It was coming up on four o'clock. The sun was dipping behind the block of flats, casting long, still shadows on the hot concrete. As he started towards the entrance, Tom caught the smell of weed in the air. He looked up. A rowdy bunch of twenty-somethings were crowded on a small balcony on the second floor, singing along to – you guessed it – Prince's '1999'. In the window directly below them, a plastic Christmas tree stood facing the glass, naked aside from a single angel on the top. From somewhere beyond the tree, a baby was crying.

On his way in, a skinny man stepped out through the doors. He was topless, with a raw, sunburnt chest and two of the sharpest collarbones Tom had ever seen. He was carrying an open longneck in one hand, and a small black-and-white TV in the other. One of Marty's new neighbours. The man glared at Tom as they passed each other. He stank of sweat and pot.

What was Tom's son doing in a place like this?

He entered the complex via a heavy steel gate, followed a narrow path between two great walls of letterboxes, then walked up a groaning flight of stairs. He stopped outside apartment four, took a deep breath, then knocked on the front door.

A scrawny kid with bags under his eyes appeared. He had a thick mess of red hair. 'Let me guess,' the kid drawled. 'You're either a Jehovah's Witness or Martin's dad.'

Mar*tin*?

'The second one,' Tom said.

'I'm just on my way out to pick up some bog-roll, but you can go on through. He's in his room. It's the big one at the back. I'm Gordo, by the way.'

Gordo gave Tom a high-five, slipped past him, and skipped on down the hallway. Tom let himself into the flat. Marty's – ahem, *Martin's* – new place was roughly the same size and shape as a shoebox. The main room combined the living, dining and kitchen spaces into one cramped area. The furniture was a flaking vinyl sofa and a tattered old armchair. There were no balconies on this floor, but there was a big window that gave a stunning view of a brick wall. It was slung open, and the warm, stuffy smell of next door's pot drifted in.

One of the bedroom doors was open. Marty was inside, unpacking his clothes into a desperate wooden wardrobe that looked like it had been dragged off the street on hard rubbish day.

'Hey, kid,' Tom said.

Marty looked up and smiled. 'Dad. Geez, did you get lost? Mum and Keiran already left. Mum's pretty pissed off.'

'I thought she might be,' he said.

'Where have you been?'

'I got caught up with some other stuff. Your new roommate let me in. He's off to buy bog-roll, by the way.'

Marty laughed. 'He's a charmer, isn't he?'

'He called you Martin.'

'That's my name.'

'On your birth certificate,' Tom said. 'But I don't think anyone's called you that for, well, ever.'

He shrugged, then returned to his unpacking. 'It's something I'm trying out. Now that I'm officially an adult, I thought, I don't know, I guess I just felt like a bit of a change. What do you think?'

Everything is temporary.

'I'll get used to it,' Tom said.

'Where's all my stuff?'

'Downstairs.' Tom sat down on the bed. 'We need to talk first.'

'You didn't leave Lil' Red unlocked, did you?'

'Sit down, Marty.' He paused. '*Martin.*'

He did as he was told. 'It sounds weird when you say it.'

'I've just come from Cassie Clarke's house,' Tom said.

Marty gave nothing away, just as he'd given nothing away when Tom had told him Tracie had gone missing a few nights ago in his room.

'Cassie Clarke?' Marty said, making a little show of trying

to place the name. 'From school?'

'When was the last time you talked to her?'

Marty pretended to think about it. 'I'm not sure I ever have. But if I did, it would have been back at Camp Hill Christian.'

'Are you sure?'

Marty looked at him. 'Pretty sure. Why?'

'You didn't see her at the roller rink four weeks ago, with Tracie?'

Marty blinked three times in quick succession.

'I don't know,' he said. 'I can't remember.'

'What about at the Camp Hill year twelve bonfire party a month ago? Tracie was there that night, too.'

Marty stilled. It was as if someone had just hit the pause button. When he could move again, it was his hands Tom noticed first. They were trembling.

'What about near the school gate at the end of most weekdays, or at the Frankston shopping centre on the weekends, or near the bus stop on Novak Street?'

Silence. Cold and heavy.

'And at the movies three weeks ago,' Tom said. 'The night Tracie disappeared.'

'I don't want to talk about this with you.'

Tom said, 'Too bad.' Then, 'This is real.' Then, 'This is happening.'

He wasn't just talking to Marty.

'Tracie knew someone was following her,' Tom said. 'She never got a look at who it was. But Cassie did.'

'... Dad.'

Tom took a long, slow, deep breath, and said, 'Points for honesty, kid.'

Marty blinked tears from his eyes. 'When Tracie disappeared, I kept waiting for the cops to come and talk to me. I was sure Cassie would have told them about me.'

'She didn't think you could have had anything to do with Tracie's disappearance, so she protected you.' He paused. 'I think she likes you.'

Marty just shook his head.

'The first time I asked you about Tracie, you acted like you hardly knew her,' Tom said.

Slowly, Marty got up to close his bedroom door. When he started to talk, his shoulders sagged. His chest deflated. It was as if something had been uncorked.

'For a while, I didn't even notice her,' Marty said. 'Then, suddenly, I couldn't stop noticing her. I'd never experienced anything like it. It snuck up on me, like in one of those nature documentaries where the lion stalks the gazelle. When the lion finally leaps out of the long grass, it's too late for the gazelle to do anything about it.'

It was a troubling metaphor. Was Marty the lion or the gazelle?

'You liked her,' Tom offered.

'It was more than that,' Marty said. 'Stronger than that.'

Tom remembered what it felt like to be a teenager in love. Tom had felt something for Sharon Guffey, once upon a time. It might have been love or lust – they were interchangeable at that age – but those feelings were raw and complicated and painful and, Tom thought, beyond anyone else's understanding. To paraphrase Nazareth: *love hurt*. It had hurt Marty. Tom could see it on his face.

'Did you tell Tracie how you felt?' Tom asked.

He shook his head. 'I didn't know how. I was a total dork back then. Me and Sean were like these weirdo loners. So I changed. I started working out, got in with some of the cooler guys and became something I thought Tracie would want.'

'Is that why you and Sean stopped being friends?'

A flash of guilt came to his face. He shook it off, then shrugged. 'Sean was an anchor. I couldn't get to where I needed to be with him hanging around.'

'And where you needed to be was with Tracie,' Tom said.

'I never worked up the nerve to tell her how I felt. Then, I don't know, I graduated. I tried to move on. To forget about her. But she just stuck. I couldn't get her out of my head.'

'So you started following her?'

'Not at first,' he said. 'First, I just watched. Her place is right on the other side of Wild Place. It wasn't pervy. It's not like I watched her get undressed and stuff like that. I just wanted to be close to her world. I don't know. Close enough to look into her world.'

Like a snow globe, Tom thought.

'The coffee can full of cigarette butts is yours,' Tom said. 'I didn't even know you smoked.'

Marty shrugged, then looked off. 'I'm trying to quit.'

'Tell me about the night Tracie disappeared,' Tom said.

'How much did Cassie say?'

'She said she saw you at the movie, sitting in the back row by yourself.'

'Halfway through the movie Cassie got up. She pretended like she needed to pee, but really she was sneaking up to talk to me.'

Cassie hadn't mentioned that to Tom.

'What did she say?'

'*You could do better.*' Marty looked at his hands and sighed. 'Then she just went back to her seat.'

Tom braced himself.

'Did you see Tracie again that night?' he asked.

Marty gave a helpless little nod, then stared at the brick wall outside the window. The sound of traffic and distant music drifted in from outside.

'Whatever happened,' Tom said, 'whatever it is. I can protect you.'

'You can't protect me from this,' he said.

Tom felt cold and heavy and frightened. 'Did you go into Wild Place that night, Marty? Were you ... watching Tracie again? Were you outside her house?'

Marty turned back.

'Actually,' he said. 'She came to ours.'

'... Tracie was at our house that night?'

'It was late,' Marty said. 'You were off at your work trivia night and Mum was already in bed. So when Tracie knocked, I answered. I thought Cassie must have told her I'd been following her. I thought she was there to confront me.'

'But she wasn't?'

He shook his head. 'She was stoned. I could smell it on her, and see it in her eyes. Then, when she started to talk, it was even more obvious. She was rambling. Talking about how she felt guilty, how it was eating her up and she had to say something.'

'Say something about what?'

'She told me, Dad.'

Tom dragged a hand across his face.

'Told you what?'

'She told me about the affair,' Marty said.

'What affair, Marty?'

Marty held his father's gaze.

'Yours,' he said. 'With Tracie.'

30

'I don't know what you're talking about,' Tom blurted. 'Marty, whatever that girl told you—'

'She didn't just *tell* me, Dad,' Marty said.

Tom felt his face contort.

From outside the stuffy bedroom came the sound of Marty's flatmate arriving home, whooping and whistling with his bog-roll. Marty lowered his voice and said, '*Hey, Mr Witter, got a sec?*'

Tom shook his head. 'What?'

Marty strained. Fresh tears welled in his eyes and spilled over. Tom put a steadying hand on his son's shoulder. Marty shrugged it off.

'*It's after four,*' Marty said. '*What are you still doing here?*'

His lip quivered. His hands turned into fists.

'What are you talking about?' Tom asked.

'*I saw your Sigma in the car park and wanted to come and say goodbye.*'

'Marty, I don't know what you're …'

Then it hit him. Tom understood.

'She recorded you, Dad,' Marty said. 'She got the whole

thing on tape.'

And there, in an ugly block of flats in Frankston, Tom's world began to end.

'What about love?' Tracie had asked him, back on that grey afternoon in his classroom.

'It takes a lot of that, too,' he told her.

'I'm not sure my parents were ever really in love. From my very limited experience on the subject, when you love someone, you don't let anything get in the way.'

'Have you been in love, Tracie?'

Tom grinned. Tracie blushed.

'Who's the lucky guy?' he asked.

'I don't know if I'd call him lucky.'

She stared at him, and he understood.

'Oh.'

'That's it? *Oh?*'

'I'm flattered, Tracie. Really. But I'm your teacher.'

'Not anymore.'

'I'm twice your age.'

'Actually, it's closer to three times.' She smiled. 'I just want to know what it's like to have something you love, even if it's just for a little while.'

'Tracie …'

'Nobody needs to know …'

Tom closed his eyes and tried to erase the memory of what came next. Locking the classroom door. The smell of her hair. The taste of her lips. Her small body against his.

For the record, it wasn't *an affair*. That made it sound like it meant something. It didn't. It was one time. One mistake. When it was over, he'd been surprised just how little he'd had to wrestle with what had happened. How easy it was to reframe in his mind, to spin it just right, hold it at the perfect angle for him to sleep at night. It was a lapse in judgment, obviously and absolutely, but a common one. It was cause and effect. A function of being a man.

And on those rare nights he couldn't justify it to himself, he had pushed it deep and locked it away. Now, he felt something like turbulence. Because Marty knew. Marty knew, and it had crushed him.

Tom stood up. Sat back down again. He put his hand to his heart. It ached. His bowels began to thrash. Bile rose in his throat. He saw everything he had – his wife, the boys, life – shattering.

'Marty,' Tom said. There was desperation in his voice. 'I can explain.'

'No, you can't, Dad.' Marty stared at him. His gaze felt hot. 'When you came home the other night with that damn poster, I didn't know what you were thinking. It was like you were trying to rub it in my face.'

'Marty, just wait—'

'Then you couldn't seem to let it go. You got angry at your cop friend for not doing enough to find her. Why did you get so obsessed? Did you actually care about finding her, or were you just scared someone might figure out your secret?'

'Marty—'

'Did you have feelings for her, Dad? Were you in love with her too?'

Tom gave an honest answer.

'No,' he said.

Somehow, that made this whole thing feel worse.

'Does your mother know?' he asked.

'What do you think?'

Small mercies.

'Thank you,' Tom said.

'For what?'

'For not telling her. For ... protecting me.'

'I was protecting *her*, Dad. If she knew, if Keiran knew, it would rip this family apart. I didn't want that on my conscience. But I wasn't going to stick around and live with it, either.'

Tom steeled himself.

'Where's the tape now?' he asked.

Marty shook his head. '*That's* what you care about?'

Tom looked at his son – not a boy, anymore, but a man. 'Tracie Reed is dead. Her body was found this morning. Someone killed her and buried her in Wild Place.'

Marty's expression turned cold.

'You don't look surprised,' Tom said.

'Nothing surprises me anymore.'

'Cassie knows you were following Tracie. It'll get out.'

'It hasn't yet.'

'Cassie didn't say anything because she thought Tracie ran away. Now that she knows she's dead, you can't count on her to stay quiet. If there's anything else you haven't told me ...'

'Like what?'

'You were angry that night. You'd just found out the girl you loved ...' Tom couldn't finish that sentence. 'You'd just had your heart broken.'

'What exactly are you asking me, Dad?'

'I can't protect you unless I know the truth.' Tom stood up. 'What happened that night?' Tom thought about the rifle slung over Owen's shoulder. 'God damn it, Marty, this is important.' He raised his voice. 'This could be life or death. What exactly happened after Tracie played you the tape?'

'I did what you should have done, Dad,' he said. 'I told her to fuck off.'

Tom wanted to believe him, but he couldn't help but notice Marty's sudden reluctance to make eye contact. The way he drew his lips tightly together after he spoke. The shiny gleam of perspiration on his brow.

When they were back at Sean's house, Owen had called those *tells*.

'Are you lying to me?' Tom asked.

'... No.'

This time, Marty was the one to twitch.

31

Sharon parked across the street from the Witter residence. She kept the engine running and the air con on. The sun was setting over Tom's split-level, suburban paradise. The sky was burnt orange, turning black. The streetlamps would soon be on. There must have been some sort of New Year's Eve bash at the big house at number four tonight, because a steady stream of neighbours filed along the footpath, drawn along by a Journey song – 'Don't Stop Believin'' – like rats following the Pied Piper of Hamelin. Steve Perry was known to have that effect on people.

Sharon could think of better ways to see in 1990.

She was still rattled from her exchange with Tom. He'd given all the right answers and said everything she'd wanted to hear. Technically, at least. But she hadn't seen him twitch that badly in years. Maybe ever. She saw a dark path in her mind, twisted and narrow, and tried desperately not to go down it.

Tom's turd-brown Sigma pulled onto the street and rolled up the Witter house driveway. Connie and Keiran got out.

There was no sign of Tom. Sharon watched them for a moment and made a silent vow: if – *when* – Connie confirmed Tom's story about last night, she'd drop it. Simple. Easy. Just like that. And if her gut told her to keep digging, she'd remind herself that the Witters were a still, peaceful pond. A stone like the one she was holding would send ripples out forever.

If Sharon believed in God, she might have made the sign of the cross. But she didn't. Without ceremony, she got out and caught the Witters as they reached the front door.

'Connie.'

Tom's wife turned. Caution flashed on her face. Sharon gave her a smile, which seemed to ease her panic a little.

'Sharon, hi,' she said.

'How did the big move go?'

'It was even more depressing than I thought. Mind if I borrow some handcuffs so I can chain this one to a radiator?'

She pointed to Keiran. He rolled his eyes, then disappeared upstairs, leaving the two women alone on the doorstep.

'Tom's not home,' Connie said.

'That's all right, I actually wanted to talk to you.'

'Is everything all right?'

'Just ticking a few boxes so I can go enjoy my New Year's,' Sharon said. 'Mind if I come in?'

Connie opened the fridge and pulled a bottle of Chandon down from the top shelf. She turned to Sharon as she started to work the cork. 'You want a glass?'

'I'm on duty,' Sharon said. 'So definitely yes.'

Laughing, Connie cleaned out two flutes with a tea towel and poured them each a glass. 'I was saving this to drink with Tom tonight. He was supposed to meet us at Marty's with the second load but he must have got caught up. I'm sure he feels terrible and is about to rush in that door, apologising profusely, in three, two, one … That never works.'

They tinked glasses and drank.

'Is it like him to go MIA like that?'

Connie shrugged. 'No, but he's a little off his game lately. I can't tell if it's a midlife crisis or a mental breakdown. Maybe both.'

'Have you talked to him about it?'

'I tried.' Connie sipped her sparkling wine. 'Marty moving out has really messed with him. I think he assumed life would go on in the exact same way forever.'

'Did you hear about Tracie Reed?' Sharon asked.

'No.'

'I assumed Tom would have mentioned it.'

'I haven't seen him.'

Sharon made a sour face. 'They found her body in Wild Place.'

'Jesus, God.' She looked off and drank. 'That's just so tragic. Her poor parents. I think we all assumed she ran away and they'd find her hitchhiking her way to Sydney or something.'

'Everyone except for Tom,' Sharon said. 'Who assumed she was kidnapped by a Satanic cult.'

Connie rolled her eyes.

'Was it a suicide or the other one?' she asked.

'The other one,' Sharon said. 'But you didn't hear that from me.'

A Bon Jovi track came on in the house down the street. It was followed by a rush of cheers. Connie gazed in the direction of the song.

'Yet life goes on,' she said.

'Sounds like quite a party.'

'It's Bill and Vicky Davis's annual New Year's Eve celebration extravaganza. Tom and I decided not to go this year, mostly because last year was horrible, but if the choice is between that and spending the night alone …' Connie sipped her Chandon. Her expression hardened. 'So I have a sneaking suspicion you're not here for social reasons.'

'No,' she said. 'Official police business, I'm afraid.'

'About Tracie Reed?'

'About Sean Fryman.'

Connie leaned back against the stove and raised both eyebrows. 'Was Tom right?'

'About what?'

'Did Sean have something to do with what happened to Tracie?'

'Sean's missing,' Sharon said.

Connie froze, then thawed slowly.

Sharon finished her drink — liquid courage — and asked, 'What time did Tom get home from the neighbourhood watch meeting last night?'

32

Owen fed loose change into one of the vending machines outside the change rooms.

'Snickers?' he asked.

'I'm allergic to peanuts,' Sean called back.

Owen selected a Mars Bar instead. He took that and the creamy soda he bought from the drink machine back over to the pool and set it down in front of Sean. The kid must have been starving because he tore the wrapper open and scoffed the chocolate. A second later came the *crack* and *glug-glug* of the soda being opened and inhaled.

Sean burped.

'Where's Mr Witter?' he asked.

'I don't know,' Owen said. 'I'm sure he'll be here soon.'

'You don't think he's gone to the cops?'

'Don't talk.'

Owen sat down in the fold-out chair and rested the rifle case across his knees.

'I'm sorry about your daughter,' Sean said.

Owen glared at him.

'I won't pretend I knew Tracie well, but I liked her,' Sean said. 'She had a warm sort of energy, you know.'

'*Don't talk*,' Owen said again. 'Especially not about my daughter.'

'Okay.' Sean chugged the can. 'Sorry.'

Owen closed his eyes. Then opened them. 'I know what you mean. About her energy. She was like that ever since she was a kid. It felt good just to be near her. Like sitting by a fire to keep warm.'

Sean was silent.

'But then I started having trouble reading her like I used to,' he said. 'It might have been the divorce talk getting her down, or it might have been, I don't know, life. But I worried that she was depressed.' He spread his hands flat on the leather rifle case. 'Two days ago, I was called to the coroner's office to identify a body. A suicide victim, roughly the same age as Tracie. Right before I went in, right before I saw it wasn't her, I felt a strange sense of … inevitability. I knew she'd been sad, and I knew I'd missed it.'

'I don't think she was depressed,' Sean said. 'I think she was scared. And angry. No more than the rest of us.'

'What did she have to be angry about?'

'Do you remember what it was like to be our age, Mr Reed?'

Owen said nothing. He could see what Sean was doing: playing nice, being polite, trying to get on Owen's good side.

'You start to realise what life really is,' Sean said. 'And it's not the one you were promised by TV and books and society and everyone. It's not depression, exactly. It's more like, buyer's remorse.'

'*Buyer's remorse*,' Owen echoed. 'Is that why you dress the way you do and listen to your sort of music?'

'Partly.'

'What's the other part?'

'There's always been a little darkness in me,' he said. 'My dad has a temper. A pretty bad one. I think he passed that down to me. He took it out on my mum. I always worried I'd end up like him. Then, I decided to own the darkness. I started listening to metal and wearing black. It became part of my identity. It stopped controlling me.' He paused. 'Pot helps too.'

Despite everything, Owen laughed out loud at that.

'I'm not a bad guy, Mr Reed,' Sean said. 'I wouldn't sell pot if I thought it really hurt anyone. I just wanted to sell enough for a plane ticket out of here.'

'Where?'

'London. I thought maybe I'd find my place over there. The crazy thing is, I saved up enough money to go months ago.'

'Why didn't you go?'

'It's lame.'

'Try me.'

'I was scared of leaving my mum. Not because she wouldn't be okay without me – she's the strongest woman I know – but because I was worried I wouldn't be okay without her.' He shifted, and Owen heard the bike chain scrape against the steps of the diving board. 'If I ever get home, I'll buy my ticket the next day. I'd be gone, Mr Reed, and I'd stay gone.' A hesitation, then: 'I wouldn't tell anyone about what happened here.'

Owen didn't say anything.

'What's the plan here, Mr Reed?' Sean asked. 'Because you either have to kill me or let me go, and I know you don't want to kill me. You know I'm innocent. You're thinking about letting me go. I can see it on your face.'

'That's not what I'm thinking about, Sean.' Owen stood. 'I was thinking about my daughter. I was thinking about how good she smelled when she was a baby. I was thinking about her first day of kindergarten, walking away after drop-off, her tiny, tiny hand clasped in her teacher's. I was thinking about Tracie in the throes of puberty, brooding and moody, but not too moody to give her old man a goodnight kiss each and every night.'

He took a step towards Sean, then another.

'You said I have to kill you or let you go,' he said. 'But there's a third option.'

'What?'

Owen rolled up his sleeves.

'I can make you tell me the truth.'

33

Keiran was coming down the stairs when Tom got home.

'Hey, Dad,' he said. 'Can I go over to Ricky's place tonight? We're going to watch the fireworks.'

Tom paused at the bottom of the stairs and tried to keep the urgency from his voice. 'Where's your mother?'

'She went to Bill and Vicky's party.'

'... Really?'

'She told me to tell you she'll be home sometime after midnight and not to wait up.'

Tom spun on his feet and started for the front door.

He needed his wife. He needed Connie to tell him how to handle all this, to tell him what to do. The longer Tom made Owen wait, the higher the chance of violence, but it was time to bring Connie in. He was dimly aware of where that conversation would lead. The idea of her knowing hurt him someplace deep and sacred and rarely visited, but there was something comforting about the thought too. He'd confess, explain, beg for forgiveness, hope their house was still standing when it was over, and if it was, Connie would help carry the load.

Tom would be unburdened. Wasn't that what marriage was all about?

Besides, she'd need him in the dark days ahead.

'Dad!'

Tom turned back. 'What?'

'Can I go over to Ricky's or not?'

'Sure,' he said. 'Just—'

'I know. Stay out of Wild Place.'

'I was just going to say be careful.' Tom ruffled the kid's hair. 'Enjoy the fireworks.'

Tom gave Keiran a hug.

'See you next year,' he said.

'See you next *decade*,' Keiran told him.

And then he was gone.

When Tom was alone again, he gave himself a beat to let out all the tics and twitching that were screaming at him from the shadows. His chin pulled to the right in a sudden jerking motion, the left side of his mouth quivered, then settled, then quivered again. His eyebrows were like dancing caterpillars on uppers.

Back out on the street, a cool breeze was stirring, a whisper of relief from the heat.

Bill and Vicky's place was lit up like an amusement park. They'd left their Christmas lights up: a twinkling, tasteless, Griswoldian explosion of red and green. They'd also set up nearly a dozen mini tiki torches on either side of the little stone path that led to the front door. A few steps closer, towards the house, was a handpainted, brightly coloured sign that read: WELCOME TO THE YEAR 1990! A few steps beyond that was a bizarre fibreglass leprechaun figurine in a pair of novelty sunglasses.

This year's theme seemed to be whatever Bill had liked at the party supply shop. But Tom had to give it to the hosts. They did not do things by halves.

The front door was propped open with a wooden Christmas tree doorstop, so Tom went inside. The living room was alive with activity. The music was loud, the conversation upbeat and lively. Tom recognised most of the faces. Cheree Gifford was performing well in the limbo. A small dance floor had formed near a long trestle table filled with pot-luck plates, apparently led by Betsy Keneally. Ingrid Peck (desperate divorcee) was locked in an intense conversation with Gary Henskee (just desperate).

Everyone Tom could see, without exception, was shit-faced.

It was as if he'd stepped into an alternate dimension, where people had small, normal problems that were easily forgotten during a night of fun and booze.

Tom started weaving through the party, searching the faces.

'Tom!'

He spun around. It was Bill Davis. He was dressed in a loud Hawaiian shirt, buttoned halfway up, over dark blue denim jeans. His *good jeans*, Tom figured. Every middle-aged man had a pair. He was carrying a glass of something blue, with several little umbrellas in it.

'Bill, hi,' Tom managed. 'About last night—'

'Apology accepted,' Bill roared over the music.

He pulled Tom in for a tight, one-armed bear hug. It wasn't entirely unpleasant. Bill held him for a few seconds too long, then released him.

'In a way, I should be the one apologising,' Bill shouted. 'I'll be honest with you, mate, last night, after our little exchange, I came home in a bit of a huff and explained the whole thing to Vicky and, well, it led to a pretty enlightening conversation. She pointed out some things about myself I needed to hear.'

Bill might have needed to hear them, but Tom didn't.

'Bill, I'm looking for—'

'Vicky compared me to a bottle of bourbon,' he went on. 'Wonderful in moderation, but too much gives you a headache. And I got it. I just *got it*, you know.' His breath smelled like 100 proof. What the hell was in that punch? 'Anyway, I'm really glad you came, mate. You're one of my best friends and this party wouldn't have been the same without you. I'm serious, you know. One of my *best friends*. Not just on the street, but in the whole world.'

'Thanks, Bill, but like I was saying—'

'How about that girl turning up dead? Can you believe it? Right over there in Wild Place. Practically our backyard. You think if she was left out there any longer, the smell might have reached us? I can just imagine Lydia getting all pissed off about it at the next neighbourhood watch meeting.' He went on in a high-pitched voice. '*Will whoever left the corpse rotting in Wild Place please do something about it? Yes, I'm looking at you, Gary Henskee. A death-free street is a happy street.*'

Vicky spotted them from across the party and swept over. Bill's wife was a small, compact woman, aglow in a lime-green dress with big, puffy shoulder pads.

'Are you doing the neighbourhood watch meeting bit again?' she asked. 'It's hilarious, honey, but you really need some new material.' She turned to Tom. 'It really is so tragic, though. She was seventeen. We thought about cancelling the party out of respect, but then I thought, people need the joy of a real Davis party now more than ever. How are you, Tom? Can I get you a drink? Have you tried the punch?'

'Have you seen Connie?' Tom asked.

'I think I saw her outside.'

He moved on fast.

The music wasn't as loud in the backyard. There were more tiki torches out here, full size this time. They formed a wide arc around the party and cast an eerie, flickering light over the faces of the guests.

Nearby, Rob Chow thrust his hand into an inflatable swimming pool filled with ice and booze. His wife Lydia was talking to Irene Borschmann. Both had a plastic cup of blue punch, and both cups had tiny umbrellas.

'Have either of you seen Connie?' he asked.

'She was around here somewhere,' Irene said. 'Is there something wrong with your eye, Tom?'

'Do you know where she went?'

Irene shook her head. Lydia took Tom by the arm and drew him in.

'You've got to hear this, Tom,' she said. 'Irene was the one who led police to the body.' To Irene: 'Tell him.'

'You just did,' Irene said. 'And anyway, he was there.'

'Do we know how she was killed yet?' Lydia asked. 'I called my friend Betty Garland, whose son works at the Frankston cop shop but, apparently, they're all being very tight-lipped about it. Betty thinks the poor girl's throat was slit. When I asked her *why* she thought that, she said that's how she'd kill someone. So remind me not to spend time alone with Betty anymore.'

She paused to drink, and to take a breath. 'Anyway, the method isn't the most intriguing part, it's what he did to her before he put her in the ground.'

Tom flinched. The *he* in Lydia's sentence referred to Sean, not Marty, but the cold knot tightened in his gut.

'God, the whole thing is just so tragic,' Lydia said. 'But, well, I'm just going to say what we're all thinking. It's also a little exciting, isn't it?'

'You're the only one thinking that,' Irene said.

'Oh, come on, Borschmann. Are you telling me you're not loving all the extra attention? You're like a Keel Street celebrity now. Oh, but you know what the *best* part is?'

'Stop,' Tom snapped.

The ladies turned to him.

'There's no *best* part, Lydia,' he said. 'A girl is dead.'

Lydia gaped and made shocked faces. Irene smiled.

Tom continued his search for Connie, but as he moved through the party the faces began to blur. The flickering light from the tiki torches cast monstrous shadows across the yard, like demons dancing in hell. Beyond them, the trees of Wild Place shifted in the breeze, black shapes on a field of more black.

'They're planning on burning him at midnight,' someone said.

He turned. It was Ellie Sipple, the only one at the party without a drink.

'What?'

'The effigy,' she said. 'Bill's going to set it alight after the countdown.'

She pointed into the yard. In the middle of the lawn, Bill and Vicky had erected a man-sized scarecrow. It was dressed in some of Bill's old clothes, a faded red T-shirt and blue football shorts. It was made of straw and newspaper, and wore the same novelty sunglasses Tom had seen on the leprechaun outside. Scrawled across the effigy's T-shirt in white spray paint was: *1989.*

'I'm looking for Connie,' he told Ellie Sipple. 'Have you seen her?'

She glanced around to make sure nobody was listening, then lowered her voice. 'I know what you did, Tom. You and Owen.'

The pit in his stomach grew.

'For the record, I understand why. I even understand the urge. But I need to live in an ordered world, and that way lies chaos.'

'I don't know what you're talking about, Ellie.'

He backed away, wandering from the party, beyond the line

of tiki torches. He paused before the effigy. It had been built on a bed of logs and straw. He sniffed the air.

'It's lighter fluid,' came a small voice from the dark. 'Bill's probably going to start a bushfire tonight. This time tomorrow, Wild Place will be nothing but ash.'

'That might not be such a bad thing,' Tom said. 'Fire is supposed to cleanse, right?'

Connie stepped out of the dark. She looked ghostly and beautiful in the wavering light of the torches. She was wearing a simple black dress and holding the obligatory cup of blue punch.

Tom gestured to the cup. 'Speaking of flammable.'

Her smile was faint and fleeting.

'What are you doing all the way out here?' he asked.

'Avoiding the party.'

'What are you doing at the party?'

'Avoiding life.' She drank.

The punch left a blue hue on her lips.

'I'm sorry I disappeared today,' he said.

'You've been disappearing for a while now.'

He looked up. The effigy loomed over them. Beyond it, a blanket of stars.

'I've made a mistake, Connie,' he whispered. 'Actually, I've made a series of them. I need your help, baby. I need your help to fix them.'

His muscles relaxed. A strange quiet fell over his senses. He reached up, touched his face, and discovered he was crying. He couldn't remember the last time that had happened. It felt like someone had turned a release valve in his head. He laid his face in his hands and let it pour out of him. Wordless, there in the dark of Bill and Vicky's backyard, Connie held him.

'Shh,' she said.

'I need to tell you some things, Con. They're going to be hard to hear.'

She kissed him on the forehead and whispered, 'No.'

'What?'

'You missed the window, Tom.' Her voice was flat and steady and final. 'Last night, all I wanted was the truth. An emotional spring-clean. But something happened today that made me change my mind.'

Tom's tension returned with a vengeance. Every muscle in his body seemed to lock and unlock. 'What happened?'

'Sharon came to see me. She asked me some questions. Where you were last night, what time you got home, did you go out afterwards. I asked her why she wanted to know, and she told me Sean Fryman had gone missing.'

'What did you tell her?' Tom asked.

'I lied for you, Tom.'

Tom tried to keep the relief from showing on his face.

'I did something bad, Con. I think Marty did too.'

She tightened at the mention of Marty's name.

'Can you fix it?' she asked.

'I don't know.'

'That's not good enough, Tom. I need you to be a man, and I need you to fix it.' She took one small step backwards. 'It's a parent's job to protect their family. Do you understand?'

Tom digested her words.

'Yes,' he said. 'I think I do.'

34

It was almost 10pm. Barely two hours before 1990. Shops were pulling down shutters – Tom couldn't remember a time when they had stayed open this late – and people were rushing off to parties to get there before the deadline.

He stood hunched in a Telecom phone booth, gripping the receiver in both hands. Earlier, at the school, he'd made a note of the phone extension in the lifesaver's station. He dialled the number and waited. He'd driven over to the Camp Hill Shopping Village to place the call. He wasn't sure if the police could trace calls the way they did in the movies, but he knew he shouldn't take any chances.

He'd already taken so many.

The glass walls of the booth were heavily graffitied. Highlights included *Lisa is a dickhead*, *This is a funny looking toilet – oh well, pissing anyway*, and the good old standard, *For a good time call* … Did anyone ever actually call those numbers and, if so, who was on the other end? Shifting focus, Tom saw dozens of youngsters milling around, drinking and laughing.

There was something mindless and goofy about it all: people going about their lives as normal. He wondered dimly if his life would ever resemble that again, and decided it probably wouldn't. Even if his plan to *fix this* worked – and at this stage that was a very big if – he had changed on a fundamental level. The shift felt permanent. Biological, almost. He had pierced an invisible barrier that surrounded suburbia and stepped through it. He could see too clearly now, from the outside looking in.

What did he see? People, for the most part, especially those who lived in places like Camp Hill, played by the rules. But Tom had discovered a big secret this week: they didn't have to. How could he ever plug himself back into that system? He pictured a chimp escaping the zoo, tasting freedom, then getting dragged back to the cage.

'Tom, is that you?'

Owen sounded tired. His throat was full of panic.

'Has anything changed?' Tom asked.

'You've been gone for hours. Where the hell have you been? What did you find out?'

'I'll tell you in person,' Tom said. 'I can be there in twenty minutes. Please don't do anything until I get there.'

'Damn it, Tom, what the hell is going on?'

'Twenty minutes, and I'll have all the evidence you need,' Tom said. 'I just have to make one quick stop first.'

Tom hung up and exited the booth. He looked at the bus shelter across the car park. Tracie Reed's face looked back from one of the missing posters Tom had stuck there days ago. When he'd first seen that picture, he'd thought her smile had looked bright and beautiful. Now it looked forced. The eyes, once warm and trusting, blazed with accusation. He stared into those eyes for a moment, letting the guilt and shame burn in his chest. He entered the booth and picked up the phone again.

When he was done, Tom stepped back into the fresh air. The car park was beginning to empty out. Tom had left the Sigma parked outside the newsagent in the far corner of the village. When he reached it, he glanced once at the car parked next to his. It was a shiny black BMW with personalised licence plates: *STVMCD*.

'Twitchy?'

Tom turned. Steve McDougal. What luck Tom had, to run into his high school bully twice in three days. That was Camp Hill for you.

Steve was holding a slab of Melbourne Bitters. The man with him was holding two, as if it were a competition. The other guy looked vaguely familiar. Tom mentally dressed him in the Camp Hill Christian colours, removed a little weight and added a lot of hair. Then he saw it: Adam Bartlett. The second member of the High School Carnivores trio. The third was Benny Cotter, who was thankfully, presumably, still in prison.

'Second time in three days,' Steve said. 'Are you stalking me, Twitchy?'

'Ha. No. Hello again, Steve. Hi, Adam.'

Adam glared at Tom as if he were a stranger. Then it

dawned on him, and a wide toothy grin spread across his face. 'Twitchy Witter. Jesus. It's been years and, whoa, still got them tics, I see.'

Steve juggled the slab and stuck his key into the boot. It swung open, and the boys stored their beer inside.

'Got a party to go to?' Steve said.

'Not really. No.'

The Carnivores exchanged an unsurprised look, then burst out laughing.

'Nothing's changed,' Steve said.

To Steve, Adam said, 'Remember that time we left him duct-taped to the kiln in the art room and turned the lights off?' Then to Tom: 'Hey, Twitchy, remember that time we duct-taped you to the kiln and turned the lights off?'

'Yeah,' Tom said. 'I remember. The night security guard found me. I spent hours in there. In the dark. I was terrified.'

Another burst of laughter.

'What a pisser high school was,' Steve said.

'Not for me,' Tom said. He surprised himself by saying it. 'High school wasn't a pisser. It was hell. I cried every day. I was scared. *Every day.* You two went after me. Tormented me. Traumatised me. Shit you did to me – shit you thought was funny – scarred me for life. You two should be ashamed of yourselves.'

The men exchanged a baffled look over the roof of the BMW.

'Do we have a problem, Twitchy?' Adam asked.

'Yeah.' The word was out of Tom's mouth before he had

time to consider the consequences. 'I think we do have a problem.'

At first, Steve and Adam looked confused, as if they were bears standing over a stream, and the tuna they'd caught had just bitten back. Then Steve came around the car to join Adam. His chest was out, elbows back. It was the classic alpha-male pose.

'You're about to get a few fresh scars, Twitchy,' Steve said.

Tom's throat filled with a giggle. Then he let it out.

Adam asked Tom, 'Why are you laughing?' Then to Steve: 'Why is he laughing?'

Tom moved to the back end of the Sigma and swung the door up. While Steve and Adam stood there, gaping, Tom lifted the strip of carpet that hid the spare tyre. He fished around for the tyre iron. Brought it out. Held it firm between his hands. It felt cold and heavy and wonderful.

'What are you waiting for?' Tom asked.

He took a step forward and swung the iron. The men stepped back. They were tiny men, Tom now saw. Physically larger, but stacked up against the events of the past four days, they were little. Two little men in a snow globe. Tom had never noticed it before now, because he'd been in there with them.

'Are we going to do this or what?'

A small crowd had gathered beneath the awnings of the bottleshop.

'He's not worth it,' Steve said. 'Come on.'

The High School Carnivores piled into Steve's Beemer and

peeled out of there, tyres screeching. Tom watched them leave. He lowered the tyre iron, got back behind the wheel of the Sigma, and drove.

Tom crossed another front lawn and knocked on another front door. He stood back and waited on the step. He caught the whiff of pot and barbeque smoke from a neighbouring yard. There was the beginning of a drunken argument two doors down, but it quickly evolved into a laughing fit.

He knocked again. There was shuffling inside the house, then finally the door opened. It banged against a chain-lock. The smell of days-old alcohol wafted out. Nancy Reed looked worse than ever. Her eyes were black pits. Her face was gaunt, stripped back to the cheekbones. Her lips were raw and dry. Her teeth were stained blue from too much red wine.

She stared at Tom a moment, trying to place him through a drunken haze. Then her expression hardened. She was wearing a short terry-towelling robe with little or nothing underneath. She tightened the straps across herself. 'What are you doing back here, Mr Witter?'

'I'm here to pay my condolences.'

'Fine. Well, consider them paid. Whatever that means.'

She swung the door shut. Tom caught it with the toe of his shoe.

'Mind if I come in for a sec?' he asked.

'It's almost eleven.'

'I know. I won't keep you long.'

She glared down at his foot, then over his shoulder, into the street beyond. Then she unchained the door and let him through.

The house had only grown untidier since the last time he was here. The stack of unopened mail on the side table had slid and toppled onto the floor. The dirty footprints on the carpet were dirtier, the cluttered living room more cluttered. The mound of broken glass, which had been swept together and left there to gather dust, had only gathered more dust. Tom could picture it going on this way, getting dirtier and dustier and heavier, until there was no room left for Nancy.

Nancy collapsed in the wingback armchair. A cloud of dirt and crumbs puffed up as she sat down. A photo album sat splayed open on the coffee table. Different generations of Tracie gazed out: the newborn, the toddler, the primary school student. Next to the album was Nancy's shrine to her daughter: the smiling photo, the dried flowers, the hideous rag doll and the TCM-100B Walkman. Also among the things was the pentagram necklace.

Off Tom's look, Nancy asked, 'Do you believe in the devil?'

'I believe there are people who believe,' he said. 'That makes them dangerous.'

'Oh, come on. Climb down off that fence.'

He raised a sad and weary smile.

'What do you believe?' he asked.

'That's what I've been sitting here trying to decide. If that boy sacrificed my Tracie to Satan, then is it better the devil exists, or doesn't? If he does, then she's down there with him right now, screaming and writhing in agony. If he doesn't, then her death really was for nothing.'

This woman was mad with grief and wine. There was a full glass and empty bottle on the coffee table. There were more empties beneath it, each one turned upside down and shoved into the magazine holder, as if waiting for a waiter to come along and collect them.

'If the devil is real, then God must be real too,' Tom said. 'And if God is real, then I'm sure Tracie's with Him right now.' Then, because that just didn't seem like enough, he added, 'Your daughter had all of God's best qualities: kindness, generosity and love.'

'Is this the same God who endorsed slavery?'

'God's much easier to believe in if you don't read the Bible.'

He looked into the kitchen. Music and party chatter drifted over from different houses on the street.

'I think I know why you're here,' Nancy said.

Tom doubted that was true.

'You want to know how much I know,' she said. 'And how much I told her.'

'Told who?'

Nancy sipped her wine. 'You want one?'

Tom shook his head and waited.

'An hour ago, the detective in charge of my daughter's case called.'

'Sharon,' he said.

'Oh, that's right, you went to high school with her.'

'What did she want?'

'She had a lot of questions about Owen,' she said. 'And a few about you.'

Tom tried to keep the panic from his voice. 'What kind of questions?'

Nancy said, 'She told me about what happened at the neighbourhood watch meeting last night. She wanted to know where Owen was last night. If I'd seen him. She also mentioned another kid is missing.'

'What did you tell her?'

More importantly: how much did she know?

Nancy guzzled wine and stared down at the open photo album. There was a picture of a much younger Owen. He must have been somewhere in his mid-twenties, with chin-length hair and a try-hard beard. He looked happy. Genuinely and profoundly happy. He was holding a fresh baby girl in his arms. Below the photo, in neat cursive, someone had written, *The beginning of a beautiful friendship.*

'Owen loved that girl from the moment he met her,' Nancy said. 'I know that might sound obvious. She was his daughter. But their connection was profound. It was something primal. I can't explain it. You're an English teacher so you might have more luck, but, for me, what they had is beyond words. Sometimes, and I'm not proud of this, their relationship made me jealous.'

'It was like that with the boys when they were younger,' Tom said. 'Both of them favoured their mother. It's hard not to feel a little rejected.'

'No matter how equal you try to be, one parent always

defaults to playing bad cop. That was me, and I'm guessing you, too.'

Tom nodded.

'I thought it would change as she got older,' Nancy said. 'I looked at it as if I was waiting my turn. Being the apple of a little girl's eye is one thing, but what happens when she gets boobs and starts her period and brings home boys.' She drank. 'But their bond just got stronger. Peas and carrots, and all that.'

She reached across the table and closed the album. The cover landed with a heavy thud.

'But that all changed when Owen and I separated,' she said. 'He insisted we tell her it was mutual.'

'But it wasn't?'

She shook her head. 'There was someone else.'

'He had an affair.'

'No.'

'... Oh.' Tom thought about it.

'Tracie knew. I told her about it the night she disappeared. The night she ...' She faltered. 'She went to her grave hating me, Mr Witter, and she had every right to.'

'Why are you telling me this?'

'I've betrayed my husband once,' she told him. 'It'll never happen again. I told the detective nothing. About either of you. I was wrong about you, Mr Witter. You had Tracie's best interests at heart all along, and you were one of the few people who did something about it. You're one of the good ones, Mr Witter.'

Debbie Fryman had told him the same thing.

Nobody really knew anyone.

Tom picked up the necklace.

'I did a little research about this symbol,' he said. 'You're right. It's used by Satanists, but it has other meanings too. In some cultures, this is a protection symbol. Maybe Tracie left it for you.'

She lifted those sorry, sunken eyes to meet him. 'Do you think that's true, Mr Witter?'

'Call me Tom,' he said. He looked at her glass. 'Does the offer still stand for that drink?'

She nodded. 'Red or white?'

'Surprise me.'

Nancy Reed went to the kitchen, poured a fresh glass of red and topped up her own, then returned to the living room. Tom was gone.

35

The sun had long gone down over Camp Hill. The bank of frosted glass had turned black. Owen couldn't risk turning on the overhead lights, but a little moonlight fell in through the windows and reflected off the surface of the pool. It was too dark to see much, but there was enough light to see the blood on his knuckles.

Sean lay in a heap at the foot of the diving board. Owen had given him a good once-over, but the kid hadn't given him anything new. Just a lot of *pleases* and *let me go*s and *I didn't hurt her*s. Owen was ready to try again, but Tom had told him to wait.

So he waited.

Sean cried quietly into his hands. His sobs echoed off the high ceiling.

'Please,' he whispered. 'Just tell me what you want me to say and I'll say it. I don't even care anymore.' He cried harder. 'I just want to go home.' Harder. 'I just want to go home to my mum.'

Owen tried not to think about Sean's mother.

'All I want is the truth,' he said.

'No, you don't.' Sean managed to sit up. 'What did Mr Witter say when he called?'

Bang!

They both jumped. It was the sound of the double doors in the hallway.

'He's here,' Owen said. 'You can ask him yourself.'

Owen waited, feeling nervous. He couldn't help but think Tom held his fate in his hands, along with Sean's. If he came in here with proof that Sean killed Tracie, what then? If Tom came in and suggested they confess, that they turn themselves in and let Sean go …

He looked at Sean in the dark.

The door opened. Owen heard the click of switches, followed by dozens of fluorescent tubes flickering on. He blinked violently against the sudden burst of light.

'Turn the lights off,' Owen said. 'People might see it from the road. What the fuck are you doing?'

Then, as the strobe effect of the tubes settled into a bright, harsh yellow, Owen looked to the door and froze. It wasn't Tom.

Fear grabbed hold.

A tall woman stood alone at the far end of the pool, her side-arm drawn. Owen lifted the rifle and aimed it at her. The woman's eyes darted between him and the shivering, frightened kid chained to the bottom step of the diving board.

'Police,' she barked. 'Put it down right now.'

'He killed her,' Owen said.

'Please,' Sean cried. 'I didn't kill Tracie!'

'Mr Reed, drop the weapon right now or I will open fire.'

'Tell her,' he said to Sean. 'Tell her what you did.'

'Mr Reed,' the detective called. 'Owen. There are more officers on their way. You're not getting out of here unless you lower the weapon.'

'Tell her what you did,' Owen said. 'Confess! CONFESS!'

Owen took his eyes away from the detective for a second to look at Sean. He was on his knees, arms slung back, head towards the ceiling, sobbing. He looked back at the cop. She was crying too.

Owen relaxed his grip on the rifle, just a little. The woman exhaled. Owen raised it again.

The detective had time to say, 'Owen.' Then, 'Don't.' Then, 'Please.'

Owen took his shot.

She took hers.

Hers punched a messy hole through Owen's chest.

His severed Sean Fryman's brain stem.

36

Tom couldn't risk pulling into the school, so he parked on Butler Avenue and went the rest of the way on foot. He walked quickly towards the main building, sticking to the unlit parts of the footpath. He looked in at the classrooms as he passed, saw empty desks and chairs, leftover lessons on blackboards, teenage art on the walls.

Camp Hill Christian College was different in the dark. It seemed wrong somehow, misremembered: a version of the place in a dream, rather than the real thing. He thought about when he had been there not as a teacher but as a student. It had been a place of horror then, and it was a place of horror now.

When Tom reached the breezeway that connected the main building to the gym and swimming pool, he stepped off the path and onto the grass. There was a steep hill that rose to an expanse of empty fields, stretching on into the darkness. When he reached the top of the hill, he walked along the ridge for forty seconds, then turned to look down.

From this angle, he could see directly through the big

bank of windows and into the swimming pool. It was already swarming with police. There'd be more soon: investigators, forensics people, crime scene photographers. Tom wouldn't stick around for all that. He just needed to see if it had worked.

He found Sharon's face in the crowd of police. Then he saw the bodies.

Tom's second call from the phone box had been an anonymous one, to the police. He claimed to have heard a young male screaming for help inside the school. A strategy that relied on Owen following through on his threat to kill Sean if the cops showed up. Tom's instinct had been right. He'd been wrong about something else, though. There was something more dangerous than a man who had nothing left to lose. A man who had *everything* to lose.

On his way back to the car, Tom dug into the pocket of his jeans and took out the cassette he'd swiped from Nancy's house.

37

Tom wound down his window as he drove slowly through his neighbourhood. Sounds of celebration drifted in. Whooping and cheering and laughing.

He pulled into his driveway, hit the clicker, and waited for the garage door to ascend. A light was on in their room upstairs. Connie was home.

He edged into the garage, hit the clicker again, and waited for the door to roll shut behind him. He sat in the stillness of the car for a while, listening to the fading *tick* of the motor, revelling in the near-silence.

He keyed the electrics back on but not the engine. He looked at Tracie's cassette in the dash light. Joni Mitchell's *Shadows and Light*. Store-bought cassette tapes always came with the little tabs removed so you couldn't record over them, but Tracie had put a small strip of sticky tape over the gap. He slid it into the tape deck and hit the rewind button. As it whirred back, he rested his head on the steering wheel and braced himself. He didn't want to listen, didn't want to relive that memory. But he had to be sure. He'd come too far.

The tape deck clicked. The cassette was ready. Tom braced himself – for, *'Hey, Mr Witter, got a sec?'* – then pressed play. Instead, he heard something different. The sound of an idling car. Then, a voice that wasn't Tracie's.

'—need a lift?'

A brief pause.

'It's all right, hon, I'm not some crazy person who drives around late at night looking for random girls to murder. Then again, if I was, I suppose I wouldn't tell you, would I?'

Tom recognised the voice. He stared down at the tape deck. His head began to spin. If he hadn't been sitting down, he might have fallen over. He stopped the tape. Pressed play again, hearing Tracie's reply.

'You're Mr Witter's wife, aren't you?'

38

'Don't hold that against me, sweetheart. And please, call me Connie. What's your name?'

'Tracie.'

'I heard you talking to Marty. I'm going to use my powers of deduction here and assume you kids had a fight. By the time I came downstairs you were gone, and Marty had slammed his bedroom door. I don't like the idea of a young girl walking home on her own in the middle of the night. So come on, get in.'

'Are you sure? I don't mind walking.'

'Get in ... Do you live in Camp Hill?'

'Yeah, but I'm not going home. Can you drop me at the motor inn?'

'How old are you?'

'Seventeen.'

'They won't give you a room.'

'No, I know. I'm going to go stay with my dad. He's sort of living there. My parents are getting a divorce.'

'Oh. Sorry.'

Tom listened to the silence that followed. He heard the *tik-tak* of Lil' Red's indicator as they turned onto another street. There was a little more background noise now. Traffic. Connie spoke next.

'How long have you and my son been dating?'

'We're not.'

'Should I rephrase? How long have you been seeing each other? Getting with each other? Going steady? Am I getting close?'

Tracie's laugh hit Tom hard. It was a wonderful, tragic sound.

'Marty's not my boyfriend, Mrs Witter. Connie. He's nice. I like him. But mostly because he reminds me of someone else.'

'If you're not his girlfriend, what was the argument about?'

'How much did you hear?'

'Just the part where he told you to get out and never come back.'

'I didn't come to your house tonight for Marty. He just happened to answer the door.'

'Then who?'

'I came to see you. But Marty made me see that when you confess to something, it usually only makes the guilty party feel better.'

'What do you have to confess, Tracie?'

This time the silence was thicker and heavier. Palpable. It sounded like Tracie was crying.

'You're so nice, Mrs Witter. Connie. You're, like, too nice, and too pretty. I thought about you. A lot. And every time I did, you were some horrible, hideous person. I had to see you that way because—'
'There's a Kleenex in the glove box, honey. Everything's okay.'
'No. It's not. I think I'm in love with your husband, Mrs Witter.'
'Oh, honey. That's what this is about? I had a crush on one of my teachers too. Mr Leng.'
'This is more than a crush.'
'I know you probably don't want to hear this, but mine felt that way too. I remember what it felt like at your age. Love cramped. It ached. But—'
'We had sex.'

At first Connie didn't reply. Tom heard only the sound of the engine thrumming. Then the shuffle and brake of the car pulling over, idling.

'Tracie …'
'What?'
'This is a serious accusation. The things you're saying are the kinds of things that pull families apart. That end careers. I need you to understand that. To feel that. So if this is some sort of prank or lie

or you're getting back at him for giving you an F—'

'My mum was unfaithful to my dad. Pretty fucked up, right? I found that out tonight, and it forced me to think about what had happened. What I'd done. With a married man.'

Silence.

'I used to think I was lucky. That Mr Witter – Tom – chose me. That he gave me something. But now I see it's the other way around. He took something from me. He didn't make love to me. He fucked me.'

'Tracie.'

'He took me.'

'Please.'

'He didn't think about you.'

'Stop.'

'He didn't think about his kids.'

'Don't you dare talk about my children … Who else knows?'

'Nobody … yet.'

Silence.

'Get out, Tracie.'

Tom listened as the car door opened, then slammed shut. The sound of Tracie's footsteps moving from bitumen to gravel. A few seconds passed – no more than three – before Tom heard the engine rev.

Then—

Tom heard Connie's voice again. It wasn't the tape this time. It was in his head.

'It's a parent's job to protect their family. Do you understand?'

—a sickening thud.

The sound of a small body slamming over a bonnet.

Tom listened to all of it. The conversation, the hit, then Connie cleaning up her mess: the car hatch opening and closing. Dragging noises. Bats chirping and possums hissing: the familiar sounds of Wild Place at night. A shovel into dirt. He absorbed every second of it. Then, when the tape ended, he listened to the white noise that followed. It was heavy and full of darkness.

Tom ejected the tape and turned it over in his hands.

Stepping out of the Sigma, he folded slowly and quietly to his knees. He placed Tracie's tape down on the cold concrete. He said a prayer. He asked God to forgive him, not just for all he had done, but all he was yet to do.

When he stood, he left the tape on the floor where it was. He lifted his foot and stomped down hard. Plastic shards flew out and disappeared beneath the car and the tool shelves. He worked the sole of his shoe against the tape, first crumpling it, then shredding it.

The job was done. This was fixed. But he went on stomping anyway.

A muffled blast outside made him jump. At first he thought it was a gunshot, then he realised the time. He opened the garage door and stepped outside. A plume of fireworks filled the sky, exploding red and blue, high over Keel Street.

39

Monday

1 January 1990

Keiran strolled home along Keel Street with a package under one arm. He'd spent the night at Ricky's house and snuck out before anyone was up. He wanted to be home before his parents woke up because, technically, he hadn't asked permission to sleep over. But it was hard to hurry. It was a warm, still morning. Rays of sunlight made all the houses look orange and magical. He wanted to take his time. Soak it up. It was 1990, after all. That was practically the future.

There was something else. He didn't really care what his parents thought anymore. There was something a little scary and weird about that. But there was something liberating, too.

On his way past Sean's place, he looked up. Debbie was sitting on the veranda, staring back at him. Her face was pale and sunken. It looked like she hadn't slept. Keiran offered her a little wave. She returned it. He tried to move off towards home but something stopped him. Debbie looked so sad. So desperate. It felt wrong to leave her alone like that.

He walked up the driveway and onto the veranda. Once

there, he stood awkwardly on the top step and said, 'Happy New Year, Debbie.'

'Happy New Year, Keiran,' she said.

Now he was closer, he could see that she'd been crying.

'Did Sean come home yet?'

She shook her head.

'Did you hear about Tracie Reed?' Keiran asked.

'Yes.'

'I was at my mate's house when I found out. I still can't quite believe it. It felt weird last night, with the fireworks. It didn't feel right to celebrate. Know what I mean?'

'I do.'

'It's been a weird week,' he said, almost to himself. 'A few days ago, I was so scared that when we'd screwed around with the ouija board, we'd ... summoned something evil. But now, after Tracie, I don't know. It feels like there's plenty of evil in the real world to be worried about.'

She smiled at him, but it wasn't a happy or funny smile. It was a strange, strained thing. 'Funny, I've been thinking about that too.'

He looked out over Keel Street. It felt smaller.

In the years to come, he'd think back on this moment. It would mark the end of something and the beginning of something else. He'd walked up those steps a child. When he left, he was ... well, not a man, exactly, but something else. Something changed.

'Sean will come home,' he said.

'You seem pretty sure about that,' Debbie said.

He shrugged. 'Wherever he is, he must know you'd be worried about him. He's a good guy.' He paused, then thought about it. 'A good *man*.'

Debbie smiled at that. Then, reading the side of the package he was holding – Frankston Record X-Change – she asked, 'What do you have there?'

'Mötley Crüe,' he said. 'Picked it up yesterday. Sean got me into them.'

A black four-wheel drive pulled up outside. Sharon Guffey got out. Keiran liked her. She'd been nice and sort of funny at dinner. There'd been something light about her, then. Today, she looked heavier.

Debbie shot to her feet. 'Is there news?'

Sharon looked to Keiran, then back to Debbie.

'Let's talk inside,' she said.

Keiran watched them go in. He waited there on the top step for a while, trying to listen. He couldn't hear what they were talking about, but when Debbie started to wail, he knew his friend was dead.

40

Tom woke early. He hadn't expected to sleep, but seconds after falling into bed last night – or should he say in the early hours of the morning – he had slipped into a heavy, dreamless unconsciousness. He got up. Connie was still asleep next to him, taking soft, delicate little breaths. He watched her for a while. She didn't wake.

He went downstairs and made coffee. The instant variety. He would never understand why Connie preferred it. The things we do for love. He drank an orange juice by the window and watched the Fryman house. Sharon's four-wheel drive was parked out front.

The street was still and quiet. Most of the neighbours were probably sleeping off hangovers. From the look and smell of Bill's blue punch last night, some of them might not wake up at all. Even Ellie Sipple's window across the street was empty.

His focus shifted then, to something on his front lawn. He leaned closer to the glass to get a better look. It was a wad of something tan and red. The patch of lawn beneath it was singed black. Now that he looked, Tom saw more of them. Two more on his lawn, and more scattered down the street.

He took his coffee outside to have a closer look. In the middle of a circle of ash was a tattered shred of T-shirt. Scrawled on it was '*89*'. These were chunks of Bill's effigy. They were everywhere. Lydia would have a lot to say about that at the next neighbourhood watch meeting.

'Witter.'

Tom looked up. Sharon had just stepped out of the Fryman house and was walking towards him, taking long, deliberate strides. She looked, as Connie might say, like she'd been ridden hard and put away wet. Tom doubted she'd slept.

'Hi,' he said. He pointed to Sean's house. 'What's going on?'

She glared at him. 'Last night, someone made an anonymous call to the police informing us that Owen Reed was holding Sean Fryman hostage at Camp Hill Christian College. When we responded, Owen Reed shot and killed Sean Fryman.' She breathed deeply. 'Owen's dead too.'

Tom pretended this was new information.

'My God,' he said. 'Jesus. Sharon, that's terrible.'

'We found narcotics in Tracie's backpack. Apparently, Sean sold a little weed to the neighbourhood kids. My superiors think she threatened to blow his cover. They think this is about the scourge of drugs and a father's revenge.'

'Your superiors think that?' Tom said. 'But what do you think?'

'I think it's too neat. Life, and death, usually isn't.' She looked off. 'I've seen Tracie's body. Multiple bruises. Blunt force trauma. No defensive wounds. Whoever killed her didn't hesitate. Maybe it was Sean. Maybe it wasn't. He's dead, so we'll probably never know for sure.'

Tom looked at the Fryman house. 'How's Debbie?'

'How do you think she is, Tom?'

He shuffled a few steps backwards. 'Sharon, if I've done something to upset or offend you—'

'When I went to the school, Owen had been expecting someone. An accomplice. What do you think of that, Tom?'

Tom shook his head and furrowed his brow.

'Maybe someone who had a key,' she said.

He held his ground, tried to smile. 'And people say *I'm* paranoid.'

'Don't gaslight me, Tom,' she said. There was hurt on her face. And fear. And outrage. 'Yesterday you were convinced a Satanist lived next door and now you're acting like I'm the crazy one. You lied. Your wife lied. I can't prove it, and some sick, twisted part of me is thankful for that. But we're done. Do you understand? We went twenty-five years without being in each other's lives. Let's see if we can break that record.'

Tom didn't know what to say, so he didn't say anything.

'You know what the most fucked-up thing is, Tom?' she said. 'I could really use a friend right now.'

She started back to the house.

'Sharon.'

She kept walking.

'Is this over?'

She turned. 'For now.'

She looked at him, then cocked her head at a curious angle. 'Well, would you look at that.'

'What?'

'You've stopped twitching.'

When he got back inside, he found Connie in the living room. She was dressed in her workout gear. She slid Jane Fonda into the VCR and hit play.

'Really?' Tom asked.

As instructed by Jane, Connie got down on all fours and lifted her right leg over and over, then switched to the left. Like a dog peeing on a tree. 'It's the best way to work off a hangover. You should try it.'

'I'm not hungover.'

'Don't you want to fit into your good brown blazer again?'

'Not that badly.'

With her eyes still on the TV, Connie said, 'I saw you talking to Sharon.'

'... It's over, Con,' Tom told her.

She paused mid-workout. A weight lifted off her shoulders. Tom could see it in her posture and her face. She exhaled. Then she returned her attention to Jane Fonda.

Tom joined her in front of the television, down on all fours, and started working out right alongside his wife.

'You're a natural,' she laughed.

'Really? Because it feels like I'm just asking for a heart attack.'

That, it seemed, was that. But could it really be that simple? Connie had known about his mistake with Tracie for weeks and said nothing. How long would she have held on to that secret? The answer, he now saw, was obvious. She'd carry his secret as long as he carried hers. He'd put it in a box and lock it, someplace deep. Connie had already done the same. Marty would too.

Loud music came on upstairs in Keiran's room. Tom and Connie looked up.

'What time did he get home last night?'

'Past his curfew, that's for sure.'

'I'll talk to him today.' He paused to take a sip of Connie's coffee. 'Ew. God, Connie, I don't know how you drink this muck.'

'What can I say? I'm a regular joe and I like my joe regular.'

'Cute.'

'I thought so. Oh, before I forget, I invited Marty to dinner next Sunday. I thought we could make that a regular thing.'

Tom was getting puffed now. 'What did he say?'

'He said yes.'

Tom sighed. It was a small relief, but a relief all the same.

'Sunday night dinners,' he said. 'We're officially old now, aren't we?'

'I was worried you hadn't noticed.'

'He wants to go by Martin now, by the way.'

'I'll never get used to that.'

They went on talking like that, working out to Jane Fonda, sprinkling dirt over the hole. Tom felt a lot of things. But, most of all, he felt surprised. The fear and guilt and shame were real and deep, but they were already starting to fade. The way his mistake with Tracie had faded. In their place, he felt the stirrings of something else: freedom.

EPILOGUE

Tuesday

23 January 1990

Three weeks later, the police returned Tracie's backpack. Detective Rambaldini hand-delivered it. He was back from holiday. Tracie had been wearing the bag when she was killed, and when she was put into the ground beneath Wild Place. The cops must have got whatever evidence they could from it.

If they even bothered to open the damn thing, Nancy thought.

Officially, Tracie's murder was solved. She was killed after buying pot from a neighbourhood boy. But that didn't sit right. Nancy tried not to think about it. She tried instead to focus on the memories. That's all she really had now. So she drifted from room to room, reliving moments. Capturing. Trying to preserve them.

Here was Tracie at four, on Easter morning, sceptically examining the half-eaten carrot left by the Easter bunny. There she was shouting out from the bathroom that her bath needed *more bubble*. Here was Owen, the day they moved in, insisting on carrying Nancy over the threshold.

Stupid, funny, silly, happy memories. The house had already

started to smell different. Tracie's scent was fading. Owen's scent – that unusual mix of leather and aftershave – had already gone. But the memories remained. They'd be the last things to go. The last things she'd let go of.

Damn, she thought. She was crying again.

Nancy looked at the coffee table: the photo of Tracie, the rag doll Tracie had found as a toddler at an op shop and refused to leave without, the pentagram necklace, her Walkman. And now, her backpack.

She unzipped it. It was packed with clothes, mostly: underwear, a handful of T-shirts. And a cassette tape. It was labelled. On a strip of tape, Tracie had written, *Mr W.* There were little love hearts on either side.

Nancy picked up the Walkman, removed it from the plastic bag and opened it. It was empty. Hadn't Joni Mitchell been in there before?

She stuck the tape in, slung the headphones on – Rambaldini had brought those back too – then took it with her down into Tracie's room. Through the big window over her bed, Wild Place was full and total beneath a setting sun.

She eased her head back on Tracie's pillow, inhaled as much of her scent as she could, then hit the play button.

'... Hey, Mr Witter, got a sec?'

AUTHOR'S NOTE

Anyone who has read my other books knows I like to stick a little note here at the end to thank you, the reader. It's sort of like a DVD extra. That makes me sound ancient, but I think you catch my drift.

Since you're here, I'd like to tell you about the inspiration behind this book. My usual writing process goes like this: take one crime trope, add a strange and interesting thing that intrigues me, blend and pour over ice. *The Nowhere Child* was a kidnap story with Pentecostal snake handlers. *The Wife and the Widow* was a murder mystery with swingers (the swingers storyline got written out because it made no sense, but who knows, there's always book number four). *Wild Place* is a *Rear Window*–style mystery. The special ingredient: 'Satanic Panic' – a wave of hysteria and moral outrage that swept the world in the 1980s and 90s.

I've been interested in Satanic Panic ever since I heard about the West Memphis Three, a group of teenagers who were wrongly convicted of murder in the early 90s, largely based on the way they dressed and the kind of music they liked. But the idea of seemingly normal, educated adults suddenly becoming terrified of roaming Satanic cults, with next to no evidence, well, it just seemed so silly. I didn't understand it. I couldn't put myself in their shoes, so I shelved it.

Then, the COVID-19 pandemic hit.

Early on in the first lockdown, I was amazed by how quickly conspiracy theories emerged. COVID was being spread via 5G broadband networks; Bill Gates was installing secret microchips in the vaccine so he could track us; Hillary Clinton was drinking the blood of children. The stories were new, but the hysteria wasn't. I was witnessing the natural evolution of Satanic Panic.

Suddenly, everything clicked into place. I understood how people might believe this stuff. It's all about fear. The more scared/angry/outraged people get, the lower their standards of evidence become. The best conspiracy theories use several facts as tent poles, then string a line of bullshit between them. But it's not your everyday bullshit. No, this bullshit is compelling, propulsive and engrossing. It usually gives you someone to blame. I pictured an average, mild-mannered suburbanite with a pitchfork, looking for someone to aim it at. That's how *Wild Place* was born.

As usual, if you want to reach out, drop me a line at christian@christian-white.com. One of the true joys of putting a book into the world is hearing from you guys. I've taken a step back from social media (because it's the Devil), which means I've been slightly less involved online, but I read every email I receive. So, keep 'em coming!

Stay safe, stay sane and see you next time!

ACKNOWLEDGEMENTS

This is my *third* book. Crazy, right? Who would have thought I'd manage to pump out *one* of these bad boys, let alone *three*? Luckily, a lot of wonderful people were around to help.

First off, to everyone at Affirm Press: thank you, thank you, thank you. Martin Hughes and Mic Looby spent countless hours making this book what it is. Keiran Rogers, Grace Breen and Laura McNicol Smith spent countless hours getting people to read it. If any of you ever needs a kidney, I'm your man.

I'm going to let you in on a little secret now. As far as the business side of all this stuff goes, I have no idea what I'm doing. Luckily, I have two incredible agents in my corner. Jenn Naughton and Candice Thom, you continue to make me feel safe and protected. I couldn't do what I do without you.

On the research front, special thanks to my bro-in-law, Jeremy Smith, who taught me more than I needed to know about puncture wounds. Originally, I conceived a scene where Tom stabs Sean, then Sean, the son of a paramedic, has to give him instructions on how to patch himself up, using items from around the house that would only be available in 1989. Jeremy gave me a list of scenarios, each more messed up than the last. Then, like an arsehole, I completely rewrote the scene, rendering all his hard work useless. Sorry, mate; I owe you a beer. Thanks also to David Mahony, who took a deep dive into the weird world of Satanic Panic for me, and no doubt got himself put on a few government watchlists.

To my dear friends and family, I love you all. You're too numerous to name (seriously, there really is a lot of you), but I'll give a few shout-outs. Maia Smith and Roy Asquith: welcome to the world! Chris De Roche, thanks for getting me addicted to Rebel Donuts while writing this.

To my parents, Ivan and Keera White – for my entire life, I've always been able to count on you for love, support, pride and praise. Even when I used to edit porn! That means everything.

To Issy: my four-legged daughter, my best friend. To paraphrase The Fauves, dogs really are the best people. Speaking of daughters, my little family has grown by one since the last book. Zee, thank you for bringing so much love, fun and wonderful chaos into our lives. Don't read this until you're fifteen. No, fourteen. Let's chat when you're twelve.

Lastly, a big, huge, giant thank you to Sum. Wife, best friend, collaborator. At this stage it will surprise no one that you came up with all the best twists and turns in this book, but you're also really good at puns. Like, freakishly good. After reading an earlier version of the dog/band pun scene in *Wild Place*, Sum came back to me with the following suggestions: The Flea Gees, The Rolling Bones, Fleawood Mac, Sonny and Fur, Phil Collars, David Bonie, Bone Jovi, AC/FleaC, Muttley

Crew, Pet Shop Boys, Barking Heads, Simon and Barkfunkel (the list went on).

Remember that scene in *Wayne's World* when Wayne looks at Cassandra and 'Dream Weaver' plays? That's life with you, Sum.

READ CHAPTER ONE OF

THE WIFE AND THE WIDOW

1

THE WIDOW

Kate Keddie stood in the airport bathroom, practising her smile in the mirror. She hated her mouth. It was several teeth too big for her head, so grinning usually made her look maniacal and deranged. She tried gently curling up the corners of her lips. She was going for confidently demure. She got Shelley Duvall on bath salts.

'What are you doing with your face?' Mia asked. Kate's ten-year-old daughter had skipped out from one of the bathroom stalls to wash her hands. She'd tied the string of a heart-shaped *Welcome Home* balloon to her wrist, and now it bobbed above her like a buoy.

'Nothing,' Kate said.

'How much longer until Dad gets here?'

'Ten minutes until he lands, then his plane has to taxi in, he has to collect his bags, clear customs … all up we're looking at about sixteen hours.'

'You're killing me, Mum!' Mia slapped her feet against the polished concrete floor, buzzing with the sort of nervous excitement she usually reserved for Christmas morning. She'd never spent this long away from her father.

John had spent the past two weeks in London for a palliative care research colloquium. Kate had spent most of that time striking days from the calendar with a fat red texta, longing for his return. She hoped that old cliché about absence making the heart grow fonder was true of John, but a dark part of her feared it might work the other way too. She had read somewhere that it only took two weeks to break a habit, and what was marriage if not a habit?

Kate took her daughter's hand and led her out into the terminal. The arrivals lounge at Melbourne International Airport was surging with people. Families gathered beneath hand-painted banners, watching the big frosted-glass doors outside customs. Behind them, drivers in black suits scribbled names on little whiteboards. There was a collective energy to the crowd that made it seem like one big entity rather than a hundred small ones, all moving in gentle, nervous harmony, like the legs of a caterpillar.

Any second now, John would emerge through the doors dragging his little blue American Tourister behind him, eyes sunken and weary from the long flight. He would see them and beam. He wouldn't be expecting them. He had insisted on catching a taxi back home, and Kate had insisted that was totally fine by her, knowing full well that she and Mia would drive out to the airport to surprise him.

She was eager to see her husband, but more eager to hand him back the reins. She was a good mother, she thought, but a nervous one. She had never taken to the role as easily as other women seemed to – her mothers' group friends, or the capable, busy-looking mums at school pick-up. Kate felt much more comfortable with John's backup.

'Do you think Dad remembered my pounds?' Mia asked, staring over at the display screen outside a currency exchange kiosk. Lately she'd grown obsessed with collecting foreign money.

'You reminded him at least two thousand times,' Kate said. 'I doubt he'd have the nerve to come back without them.'

'How much longer *now*?' she groaned.

'Five minutes. Watch the flight board. See?'

Qantas Flight QF31 from Heathrow (via Singapore) landed on time and without incident. A silence hung over the waiting crowd that soon enough gave way to shouts, tears and laughter as the first passengers exited into the lounge. Some people poured into the arms of their loved ones, while others beat a path through the crowd to their waiting drivers or the taxi rank beyond.

A pretty woman with a corn-coloured ponytail collapsed into the arms of her waiting man. Then, temporarily forgetting where she was and who was watching, she kissed him passionately on the mouth. Nearby, an elderly Asian couple waved frantically as a man pushed a pram towards them, twin boys dozing inside. Kate watched them, waiting for her turn.

She was a little surprised John wasn't among the first passengers to arrive. He always flew business class, which gave him access to express lanes and priority service.

Mia went up on tiptoe to scan the crowd. 'Do you see him?' she asked.

'Not yet, monkey,' Kate said.

They watched the big glass doors keenly. They slid open again. This time, a smaller group of passengers paraded out.

'I see him, I see him!' Mia squealed, pulling her balloon down and facing its message towards the door. Then her shoulders sank. 'No. Wait. That's not him.'

The second wave of passengers dispersed. There was still no sign of John. The glass doors closed, opened. An elderly gentleman hobbled out, holding a cane in his left hand and a dusty old Samsonite in his right. The corridor behind him was empty.

Kate checked the flight board, double-checked they were in the right place at the right time, then triple-checked. Surprise gave way to concern.

'Mum?' Mia said.

'Keep watching, monkey. He probably just got caught up at baggage claim or he's being hassled by a fussy customs officer. He'll be here. Just you wait.'

They waited. Eventually, trying to keep the alarm from creeping over her face, Kate found her phone and dialled John's number. The call went straight to voicemail. She tried again. Again, voicemail. He had probably forgotten to switch his phone out of flight mode, she told herself. Either that or he had left his charger plugged into the wall of his hotel suite and arrived in Australia with a dead battery.

She began to chew her nails.

The glass doors opened. Kate drew in a tight breath. Three stragglers emerged: a middle-aged couple, who seemed to be in the middle of an argument, and a young backpacker with dirty skin and a tangle of dreadlocks falling across one shoulder. Nobody was waiting for them. The doors closed, opened. This time the flight crew wandered out, chatting casually to one another, happy to have reached the end of their shifts.

Where are you, John? Kate thought.

If he'd missed his flight, he would have called or texted or emailed, wouldn't he? He may not have known she'd be waiting at the airport, but he did know she'd be waiting. She tried calling him again. Nothing. She looked around the terminal. Most of the crowd had gone, aside from a few passengers at the car rental stalls and a man in a grey coverall vacuuming the strip of carpet by the front doors.

'Where is he, Mum?' Mia asked.

'I'm not sure, monkey. But he'll be here. It's fine. Everything's fine.'

With her eyes trained on the glass doors, Kate reached out and found Mia's hand. She held it tightly. They continued to wait. Five minutes passed, then fifteen more.

The last time they spoke was over Skype, the morning John's flight was due to leave London. Kate and Mia were sharing an armchair in the living room, leaning over the screen of the MacBook. Seventeen thousand kilometres away, John sat on the bed in his hotel room. It was a typical suite, wallpapered in soft greens with a minibar to his left and a room-service menu to his right. His passport, wallet and phone were stacked neatly on his suitcase by the door.

'Are you all set for the flight?' Kate asked.

'I've got the three things all seasoned travellers should carry,' he said. 'Earplugs, valium and Haruki Murakami.'

'Is valium drugs?' Mia asked.

'Yes, honey,' he said. 'But the good kind.' He laughed, but their connection was weak and time-delayed. The screen froze and skipped, making the laugh sound like something out of a fever dream.

John was three years older than Kate but looked five years younger. He had a youthful head of hair and neat, symmetrical features. He was naturally trim and athletic. On the screen, his face seemed to have a little more colour than usual. It was summertime in London, after all.

Mia slid forward onto her knees so her face was centimetres from the screen. 'When you get on the plane make sure you sit behind the wing,' she said. 'That's the safest place to sit if it crashes.'

'Business class is right up front,' he said.

'Uh oh. In most crashes the first eleven rows get *pulverised*.'

'Mia, your father doesn't need to hear about being pulverised,' Kate said. 'How do you even know what *pulverised* means?'

Mia shrugged. 'Internet.'

'She figured out how to switch off the parental lock again,' Kate said. 'Our daughter the hacker.'

John leaned back on his elbows and looked over to his left, beyond the screen of his laptop. Kate was struck with an odd and completely unfounded impression that he wasn't alone. She put it down to paranoia.

'Leave the safe search off,' John said, after a moment. His tone had turned flat. Kate couldn't tell if he was joking or not. 'Life doesn't have a filter, so why should the internet?'

'Wonderful,' Kate said. 'Well, tonight I can show her *The Exorcist* and tomorrow we'll watch all the *Rambo* movies.'

He didn't laugh.

'We try to protect the people we love from certain truths,' he said. 'But I'm not sure that's always right, or fair. If we don't talk about the monsters in this world, we won't be ready for them when they jump out from under the bed.'

Kate had wanted very badly to reach through the screen and touch his face. What kind of monsters?

'Are you alright, John?' she asked.

'I think so,' he said. 'I think I'm just ready to come home.'

'Kate?'

'Yes,' she said. 'Kate Keddie.'

'Oh, *Kate*. John's wife. Oh, jeez, it's been a while, how are you?'

Chatveer Sandhu was the administrative assistant at the Trinity Health Centre for Palliative Care, where John worked as a physician.

'I'm sorry to bother you,' Kate said. 'But I'm having a little trouble getting a hold of John and thought you'd be the best man to ask. I'm assuming his flight from London got changed or his schedule moved around and someone forgot to contact me?'

There was a pregnant pause, and Kate had to fight hard against the urge to fill it. She looked over at Mia, who was sitting in a plastic chair next to the information booth. Her eyes were desperate and sullen. Tears were welling in them.

'Are you still there, Chat?' Kate asked.

'Yes,' he said. 'Sorry. I'm just … I'm not exactly sure what you're asking.'

'I'm at the airport and my husband isn't.'

It seemed fairly straightforward to her, but after another brief moment of silence, Chatveer said, 'I'm going to transfer you over to Holly. Hold the line for me.'

'Transfer me? No, Chat, I just need—'

Too late. She was on hold. While she waited, she continued to bite her nails. She chewed too far, winced at the pain.

Classical music drifted down the line: Henryk Górecki's ominous Symphony No. 3. One of John's favourites. A neglected masterpiece, he called it. Before they were married, Kate had been happy to leave classical music to the pretentious intellectuals. She had felt far more comfortable in the company of Mariah Carey than of Claude Debussy. But after John spent a good part of their first date discussing Wolfgang Amadeus–this and Ludwig van–that, she had gone out the next day and bought a best-of-classical deluxe double CD collection and forced herself to listen to it. She liked it now – at least, she thought she did.

'What can I do for you, Kate?' Holly Cutter asked suddenly in her ear, her tone sharp, already impatient.

Holly Cutter was frustratingly successful. Along with being Medical Director of the Trinity Health Centre, she was also a qualified nurse, spiritual counsellor, medical educator, clinical researcher, an honorary professor at the University of Melbourne and a board director of the International Association for Hospice and Palliative Care. A typical overachiever.

'Hi, Holly,' Kate said. 'I'm not sure why Chatveer transferred me, but I'm at the airport with Mia, and John's flight has landed but he's not on it. Is it possible he got caught up at the conference, or his trip was postponed or delayed or—'

'I don't know anything about that, Kate,' Holly said.

Kate felt like tossing her phone across the terminal.

'In that case, would you mind transferring me back to Chatveer?'

'Chatveer doesn't know anything about this either.'

Kate felt flushed and foolish, mad and sticky. And Mia was still crying.

'I'm not exactly sure what's going on here,' she said. 'But I think there's been some sort of a miscommunication. John has been in London for the past two weeks, at the palliative care research colloquium. He's supposed to be coming home today and—'

'Listen,' Holly said. 'I don't know what you know or don't know, and I certainly have enough on my plate without getting in the middle of anything here, but if John attended the research colloquium this year, we wouldn't know about it.'

'I don't understand,' Kate said. 'Why not?'

'Because John hasn't worked here for three months.'

Also Available by Christian White

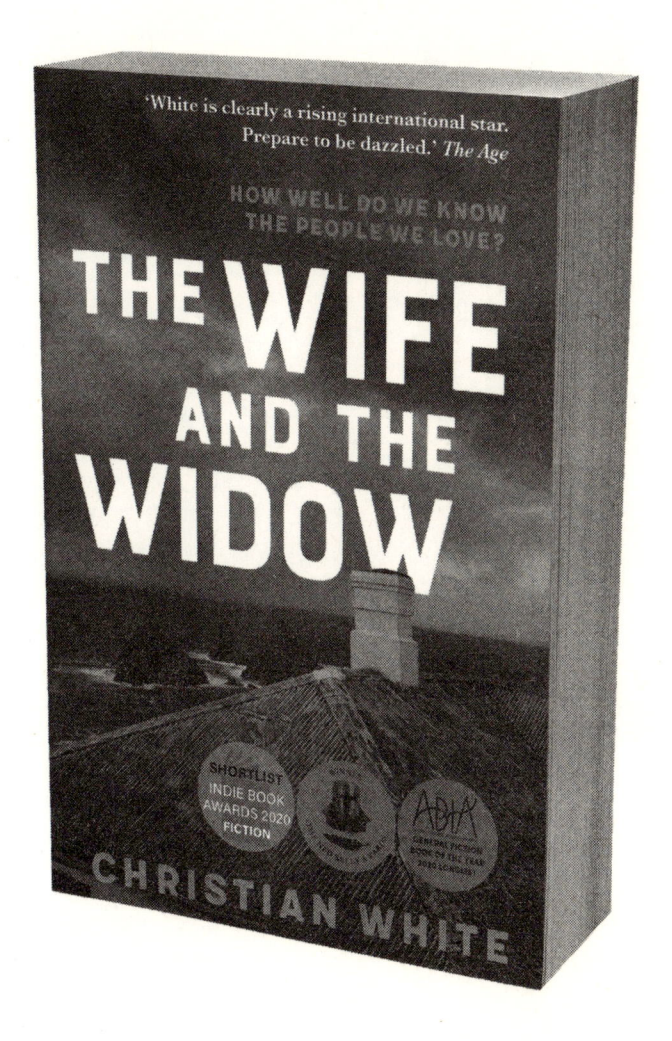

Set against the backdrop of an eerie island town in the dead of winter, *The Wife and the Widow* takes you to a cliff edge and asks the question: how well do we really know the people we love?

Paperback RRP $16.99

Also Available by Christian White

'Her name is Sammy Went. This photo was taken on her second birthday. Three days later she was gone.' *The Nowhere Child* is a combustible tale of trauma, cult, conspiracy and memory.

Paperback RRP $16.99